THE ROSE AT HARVEST END

ELEANOR FAIRBURN

THE ROSE AT HARVEST END

London, England, 1461

The handsome young heir of the House of York has wrested power from Lancaster, and is finally crowned King Edward the Fourth. Yet, amongst this triumph, Edward secretly marries the beautiful and scheming Elizabeth Woodville: an impoverished widow – and a rumoured witch. In a sea of shifting alliances, the Wars of the Roses continue, more ferocious than ever.

The Rose at Harvest End is the third book in Fairburn's renowned Roses Quartet, and features Cecily Neville, powerful matriarch of the House of York, as she tries to settle the passionate family conflicts that will decide England's fate.

The Rose at Harvest End

BOOK 3: 1461-1483

ELEANOR FAIRBURN

First published in 1974 by Robert Hale, London

All rights reserved
© Eleanor Fairburn 1974

This paperback edition first published in 2022
by the Fairburn Estate

Produced by KB Conversions, Norwich, United Kingdom

Cover Illustration & Design copyright Patrick Knowles 2022

The right of Eleanor Fairburn to be identified as author of this work has been asserted in accordance with Section 77 of the Copyright, Designs and Patents act 1988 This e-book is copyright material and must not be copied, reproduced, transferred, leased, licensed or publicly performed or used in any way except as specifically permitted in writing by the publishers, as allowed under the terms and conditions under which it was purchased or as strictly permitted by applicable copyright law. Any unauthorised distribution or use of this text may be a direct infringement of the author's and publisher's rights, and those responsible may be liable in law accordingly.

ELEANOR Fairburn (1928 – 2015) was born in Westport, Co. Mayo, Ireland. She was educated at St. Louis Convent, Balla and went on to train in Fashion, Art and Design in Dublin. After moving to England, she supplemented her income by writing articles and stories for newspapers, as well as producing knitwear designs for Vogue and Harper's Bazaar.

She settled in North Yorkshire with her husband and daughter, and began her career as a novelist in earnest. Her first book, 'The Green Popinjays' was published in 1962, followed by her most successful book 'The White Seahorse' (1964) about the infamous pirate queen Grace O'Malley.

In all, she wrote 17 works of historical fiction as well as crime thrillers under various pseudonyms, including Emma Gayle, Catherine Carfax, Elena Lyons, and Anna Neville. Alongside her work as a novelist, she taught a writing course sponsored by the University of Leeds, and was also a founding member of the Middlesbrough Writers' Group.

After the death of her husband Brian in 2011, she moved to Norfolk to be closer to her daughter, Anne-Marie. Eleanor Fairburn died peacefully in Norwich on 2nd January, 2015 at the age of 86.

FOR
C., J. & F.

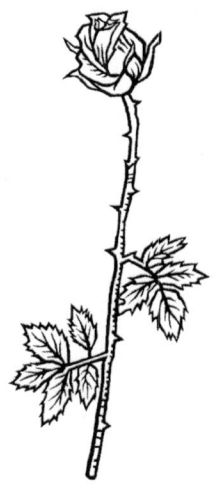

1

June, 1461

THE INTERIOR of St Paul's church was quiet, this last Sunday evening in June of 1461 – doubly quiet by contrast with the city's tumult all about, where crowds were celebrating the coronation of King Edward the Fourth.

It had been a splendid summer's day, hot sunshine and blue skies. Now the light was fading so that only the high clerestory windows retained their outline. Lower down, there was a blurring of the Norman nave and choir and transept; a massing of shadows in the side chapels except where a pool of candlelight, yellow-gold in the greyness, lapped out from before the Lady Altar. Eighty pounds of wax burned there around a memorial catafalque whose draping cloths were powdered with the White Rose, emblem of York, and the Golden Sun that was the emblem of the new King.

The catafalque commemorated the King's father, Richard, Duke of York, slain six months ago near Wakefield by Lancastrian troops. It did not contain his body: that was still in a temporary tomb at Pontefract – the severed head, recovered from a spike of Micklegate, sewn back onto the powerful neck. Richard of York might have worn the crown of England if only he'd outlived the Lancastrian Henry the Sixth.

Richard's widow, Cecily Neville, was kneeling by the catafalque. She wore a black silk mantle that curved like wings from her shoulders and covered her feet. The mantle had an upright collar, gold fastened, but no hood: hoods were quite out of fashion this summer of delicate, soaring headdresses with veils floating from their steeple-points.

Cecily, Duchess of York, had always been a leader of fashion. This morning, at her son's coronation, she'd been one of the most striking-looking women in Westminster Abbey – tall and slim, her hair fair silvering now but her eyes still intensely blue, her skin flawless; and that vital warmth and courage which had carried her through life's turbulence so far, still irradiating her personality. In her youth, her beauty had brought her the popular title of 'Rose of Raby'. Today, at forty-six, she was amusedly aware of being more often referred to as 'proud Cis'.

Certainly she was proud. Of her great Neville family background. Of her Plantagenet children. But, most of all, of her position as first lady of the realm and councillor to her eldest son, King Edward, who'd been proclaimed in March and this day crowned. Yes, let everyone see the swelling maternal pride! But not the fear – *never* the fear that lay like a lance-tip throbbing in a hidden wound. At no time must she speak to anyone, except to Edward himself, of that. Although the King turned, coldly angry from her, every time she broached the subject of his marriage. It was the one disruptive element between them. Yet the one she had to introduce again and again into their conversations, to make him do what was right by sheer frequency of talking.

'Edward, this matter must be settled one way or the other. Else it will destroy both you and your children.'

Cecily could hear her own voice, threatening, pleading with her obstinate son, through all the weeks since the disturbing news had reached her: that Edward had secretly wedded the Lady Eleanor Butler in Wigmore castle's chapel last Christmastime. There had been no witnesses to the ceremony. But it had been conducted by a priest, Dr Robert Stillington; and the lady was now carrying the child of the union. Yet Edward would not acknowledge her, not even for the purpose of seeking an annulment of his contract with her. He maintained that the Wigmore ceremony had been a mere charade, to get a stiff-necked young widow to his bed when he'd been only Earl of March, not King of England. Now that he *was* King, he'd be hanged if he'd parade this little dalliance before priests and lawyers, to beg them for his freedom.

Freedom was his already, he'd argued. It was only the lady's word against his that they'd ever stood together before a consecrated altar. Stillington wouldn't talk: the good doctor valued his position too highly as Dean of St Martin's-le-Grand. If he were discreet, he might be given a bishopric one day.

So there was no one else who would chatter. Except the lady's mother, of course. Although *she'd* only heard of events second-hand.

'As you have also, madame,' Edward had growled at Cecily. 'I tell you, there was no legal marriage between myself and Eleanor Butler. We quarrelled within a few days – she was an insufferable woman, demanding and proud – and we parted with no arrangement to meet again... Anyhow, the snow was lightening by then so I rode with the Welsh levies to join my father.'

'You joined him too late, Edward! Because of this reckless lust of yours, he died unaided – great Richard of York who never failed a friend nor broke his marriage vows to me.'

Edward had gone white to the lips while his mother spoke and a curious stillness had come over his body, like a lion's in the instant before the spring.

'Madame, were you as faithful to him?' he'd asked softly then. 'Remember, I've grown up with the label of "the archer's son" about my neck.'

Her hand clenched to strike him. Not for her own honour questioned but for the memory of a tall archer who'd gone to his death rather than take his commander's wife. A little of Cecily's innermost being had died with John Blaeburn in France all those years ago. She'd been carrying the heir of York at the time. Her body was Duke Richard's but her soul was John Blaeburn's. People had noticed how she'd favoured Blaeburn. They'd talked. And so had commenced the rumour that the handsome child, Edward, had been sired by a captain of archers.

Cecily said quietly now to her husband's empty memorial:

'Richard, you know that if Edward had been conceived in sin and born with nothing of Plantagenet royal claim in him, I would not have allowed him to take the crown of England from King Henry. I would have spoken out – denounced my own blood rather than let the holy oil be desecrated. But what now, if he weds anew by demand of the lords and commons, without first gaining quittance of his contract with the Lady Eleanor Butler? His Queen-consort will be but his harlot; their offspring unlawful born, never to inherit the crown.'

She stared intently at the candle flames, as though listening rather than looking. Then the pointed headdress bowed a little, as in a nod of acquiescence... 'So I shall speak,' she whispered, 'if he will not, before any such new marriage can take place.'

There would be time. Royal alliances were always a long while in the arranging and none had even been suggested yet for the new King. Cecily would use the intervening months or years to prevail upon Edward to set his affairs in order. And, if he still would not do it of himself, then she would override him by going to the lawyer-bishops. He would thank her in the end although the action would certainly cause a serious breach between them. This would wound Cecily because she loved Edward more than any of her other five surviving children. But a flawed marriage in the new royal line must be avoided at whatever cost. For the House of York had enemies aplenty, both in England and abroad, who would use any weakness of Edward's position for an attempted recovery of the throne by Henry of Lancaster. And Henry's Queen would never relax her baleful stare at Edward – would never miss one opportunity to attack him through Scotland, where she was now living in exile, or through France. Margaret of Anjou was an implacable enemy; a deposed Queen defending a weak consort and a younger son. Cecily understood Margaret very well. She'd known her for nearly twenty years and their ambitions were alike: to see their sons on England's throne. It was a contest which Cecily had won but in whose victory she could never relax while Margaret lived.

She stretched out her hands now to her husband's catafalque and laid her forehead on its White Rose emblems.

'Richard, when you come into Christ's Kingdom, pray

for Edward. He is young yet – careless, arrogant and reckless. He has too much belief in his luck and his popularity; too little understanding of human feelings. But I beg that your spirit may guide him to maturity. For my own part, I now make a vow of lifelong widowhood, so that no other love may distract me from the care of all our children. I hereby swear, in this House of God and before the altar of the Virgin Mary, never to remarry – for the children's sakes.'

There, it was done: the hot blood of her life dammed behind a wall of promise, never to seek the answering pulse of other blood outside the family of York... Many men had desired to wed her since Richard's death. Her sister, Katherine of Norfolk, had repeatedly urged her to accept one of the proposals. And she had passion enough yet inside herself to be kept sleepless by it in a lonely bed. But she believed that the magnitude of her sacrifice would somehow save Edward; and with him, his brothers George and Richard, and his sisters Anne, Elisabeth and Margaret, from the full exactions of life.

If she lived only for them, her maturity buttressing their youth, they might grow strong and wise. In them, too, she could forget herself; retreat into unaccustomed obscurity while they moved in the blaze of public life. She could become utterly absorbed in those other beings who were still a part of her; their minds understood; their responses anticipated; and their confidences often enough received to make it believable that she was their friend...

Crossing herself, she got up from her knees. Her black mantle fluttered open at the front to uncover the magnificent gown she'd worn at the coronation banquet in Westminster Hall this afternoon. She'd promised Edward to return there again this evening, for the festivities which would go on past midnight. But suddenly, the peace of her own home in Blackfriars seemed more attractive, and she realised how much the great day had drained her energy.

To look her best, she must rest for tomorrow, St Peter's feast, which was going to be another long morning of ceremonial. The King would wear his crown again in Westminster Abbey, and would then progress to the Bishop of London's palace at Lambeth, where he would bestow titles on many of his friends and kinsfolk. Sir William Hastings would become Lord Hastings. Wizened little William, Lord Fauconberg – one of Cecily's brothers – would become Earl of Kent. While Henry Bourchier, the King's cousin on his father's side, would be the new Earl of Essex.

But Cecily's greatest interest in tomorrow's affairs lay in the fact that her second surviving son, George, aged twelve, was to be endowed with the estates and Dukedom of Clarence... She'd hoped that her youngest boy, Dickon, would have received *his* promised Dukedom of Gloucester tomorrow also. But the King had decided at the last moment to withhold this gift for a few months, to avoid upsetting George who was always prone to fits of jealousy – indeed, he'd not been over-pleased on Friday last, at the Tower, when his small brother had been knighted alongside him in the royal chapel there. George's light blue eyes had bored into Dickon's grey ones all through the following meal at the King's table, with a hostility which had riveted Cecily's attention.

Clearly, this Dublin-born son of hers (big and softly handsome in the gold-fair Neville mould) had no affection for the thin dark boy who'd first seen daylight at Fotheringhay Castle eight and a half years ago. Perhaps it was as well, their mother had thought as she'd left the Tower with a great company of blue-clad knights bound for the Abbey, that young Richard was soon to travel north. He was to begin his training-in-arms at Middleham Castle in Yorkshire, in the household of his mighty kinsman, the Earl of Warwick, who had steered Edward to the throne... George would remain here in London as part of the royal entourage. Then he'd journey to Wales with the King later in the summer.

Two of Cecily's household ladies were waiting for her outside St Paul's church. There were also six men-at-arms in the splendid livery of York, and four litter-attendants.

'I wish to return to Baynard's Castle,' she said to the sergeant-at-arms. 'Tell the barge master that I shall not be going to Westminster again tonight.'

'Yes, Your Grace.' He held the litter door open while her ladies unpinned her hennin so that she could get inside.

The litter set off on the short homeward journey, through throngs of people drinking and dancing and shouting 'God save Edward' in the streets, around the leaping bonfires of this coronation evening.

The entrance-yard of Baynard's Castle seemed very quiet by contrast. For a moment, Cecily wished she'd gone on to Westminster after all. She had a sudden sense of isolation; of retreat from a life whose centre she'd been for so long. Dear Lord, it was hard to accept the physical limitations of middle age and the essential loneliness of widowhood! For the first time, she fully understood how lost her own mother had still been, long after Earl Ralph's death. Once, as a girl, she wondered idly and dispassionately what it felt like. Now she knew.

Abruptly dismissing her attendants and not enquiring what visitors might be in the Hall, she turned in at the little private door from the court that led to her solar in the southwest tower. At the top of the steep circular stair, she opened the door into the twilit room. It was a moment before she became aware of the slight figure sitting by the flower-filled hearth. Then—

'Beth!' she cried. 'No one told me you were here. I thought you were remaining at Westminster with Anne and Meg.'

Her daughter Elisabeth, Duchess of Suffolk, ran forward and kissed her. Even in the half-light, Cecily could see the shadows under the wide eyes; and her heart contracted with guilt for the unhappy marriage into which this girl had been forced ten months ago. Beth had become just one more sacrifice to Yorkist ambition. She'd been given to John de la Pole, the wild young Duke of Suffolk simply to keep him quiet. John was a restless, quarrelsome, unpredictable youth; son of the once-powerful Duke who'd been executed at sea, and of Alice Chaucer who was yet most troublesomely alive…

Elisabeth said, with her nervous stammer which was growing more pronounced lately: 'I c-came b-b-back alone. I wanted to s-spend a little t-t-time here again where I used to be s-so happy.'

Cecily busied herself with wine-cups and a flagon. She knew there was no advice she could give her daughter other than to accept God's Will in the persons of an impossible husband and an overbearing mother-in-law, both of whom hated the House of York because York had deposed their Lancastrian King and Queen…

While Beth talked in a halting monologue of her domestic troubles – not least of which was her inability to become pregnant – Cecily was thinking:

This is the second of my daughters to make a miserable marriage. Her eldest girl, Anne, had deserted the Duke of Exeter when he'd sided with Lancaster against York; then she'd wedded an obscure lover while her child's lawful father still lived in exile abroad. *Sweet God* – Cecily added to her thoughts now – *let us do better for Meg!* Margaret was her youngest and the most beautiful of the York girls. She usually lived with her mother here in Baynard's Castle, and Cecily adored her.

'I m-must g-g-go now.' Beth stood up abruptly. 'J-John will be angry if I d-do not return s-soon to Westminster.'

Arrogant young John de la Pole, great-grandson of a merchant, liked to display his Plantagenet-Neville wife in public. Her presence by his side proclaimed to everyone that his loyalty had had to be bought by the House of York for the price of one of its daughters; and that York was still nervous of former supporters of Lancaster. These facts amused John. His amusement did not endear him to his brother-in-law, King Edward.

Cecily went down to the water-gate with Beth, and remained there to watch the ornate Suffolk barge until it was out of sight among the jostle of other craft on the river, where thousands of lanterns had been lit and the bonfires reflected themselves in the dark water. She was suddenly conscious of her own ultimate helplessness to aid any of her children. Their destinies had been marked out too long ago by the strife which had rent England for years, York against Lancaster. Now all their lives would have to be spent buttressing the Yorkist victory. They would move further and further from their mother's influence as they grew older. But Cecily's concern would remain with each one of them on all their journeys.

2

October, 1461

GEORGE, Duke of Clarence, heir apparent to his royal bachelor brother's throne, rode sweltering in his pleated surcoat of blue velvet. Its belt was very tight about his waist, and the padding of the doublet underneath was thick over his chest and shoulders to make his young figure more like an adult courtier's. Everyone at Court was either bolstering or cinching themselves these days to alter their shapes. But George wished that he'd taken his mother's advice to choose simpler garments for the long royal tour. He'd suffered every day since August thirteenth, when he'd first ridden out with the King to Canterbury, as the sun blazed down on Salisbury, Bristol, Gloucester, Hereford, Ludlow... Now, at the beginning of October, with the cavalcade slowly making its way back towards London, and with Stony Stratford ahead, the heat was still intense.

George loosened his embroidered collar, then took off

his coxcomb hat and fanned his face with it. He felt irritable. *Everyone* was irritable today, saddle-sore and plagued by flies. Except Edward, of course – Edward seemed immune from all discomforts. He was riding gaily ahead, animatedly discussing ships and trade with cousin Harry Bourchier, the new Earl of Essex... Edward's mood had been growing better and more expansive for weeks. Ever since he'd heard of the death of the King of France, in fact.

George had heard plenty about the late Charles the Seventh, King of France, How he'd been led to his crowning, long ago, by Jeanne d'Arc. How he'd abandoned the Maid afterwards for the English to burn. And how he'd hated and feared his own son, the Dauphin Louis.

But Louis was King now since July: Louis the Eleventh. And this seemed to be a matter of great satisfaction to Edward of England. George had heard Edward say, laughing,

'Let Margaret of Anjou try to get help out of Louis against *me* – she might as well squeeze a stone!' Then he'd added: 'Oh, I shall attend a Requiem Mass for poor Charles, of course. Though I shall be hearing the words of the *Te Deum*.'

Jubilantly then, Edward had ridden on westward; his fears of Lancastrian insurrection there melting away as, one by one, the rebel-held Welsh castles surrendered. At last, there was only Pembroke and Harlech holding out for Henry the Sixth. And the latest news, delivered by relay messenger but an hour ago, was that Pembroke Castle too had fallen.

The messenger had waited to take back a message to Wales. Edward had beamed, 'Congratulate my Lord Herbert on the capture of his strong fortress, though 'tis pity he failed to net Jasper Tudor at the same time. However, you say he has the boy – the Tudor's nephew who is called Henry?'

'Yes, Sire. A child of about four years, found within the walls with his nurse.'

'Ummm.' Edward made that peculiar purring sound through his nose which betokened deep thought. George, standing interested nearby, wondered why the small boy under discussion should occupy his royal brother's mind. *Both* Tudors had been but half-brothers to the deposed King Henry.

'Well, he's of little importance,' Edward was saying then. 'He comes of a doubly bastard line anyhow. Tell my Lord Herbert that he can have the lad's custody and marriage for a small consideration.'

'Aye, Your Grace.' Walking backwards for six paces, the messenger went off with a clerk who would swiftly write everything down and obtain the King's signature.

George was remounting when he heard the Earl of Essex say thoughtfully to Edward: 'What about the child's mother though, my lord? Might she not petition against the custody order?'

The King raised a sardonic eyebrow. 'The Lady Margaret Beaufort has enough petitioning to do as it is for her new husband. Remember that I haven't pardoned Harry Stafford his support of Lancaster yet! In any case—' a golden spur in the horse's flank '—the lady gave up her son long ago to his rebel uncle Jasper.'

George closely followed the King's mount but lost the rest of the conversation... Now, as he jogged on under the copper sky, he squinted ahead towards the town of Stony Stratford and saw it lying like a heap of old bleached bones to eastward of Whittlewood Forest. Edward would be collecting money there, no doubt, just as he'd collected it from all the towns and abbeys along his route – people had gone wild with joy and generosity for the very sight of him! Everyone had dressed in their finest to receive him; and even small villages had staged pageants and spectacles for the entertainment of him who was said to be the handsomest and most popular king England had ever known.

George felt no jealousy of Edward. That would have been absurd; like envying a mountain peak. But sometimes, when he'd set out deliberately to please or impress the King, and Edward simply failed to notice that he existed, a kind of drumming would begin inside his head and he'd have difficulty in stopping himself from screaming: 'Ned, look at me! Remember I'm next in line to the throne until you get a son—' In those moments, he almost hated his royal brother.

Afterwards, he'd feel sweat trickling his spine at the idea of outraging the King's Grace. For Edward could be swift and cruel with punishment: a hand lopped here, a head there, a body stretched on the brake... Edward had vowed to discipline a realm that had grown too used to lawlessness. In Bristol on September ninth, he'd had Sir Baldwin Fulford executed for trying to raise men for Henry the Sixth. Sir Baldwin had been hanged, drawn and quartered in the market place, under the scorching sun. George still remembered how quickly the blood had dried on the scaffold steps. And how, in a kind of panic in case he was going to vomit during the disembowelling, he'd kept reminding himself that he was a royal Duke and brother of the King. Nothing like this barbarous thing could ever happen to him. He was inviolate. He would never know the agony of execution for treason.

He'd forgotten that panic now. His main fear, as the

cavalcade lumbered towards Stony Stratford, was of impending boredom. He was tired of tawdry pageants – they were all so much inferior to the entertainments he'd seen in Burgundy last year. And he was weary to death of mayoral speeches at banquets, and silly women wanting to kiss Edward. Above all, he was tired of having to be charming, by the King's express order.

'Smile, lad!' Edward would give him a hearty thump between the shoulder blades. 'Don't you know the Treasury's still empty? All we have to give the people in return for their gifts is the pleasure of seeing our faces; so *smile*.'

George had smiled – showing his even white teeth – until the expression had become moulded to his public face. He believed, now, that he'd be able to go on smiling through lies, nausea and even tedium for the rest of his life.

Why, he believed he could smile at his younger brother Richard, though he still disliked him as heartily as he'd begun to do in Burgundy where Richard, being the younger of the Yorkist exiles, had received all the comforts and petting... A curse on that thin dark face and on the choir-voice that sang like an angel's! But thank heaven, both were well out of the way presently, up in the barbarous north. George hoped that brother Dickon would remain in Middleham Castle with Warwick for a very long time. Jealousy was a wearing emotion...

He felt for the jewelled flask at his belt which had been a gift from his mother after his knighting. He was about to take a quick gulp of the sweet wine from it when he caught Edward's eye upon him – Edward had swung around in his saddle and, because of his great height, could see over everyone's head. He was beckoning his brother up alongside him. George obeyed with alacrity, refastening his collar as he rode.

'Yes, my lord?' He looked up into Edward's tanned face. He noted how the freckles were scattered across the straight royal nose and the wide cheekbones; how the brow glowed with health in the sunshine. And he thought, in sudden despair: *We resemble one another, they say. And yet I can never be like that, easy and commanding...* All at once, he felt trapped between his two brothers, Edward and Richard – who resembled one another less than any two beings on earth.

'Ah, Clarence—' the King always gave him his new title in public '—we will soon be in to Stony Stratford. Here come the civic dignitaries now to greet us.' Edward nodded casually along the shimmering white dust of the track that led to the distant gates. George saw a brightly-hued throng advancing with flags and banners. His heart sank. The speeches of welcome would drone on for an hour. Then there'd be the tableaux mounted on carts, and the long-drawn-out presentation of gifts... All at once, he craved for London, which at least went so much more briskly about its receptions! Ah well, by tomorrow morning the royal party would be quickening its pace towards the capital—

'We shall be staying here for two or three days,' Edward said.

George blinked in dismay. Two or three *days?* – in this odd corner of Buckinghamshire?

'There is some private business must be attended to nearby,' the King was continuing. 'In my absence, Clarence, I shall require you to be available for whatever demands the townsfolk make upon your time and interest. You understand?'

'Y-yes, Sire.' Edward had delegated such duties to him a few times before, but always with an air of regret for missing something – the King loved a good tournament, a pageant, a band of well-trained minstrels or acrobats. Now there was a totally altered tone in the royal voice; a subtle urgency, a note of anticipation for pleasures elsewhere.

When the leading dignitaries of the town galloped forward and commenced their extravagant greetings, the King wore his usual radiant smile. But – George noted with a vague unease – the blue gaze which normally held people spellbound by its intensity was wandering absently off into distance. Even the smile had a tight and secret impatience.

SHADOWS WERE LENGTHENING by the time Edward was ready to leave Stony Stratford. He'd bathed and shaved and changed his linen before mounting a fresh horse and setting off along the five-mile forest track to Grafton-Regis.

It was a journey he'd made once previously, four months ago. That had been on his way towards London from the north just before his coronation. He'd ridden over to Grafton Castle then to assure himself that the Woodville menfolk – father and five sons – were not still active Lancastrian supporters.

After they'd all assured him of their loyalty, he'd granted pardons to the three who'd borne arms against him for King Henry: to Richard Woodville, Lord Rivers, the blond and handsome head of the household, and to his sons Anthony and Richard – the names of the other three Edward didn't even remember now.

Neither could he recall much about their five unmarried sisters except that they'd been poorly dressed and had had a starved birdlike appearance as they'd fluttered about the dilapidated Hall, trying to hide the lack of servants and the bareness of the tables... Their mother, Jacquetta Woodville (who was reputed to be a witch) had maintained a sinister dignity, to remind her visitor that she had royal French blood in her veins. 'I, my lord, who am of the blood of St Pol—' had been her absurd preface to several remarks during the meal.

Edward had felt no great interest in the genealogy of the Woodvilles. All he'd wanted to ascertain was that the males of the family would give no more trouble as rebels. The obvious poverty of the household had reassured him on this point: the Woodvilles could not afford to back the losing side again. So they'd stay loyal. And, even if they still nourished a spite against him for certain humiliations in Calais long ago – well, Jacquetta had had the satisfaction of publicly cursing him at the time! What was it she'd screamed across the bonfires' flare? 'You, Edward of March, will spend the rest of your life making amends to the name of Woodville for this night's insults!'

He could smile at the old witch's remembered mouthings. And he could remain indifferent as to whether the Lancastrian Woodvilles survived or not in Yorkist England. Or as to whether their five pathetic girls would ever find husbands.

Yet, as he and his attendants had eaten the frugal fare of Grafton Castle last June, a thought had kept nibbling the fringes of his mind: where was the sixth daughter – she who *had* found a husband while she'd been one of Queen Margaret's ladies-in-waiting? John Grey, Lord Ferrers of Groby, had taken her to wife. Edward remembered the obscure knight's name only because it had been one of the very few on the list of Lancastrian dead after the second battle of St Albans – that nearly disastrous defeat for the whole cause of York last February. However, when York finally triumphed, John Grey's widow would have had all her property confiscated. Therefore, the odds were that she was again living here with her parents – straining the family resources still further because she'd be unable to make any contributions towards her own keep or towards that of any children she might have.

Edward recalled then her mother saying to him, as she'd presented the other five girls: 'I regret, Sire, that my eldest daughter Elizabeth is ill and cannot descend to the Hall.'

He'd hardly noted the remark at the time. But, a few measures of ale later, he'd begun to wonder about Elizabeth Woodville-Grey. Was she genuinely ill? Or was she a rebel Lancastrian still who refused to meet her Yorkist King?

Edward had been concerned for his own popularity last June, before the crown was firmly on his head. And the sensation of being able to withhold or bestow favours had still been new enough to excite him. Lord Rivers had craved him for a pardon the moment he'd entered Grafton Castle. So he'd later instructed his Chancellor to apply the Great Seal, not only to a pardon for the senior Woodville but for his two erring sons as well, and to a reversion order of all their goods confiscated. *That* should show the absent daughter that she too might regain possession of her dead husband's property, if she were to make humble petition for it from her lawful sovereign.

Her refusal to meet him had rankled with Edward. He'd wanted her to come down to the Hall, to assure him that she was not a skulking Lancastrian. But he wouldn't order her to do so. She was of noble blood, at least on her mother's side, and she was but lately widowed. It was possible that she was still ailing with grief. Many fine-born ladies ailed a whole year – or until they could appear in public without the unflattering mourning barbe! Edward understood widows. Furthermore, he liked them. They were easily got to bed and, once there, had far better manners than untaught virgins. Even the obstinate Eleanor Butler had greatly pleased him for a few nights – although he couldn't bear to think of those nights after she'd slighted and quarrelled with him. He'd given her so much; shown her so much of his true self...

Now there was this widow of John Grey's and he did not know if she were friend or foe to him. Well, perhaps he'd return to Grafton Castle some other time; receive her submission after she'd endured a year or so longer of personal poverty, and seen how complete was his clemency to her father and brothers.

Yet here he was, after only four months, riding again towards the Woodville home. He'd left his brother George and most of his escort, at Stony Stratford. With only a few attendants, he was leading the way through the autumn woods towards the castle. How beautiful everything was! How wonderful was the tingle of life through one's entire body—

He said, laughing, to Essex: 'At least old Rivers should be able to feed us all a bit better this time.'

'Aye, my lord,' Essex replied with the usual Bourchier-family gravity, 'his pardon was passed on July 12th, with a re-grant of all goods and rents forfeited last March.'

'Then, by the mercy of God and our Chancellor,' Edward grinned, 'he might have refurbished his Hall and re-clothed his daughters by now.'

Re-clothed... The King's heart gave a strange double beat under the gold lacing of his tunic. There was one woman at Grafton whom he wished to see less rather than more clothed. Indeed, the idea of her total nakedness had raced his pulse many times since last June. He'd only glimpsed her then, just as he'd been leaving. But the tantalising vision had remained in his mind, superimposed upon an older, stranger dream...

She'd been standing in the gloom at the top of the stairs. The door of a heavily-shuttered chamber had been open behind her so that her paleness had seemed to float against the smudged black... She was all pale; her skin; her loosened hair that flowed like a white-gold veil. And she was holding some kind of loose robe around her as though she'd pulled it on quickly over her bed-nakedness. The unarranged robe had left neck and shoulders bare, with the fine skin gleaming over the chiselled contours.

Almost as soon as he'd glanced up at her, she'd melted back into the darkness of the chamber. Without sound, apparently even without movement. It was uncanny. The King was half inclined to believe he'd seen a ghost. Or some troublous apparition which the witch Jacquetta might have called up to inflame his mind with sudden feverish desire... He'd rounded on Jacquetta and discovered that she was watching him, sidelong, out of her slanted eyes. But she'd said nothing. And he had not asked her to verify that the pale lady was her daughter Elizabeth...

For him, the gilt-fair figure at the head of the stairs was like a memory made flesh from other lives he'd once lived; the life of a child, in France and in Ireland; the life of a youth on the Welsh marches, and of a young man exiled abroad. Through all these changes, the vision had remained unaltered in its basic detail: of a woman's fairness accentuated by a dense darkness behind her... he'd spoken tentatively once to his mother about this dream. The Duchess Cecily had tried to convince him that it was a figure from an old tapestry he was recalling; and he'd pretended to believe her because she'd been so deeply disturbed.

But he'd put the matter into plainer terms for Will Hastings. They'd been roistering together in London just before the coronation when Hastings had asked: 'Your

Grace prefers fair woman to dark ones?' And he'd replied, with fire shooting through his veins: 'Aye. It is the white-gold kind that enliven my dreams! I imagine them, draped only in their own gilt tresses, waiting for me by an altar of black velvet...'

He'd spoken these words out of a mind tingling with sensuality just a few days after his first visit to Grafton Castle. Now it was four months since he'd been here, yet still there was this fever in him — this physical response to an abiding mental vision.

The Woodvilles had been told, two hours ago by royal messenger, that the King was coming to Grafton-Regis. So they were all assembled on the terrace by the main gate to greet him when he arrived.

Edward dismounted and strode forward. He accepted the profuse welcome of big blond Lord Rivers. Then of the diminutive Jacquetta, Dowager-Duchess of Bedford. Then of their five sons and five daughters...

The sixth daughter was waiting a little way apart from the rest. She wore widow's black and violet; and the white linen barbe that covered her chin was pinned to a black, heavily-veiled hennin. Behind her was a nurse holding two small boys by the hand.

As Edward approached her, Elizabeth Woodville-Grey dropped into the deep head-bent courtesy she'd learned at Margaret of Anjou's court. It was a pose she could hold indefinitely, without a muscle-quiver.

Edward stooped towards her, took her hands and raised her. For the first time, he could see her face clearly; and the hardness of her eyes was like a physical blow between his own. The neat little mouth above the linen band neither smiled at him nor spoke.

'Your sons, my lady?' Awkward almost, he nodded at the two boys who were still kneeling beside their nurse.

'Yes, Your Grace. The orphans of John Grey, late Lord Ferrers of Groby.' Her voice was very low. Without its controlled hostility it might have been sweet. 'They do not inherit?' he asked. 'No, Your Grace. No more do I.'

He waited for her request. None came. He looked again into her shuttered face: it reminded him of an alabaster saint's in a Lenten church. No sign of the wondrous hair. No glimpse of the slender neck with its gleaming skin and the cleft of the breast below—

By the Rood, she was more covered up in shapeless folds than his Aunt Jane in her Barking convent! And even the hand which he still held was unadorned: the very slender fingers wore no rings. Yet many rebels' widows had managed to keep their personal jewellery.

He waited another moment, giving her time to beg for possession of her late husband's goods. In that moment – tense, uncomfortable – he noted the surprising darkness of her eyes under their fragile, arched brows; and the tip-tilt-edness of her nose in her little cold, carved face. There was nothing else visible for him to notice about her. Except her height measured arrow-straight against his own – she was not over tall, just average.

'Good day to you, my lady,' he said; and passed without another glance at her, into the Hall... Her unyielding frigidity, her total lack of response, had shattered his dreams. He felt angry and cheated.

He would come no more to Grafton Castle. The King of England had more important things to do... he had ships to buy, trading ventures to set afoot in order to help pay his enormous expenses – the gifts of the abbeys and the towns were but drops in the ocean of his debts... He had to open the first Parliament of his reign and have it impeach Henry of Lancaster, Margaret of Anjou and all their adherents... And he had to bring the north-country to subjection. Many great castles there were still holding out for Lancaster despite the continuous assaults of the great Earl of Warwick from Middleham – Edward's Neville cousin who had carved a path to the throne for him.

3

September, 1463

Richard, the eleven-year-old Duke of Gloucester, never felt cut off here in Middleham. Indeed he'd often thought, during the two and a half years since his arrival, that the busy town and castle was much more the hub of the realm than London was.

Still, he always felt angered by the suggestion that his powerful cousin and tutor-lord, the Earl of Warwick, was the real ruler of England; King Edward only its sovereign by the Earl's will and guidance. Everyone at Middleham except himself had laughed at the reported remark of sly French Louis:

'They tell me there are two rulers in England now: Monsieur de Warwick and another whose name I forget.'

It was impossible, Dickon had inwardly raged, that anyone should ignore or forget golden Edward, his brother! Just because the bachelor King enjoyed life didn't mean that he was an idler. Far from it. And if he'd never fought a battle in the north since his coronation – well that was simply because the mighty Nevilles had always crushed his enemies for him before he'd even reached York...

Dickon knew by heart every detail of every campaign which he'd seen prepared here within the walls of Middleham Castle. In the February of two years ago, he'd been allowed into the torchlit Hall late one night while his awesome cousins, Warwick and Montagu, were planning the naval defences of the realm with Uncle William Fauconberg, the Earl of Kent. Dickon would never forget the drama of that night. How the torch flames had streamed in the draughts from the high windows. How the immensely long shadows of the Neville brothers had contrasted with the little hunched one of Uncle William. And how the High Table, stripped of its linen, had been strewn with papers relating to ships, men, food supplies, guns... Everything which could be spared from the quarrelling of Lancaster-inspired riots and uprisings on land was to be diverted to sea defence. Because it was reported that ex-Queen Margaret was bringing invasion troops from abroad and, if she were successful, King Edward could lose his crown – maybe even his life.

That stormy February night in the Hall, as he'd stood with the other boys who'd been chosen to attend the Neville commanders, Dickon had offered his own life to God that Edward's might be saved from the terrible Margaret of Anjou.

Every Yorkist, from the highest to the lowest, feared the deposed Lancastrian Queen. Castle nursemaids could get their charges instantly indoors and to bed with threats of: 'The Frenchwoman is coming!' And the north wind howling down on Middleham was a reminder to all of the way in which her undisciplined troops had once ravaged this land – and might do so again if the news were true that she was forming a great European league against the House of York which had exiled her with her consort and her son. It was accepted that Margaret would fight to the death for the restoration of Lancaster.

As it had turned out in this particular case however, the Queen's invasion fleet had been scattered by a great storm off Holy Island last autumntime. Margaret herself had only just managed to escape northward with a few companions. Since then, news of her had been scarce. But Warwick had ridden boldly into Scotland and demanded from the council of young King James the Third that Scotland should no longer provide a bolt-hole for rebel Lancastrians if that country wanted peace with England! Soon after, Margaret was said to be in Northumberland where the Lancastrians still held three strong fortresses. But the many attempts of the Nevilles to capture her there had failed, and it seemed that she'd now slipped away abroad again, to foment more trouble for York...

Anything which threatened Edward's dignity or safety was a matter of almost painful concern to Dickon, although he himself derived little advantage here at Middleham from being the King's brother. Indeed, the only great benefit which had come to him was that, instead of sharing crowded quarters with the hundreds of other young knights, squires and pages, he had a small room to himself, tucked up near the eaves of the west wing.

The room contained a straw mattress, with blankets; a wooden chest containing his best clothes which his mother had sent up from London with him – clothes he only wore in the Hall on a feast-evening, or on the rare occasions when he was summoned to attend the Neville ladies in their solar; a petch where hung his everyday outfits of leather tunic, rough shirts and hose; and a book support at which he could stand to read, pray or study his music-sheets.

The walls of the room were of rough stone, unsoftened by any hangings and wainscottings. In the mornings they were a forbiddingly dark grey, as were all the shadowed stones of the castle. But by evening light they took on an almost rosy tone, just as the main entrance side of the fortress did when the dawn came up and lit it for a while. The town-facing side of Middleham Castle never looked grim early in the morning. It was only as the day wore on that it frowned in near-blackness at anyone approaching it up the steep road from the market square... But Dickon was happy with his own private evening light, spilling in through the little window that looked up onto Middleham Moor. Up there on that wide, windswept space, troops were trained in the marching disciplines which the Earl of Warwick sternly enforced. There too the monks of Jervaulx and Coverham Abbeys grazed the fine horse which they bred for sale.

'Some day,' he'd once vowed to his particular friend, Francis Lovell, as they stood together at this window, 'I'll have a white destrier, high and strong, from the Jervaulx breed.'

'Not *too* high—' Francis had choked a crow of laughter '—else you won't be visible when you're mounted!'

Dickon, grimacing, had pummelled Francis in a mock attack. But the truth was that he no longer minded being small for his age. Contests in the tiltyard had proved to him that he was tough, quick and a match for the best of the other boys. So he'd resigned himself to being slightly built and a little undersized. After all, look what a reputation for valour Uncle William Fauconberg had gained! Yet *he* seemed like a wren beside the Neville eagles, Warwick and Montagu...

Eagles indeed were those two eldest sons of great Salisbury. They soared above all the other nobles of the realm in wealth, handsomeness and courage. And if they were arrogant, it was because they knew their worth, on the battlefield for the White Rose of York or in the council chamber of the King, their cousin.

Dickon had often watched the Neville brothers ride out from Middleham at the head of troops for northern warfare or of gorgeous retinues for display in York or London. And he'd never forget the first time he'd been allowed to accompany them... That had been in the January after his arrival here, when he'd ridden as helm-bearer to Warwick in the magnificent funeral cortege of the Lady Alice Montacute, Countess of Salisbury. The Countess had never recovered from the shock of learning that her husband and her son Thomas had both been slain at Wakefield along with Dickon's own father and brother, the Dukes of York and of Rutland... No one at Middleham Castle had been surprised when the mother of Warwick and Montague had died, aged sixty, this Christmas Day past.

Her body was taken with great pomp to Bisham Abbey, a religious house of Neville foundation. And thither to join it were brought the bodies of her menfolk from their temporary resting-place near Wakefield: all three to be interred together in the Abbey where the late Earl of Salisbury had often expressed a wish to lie at the last.

Dickon had overheard Warwick sigh to his brother, Lord Montagu, as Bisham Abbey came in sight: 'Here too, John, will we be brought one day.' And the boy had soberly pondered an England without Warwick, and found it unenvisageable.

Later, amid the funeral crowds at the Abbey, he'd had the excitement of meeting his own brother, George. The thirteen-year-old Duke of Clarence was representing the King. There was so much Dickon wanted to tell George that he could hardly wait for the cold-meat banquet after the service, when they could sit together.

But George showed no great desire to linger in conversation with his younger brother. As they walked towards the Abbey's refectory, Clarence's air of condescending attention gave way to one of abstraction and, finally, of impatience. By the time they'd almost reached the dais table, Dickon understood that the King's lieutenant had more important people to attend to than his own immature and provincial self, prattling on about petty matters. He came to an abrupt halt of both step and speech, and let Clarence mount the dais alone.

Silly of him not to have noticed straight away that George, with whom he had once shared ship and exile, had altered from a frightened, dependent little boy into a poised young man; handsome; beautifully dressed and groomed. Why, even his fingernails were polished while Dickon's were – well, pared short and brushed clean but that was the best that could be said for their state!

Dickon thrust them behind his back, under his travel-stained mantle. He lowered his head until his chin was resting on his chest. He carefully studied the floor-rushes in which his left foot was describing half circles.

People jostled past him. Several spoke to him. But he dared not look up for fear that the tears would spill past his black lashes.

A lady's perfumed scarf was thrown over his eyes.

'G-g-guess who?' said a soft voice in his ear.

He spun around, shouting at once, 'Beth – oh, *Beth!*' – and flung himself into the embrace of his sister Elisabeth, Duchess of Suffolk...

While she held his small body against her, Beth's fingers found the dampness of his tears on her scarf. But she asked no question about their cause. Weeping was a private matter: that was a rule she'd had to apply to her own life since her marriage to John de la Pole. She was miserably unhappy but resigned to the Will of God. She knew she'd been wedded to vicious John merely to keep him quiet, lest he raise further trouble for the House of York. So she prayed for babies to love; and she wept alone; and smiled her gentle smile at all other times.

'C-come, Dickon,' she said now, 'sit by me. For I have many loving messages for you from our m-mother and from sister Meg.'

As she steered him into a bench-seat between herself and the Lady Montagu at the Abbot's table, Beth wondered if a marriage had been arranged yet for sixteen-year-old Meg who was still living with their mother at Baynard's Castle. Beth had few opportunities to visit London nowadays – the King disliked her husband and never invited him to Court – but she'd been there briefly before Christmas and had marvelled at Meg's maturing beauty.

Yet she supposed that Edward himself must wed first. Stabilise the new dynasty by fathering at least one legitimate son. After that, he'd be in a stronger bargaining position with any European prince who might seek the hand of his youngest, and loveliest sister.

Beth knew that Warwick and the members of the Great Council and all the bishops were urging the King to marry soon – his profligate bachelor ways were scandalising many. But she did not know her royal brother's mind on the issue. He always seemed to evade it – even the Duchess Cecily admitted that! Which was one oddity upon the next, since he normally confided all things to his mother. And there could be no doubt about his fondness for women in general...

Pondering these matters anew now while the food was being served, Beth came to the conclusion that Edward was secretly in love. He was still – against all recent evidence to the contrary – a romantic. She, as his sister next in age, remembered him so as a youth. Therefore he'd find it hard to discuss dynastic marriages which could cause no pleasant fever in his blood.

∼

SOMETIMES IT SEEMED to King Edward that every duchess and princess in Europe wanted to become Queen of England. But he was in no hurry to reach a decision about marrying. He could have the company of any woman he wanted (including that of his faithful mistress, the Lady Lucy, who'd just borne him another natural child – a daughter this time). Also, there was the problem of his undissolved contract with Eleanor Butler. Although that lady's giving up of her son to foster-parents and her retirement to a convent, had now reassured him of her continuing silence.

But there was another element: a total lack of enthusiasm on his part for the notion of taking a wife. Marriage was so permanent, so static! And he was always restless for change, new experiences, the challenge of an unknown woman who might be revealed as the ideal he'd always sought and never found.

Well, likely she did not exist. And he'd end by wedding one of French Louis' offerings: Bona or Maria of Savoy, or even the child-Princess Anne de France – Warwick was urging all of these for his consideration. Then there was Henry of Castile's sister, Isabella: a union with her would be good politics, reopening England's claim to the throne of Castile. And there was Philip of Burgundy's female kin, a marriage with any one of whom would be a boost to the English cloth and wool trade. While the daughter of the Count of Foix would unlock the highway for England into Spain.

Edward felt that he might just as well choose with dice or with the turning of a painted card. No matter what name came up, he would view it unemotionally. His heart would not be involved in the business of siring legitimate heirs. That would be merely a duty laid upon him by ritual of the Church which was so generous to him with its money... he realised that he must keep the Church sweet towards him, just as he kept the towns and the great merchants. And the only way to do that – to silence the growing censure about his wild private life – was to wed, and to give his consort a child every year... But oh, by the Nails of God, if he could also love the woman – find her exciting and enigmatic – a match for his mind as well as his body! Though doubtless that was asking too much of a destiny which had already lavished on him St Edward's Crown, success in battle and in trade, and the worship of his common people.

Still, riches always came to the rich, luck to the already fortunate. He felt full of good cheer as he rode north from St Albans for a campaign against the Scots. He had his cousins Harry Beaufort and Ralph Percy on either side of him – both former Lancastrian rebels whom he'd wooed back to York.

The early September sky was blue over the rich harvest fields. Blackberries were ripening in the hedges. There should be good hunting in Whittlewood Forest this year, with the game so well fed... He decided to snatch a few hours there tomorrow morning, after the halt in Stony Stratford. But he would *not* visit Grafton Castle, to see the proud and frigid eldest daughter of the Woodvilles.

4

Autumn, 1463

In the grey hour before dawn, Elizabeth Woodville opened her shutters and leaned out through the casement. Mist lay thick in the park, and the sweet leper-scent of decay rose from all the damp places around Grafton Castle.

She'd awoken with a headache. Or, rather, with that sense of pressure inside her head which grew worse each desperate month of her poverty-stricken widowhood. Her parents provided food and shelter for herself and the two orphan sons of John Grey but they provided little else – certainly no new clothes when there were still old ones of Jacquetta's waiting to be unpicked, recut and remade. Elizabeth had an attack of nausea every time she smelt the dust of worn velvet with its ineradicable stink of mildew and sweat.

What a fool she'd been two years ago not to have thrown herself upon the mercy of the King when he'd come here to Grafton. He might have restored her property then, whilst he was still new to office and eager to please everyone – even rebels' widows! Now this widow was two years older; and the King, it was said, had grown hard in his dealings with suppliants. Yes, everything would have been simpler two Septembers ago.

But it had not been mere obstinate pride which had prevented her from asking favours of him then. It had been something she'd been unable to define at the time: a trained sense of loyalty to that other pathetic goodly King, Henry of Lancaster, and to Queen Margaret whose lady-in-waiting she'd been... Although Margaret had never commanded the love of her ladies, she'd always had their respect, their grudging admiration. And, so strong had been her hold upon their minds, they'd been incapable of disloyalty or indiscretion in her service. Margaret demanded total integrity. It was surprising how few people, men or women, failed her once their bond with her was sealed...

That day when the new King had come to Grafton, Elizabeth had realised that, to ask a boon of him, was to acknowledge his kingship. And to acknowledge him was to fail Margaret. So she had not put both knees upon the ground; nor had she spoken of her necessities even when he'd paused to give her time to do so. Her mother had railed at her for it afterwards and had been railing ever since. There were constant violent quarrels between Jacquetta and Elizabeth; petty arguments and squalid scenes...

Elizabeth had come to accept that she was diminished now within herself by poverty and dependence. To slip one more notch in her own esteem would make little odds. So, if opportunity ever presented itself again, she'd kneel to the man who had become King in pious Henry's place.

He and his entourage had arrived last evening in Stony Stratford. Grafton servants who'd gone into the town to gawp at him had been full of the news at suppertime and Elizabeth had listened carefully to their gossip... Yes, some of the royal attendants had told them that the King would hunt in Whittlewood tomorrow early if the weather held. The main body of the army hadn't caught up with him yet so he'd have to delay a few hours to see that all his troops were in order before pushing on. Northampton town's recent attack upon his cousin, Harry Beaufort, had taught the King a certain caution of his subjects!

Elizabeth had felt her lip curl at the reminder of Beaufort, Duke of Somerset, riding now as friend of York when not so long ago he'd been Margaret of Anjou's champion. But let Edward of York take care with such turncoats. Maybe he was wise to wait for the army; he might need it to protect himself.

Sniffing the air, Elizabeth studied the brightening sky above the trees and formed the opinion that it was going to be another splendid September day. So the King *would* ride into the forest...

She moved quickly then away from the window and began to harass her old serving woman with a hail of swift orders. Fetch her washing bowl. Lay out her few jewels and cosmetics. And tell the children's nurse to get the boys dressed quickly and neatly this morning because they were about to be taken for a walk by their mother.

When the old servant had washed and towelled her, Elizabeth fingered through the shabby out-dated gowns that hung from a petch against the bare wall. She chose the one whose russet fur was least moth-eaten around neck and hanging sleeve and hem. It was a tawny-green gown which matched her eyes. It fitted tight – having been made for her virgin figure – and it had a high neck, dating as it did from the chaste days of King Henry when no woman at Court might display her shoulders or her bosom. But Elizabeth could still get into the gown – a Lenten diet all year round was a wonderful shedder of maternal fat!

She drew on her hose and tied them to the points of her shift. Then she stepped into the back-laced gown and pulled it up over her slim hips.

'Alys, Alys,' she called, 'lace me; then bring my brown mantle from the cedar chest, I feel cold this morning.'

While she waited for the mantle, she looked closely into her mirror and saw in its fogged surface that, chilled and unadorned, she looked all of her twenty-seven years. So Edward would consider her too old for the kind of sport he was reputed to put second only to the hunt. Well, no matter: she had no ambition to become one of the royal whores. So she would be dignified in her mature motherhood. She would appeal only to the King's sense of justice.

Alys brought the mantle and began shaking it out. It was far from new but its top fabric and its lining still held a beech-coloured richness and its old-fashioned hood had a depth of dark fur. It had formed part of Queen Margaret's contribution to Elizabeth Woodville's trousseau. She shivered now as she put it on and tried not to think of the former Queen – exiled – hunted – shipwrecked—

The nurse came with the two boys, Thomas and Richard Grey. They'd been loudly rebellious of their 'best' clothes until they'd reached their mother's door. But they'd ceased their squirming and complaining the moment when that was opened and they'd found the coolly critical maternal gaze upon them.

'Good morning, madame,' they chorused dutifully.

'Good morning, my sons.' She nodded dismissal to the nurse and the serving woman; then said without further preamble, 'Today you will conduct yourselves as gentlemen whose great-granduncle was of the royal blood of France.' It was the only trump card of the Woodville family, that Jacquetta had been a niece of the Count of St Pol.

The boys nodded, apparently stricken dumb by the realisation that their mother was wearing an unfamiliar gown. She smiled at them, one of her rare sweet smiles, then she held out both her slim hands. Self-consciously they grasped them, hiding their plump warm fingers in her cool palms... Thus joined into a family group, the Greys proceeded downstairs and out through the deserted Hall. Only a few servants were about as yet, for it was barely light; but there had been the sound of a hunting-horn from the forest a few moments ago.

Elizabeth led her sons away from the castle by an overgrown path. Every now and then she paused, listening to the sounds of the hunt that circled and grew distant and approached again. She said: 'We will go to the Oak Glade and wait there.' The boys did not know what it was they were to await...

Elizabeth's face felt hot high on the cheekbones, and she was breathing fast and shallow in the tawny-green gown whose tightness across her lower ribs lifted her breasts.

'When the hunt comes by here,' she said as they entered the glade, 'you will bow low as you have been taught to do. It will be the King.' Then she made them rehearse their bows until they were near dropping from hunger and fatigue.

With relief, she noted their exhaustion. That should curb their animal spirits and ensure their good behaviour when His Grace arrived. If indeed he *ever* arrived — the hunt seemed to have gone away westward now... Yet this glade here, with its ancient oak tree around which strange rites were said to have been performed in distant times, was a kind of crossroads of the forest. Every hunt came this way eventually – the quarry was reputed to be drawn to its own death by the power of antique sacrifice.

Edward rode alone into the clearing. Somehow he'd lost both his companions on his way. Then his horse had taken a kind of fit and carried him here unwilling – the big beast simply would not be halted until this moment when it had stopped dead, almost unseating him.

'Devil take you,' the King muttered, breathing hard. He dismounted and moved forward hesitantly. There was a strange silence here—

He saw the woman with the two small boys under the gnarled oak. All three bowed, then sank to their knees at his approach.

'My Lady Grey?' His gaze focussed on her with a radiant attention which excluded the boys.

'Your Grace, I most humbly beg a favour—' How sweet her voice was! '—that my late lord's property should be regranted to me and to my sons.'

There was a drumming in his ears which he thought must be the other horsemen approaching but no one came into the glade. He wiped his sweating hands on his tunic, then held them out to her to help her rise. But she took hold of the fingertips and kissed them. At her touch, the drumming sound nearly deafened him.

'Your request will be granted,' he heard himself say in a queer strangled voice. 'But such things take time. You will remain here at Grafton until – until the spring at least?' Blood of God, he should have finished with the Scots by then!

Still kneeling, her expression was unfathomable, she looked up at him and nodded. He saw the gilt hair within the darkness of the fur hood. He saw the perfect skin over the fine bones, and the delicate moulding of the chin which had been hidden by the widow's barbe at their last meeting. He saw how the bodice of the tawny-green gown was pulled taut over small high breasts so that the nipples showed. All at once he wanted her as he'd never wanted another woman in his life. But the calm aloofness of her bearing said, clearer than words: 'All *I* desire, Your Grace, is the return of what was jointly mine.'

No other favours of the kind which he was always so quick to bestow on any woman who took his fancy were required by Elizabeth Woodville. And there was a further withdrawal in her manner when, to help her upright, he hungrily slipped his fingertips inside her sleeve.

'I thank you, Sire, for granting my request.' She backed away, holding the boys close against her thighs. Then all three kneeled again on the damp grass and waited, heads bowed, to be dismissed. He could think of no reason for delaying them which this cool clear-eyed woman would not see through and despise him for...

The King was standing motionless and alone by the oak tree when his anxious attendants came seeking him.

'Let us set out for the north,' Edward said then impatiently, throwing his hunting-belt to a servant. 'The sooner there, the sooner back.'

For three months, he tried to forget Elizabeth Woodville. And indeed, the press of events in the north often drove her memory to the back of his mind.

Early in December he rode to York city from his castle of Pontefract. There he met the Scottish envoys who signed a temporary peace treaty, thus releasing him from the obligation of making war upon them for the present... Edward was satisfied with this arrangement; and with the report that Mary of Gueldres, the Scottish Regent, had just died, leaving her son the boy-King James the Third to complete his country's ruin. Edward now knew that Scotland was politically doomed; that times and national prosperity were on his own side; and the ex-King Henry, whom Warwick had tried to buy from the late Mary of Gueldres, was now back in England anyhow, being hidden by Lancastrian loyalists. So why waste resources on where the danger was not? Danger was *here*, in England.

Yet when it showed itself, it stunned the King. That rebel cousin of his, Harry Beaufort, Duke of Somerset, whom he'd pardoned and entertained, trusted and laughed with and finally packed off to Wales for safety – *he'd betrayed him*. The news was that Somerset had stolen out of Wales with a secret army of Lancastrians to rejoin their former sovereign whom, Somerset predicted, would soon be restored to England's throne.

Furious at having been duped, Edward reacted violently. He sent a strong force to Newcastle with orders to take Harry Beaufort dead or alive. The rebel Duke was almost caught there in his bed. But he escaped, barefoot, clad only in his shirt, and reached Bamburgh Castle – that fortress which Warwick had retaken only last year but which had been lost again by the treachery of Ralph Percy, the other pardoned rebel.

Edward raged against those two cousins of his whom he'd treated so generously and who had betrayed him. From the Bishop's Palace in York, he glowered out at the December sleet half-obscuring the windows. It was no season to take troops on a march further north, even if he had somewhere to garrison them at the end of that march. But to encamp them on the wild Northumbrian shore – *that* would be foolish generalship indeed. Yet his every instinct was to fling all his force against Somerset and Percy in Bamburgh – to have the traitors torn limb from limb when they were dragged out.

As calmly as he could he discussed the situation with

his Council. As he'd anticipated, the members' advice was: 'Your Grace, leave northern matters to the Nevilles.'

But his dependence upon his mother's kin was beginning to irritate him. Often, he'd wish that he could act independently of Warwick and Montagu. Yet he knew that he could not — not in a matter like this anyhow, which needed years of experience in northern campaigning such as only the Nevilles had: it was bred into their bones, damn them. And they'd go on being indispensable to the Crown. Especially Warwick — arrogant, patronising, didactic—

Suddenly Edward's furnace of rage, stoked against Somerset and Percy, blazed up around the inflexible figure of the Earl of Warwick, who told the King what to do and was always quite certain of being heeded — why, he'd even tell him in the end which wife he must wed! Well, Warwick could go to hell.

Edward remembered Elizabeth Woodville's lips brushing his fingers; the softness of the skin of her forearm, above the wrist, under the buttoned sleeve. He remembered also his envy of the two small boys pressed against her slim flanks — how much would he have given to be so close to her! These lustful memories became all one with his passion of rage against Warwick. He shook with the buffetings of his own emotions, and yet managed to hide them all behind an easy smile across the council table...

The arrival of an attendant in the chamber brought him back to present realities. The attendant carried in dispatches which had all arrived simultaneously in York only a few moments ago although sent out from three different parts of the realm.

The first reported an uprising in Wales, in those parts from which Somerset had drawn his secret army with whispers that 'the Lancastrian revival is nigh.'

The second told of severe disturbances in Gloucester; which county had, apparently, caught the Welsh fever of revolt. And the third detailed risings throughout Cambridgeshire...

'We ride west, then south,' the King said tightly, 'where we can handle matters without the Nevilles.'

Calling all loyal men to his side, and hunting out rebels left and right, he blazed through Denbighshire. Then leaving his kinsman, the Duke of Norfolk, to punish offenders there, he thundered over into the midlands.

Demons seemed to be urging him on. Through the worst of the January weather he rode from Coventry to Worcester in twenty-four hours; spent two feverish days in that city with his chief justices, whom he then hustled with him to Gloucester to conduct further trials of rebels.

Edward did not wait to see the execution sentences carried out. By February eleventh he was speeding over to Cambridge, to fall like a thunderbolt on the risers there against his peace. After that, even the new convulsions of revolt in Lancashire and Cheshire died down as the realm began to appreciate the fact that its amiable, handsome young King was ferocious when aroused.

In the sudden hush of restored order, Edward paused and looked about him. Spring was stirring; the weather mild – bright with a tender kind of radiance. St Valentine's Feast had come and gone without his even noting it. But now, all at once, he thought of love.

The thought took hold of him, totally. He became as obsessed by it as, for the past few months, he'd been obsessed by martial energy. He must see Elizabeth Woodville again. He must discover at least the mind behind that perfect face even though she should withhold her body from him. But maybe the surge of spring had touched her also and she would respond to him at last.

Taking only two gentlemen of his household with him, he rode over from Cambridge to Buckinghamshire.

Elizabeth Woodville had altered subtly. For one thing, she dressed fashionably now in gowns whose fur-trimmed necklines plunged to a point just above the high, tight cincture. For another, she was more confident and relaxed: suitor after suitor had found the path to Grafton Castle since she'd begun drawing rents from the late John Grey's properties, and this masculine attention had improved her outlook and appearance – even though she knew full well that, without the worldly goods which the King had restored to her, the suitors would be as absent as hitherto. This fact amused her. She had no intention of remarrying unless – unless an altogether unlikely proposal, of which she hardly dared think, came her way. Though no, it was impossible…

Yet the King had arrived here again today. And one of Elizabeth's' sisters – Catherine – had read his intent with probable accuracy.

'Saints, Bess,' Catherine had whispered while Edward was talking to their father, 'I do believe His Grace would like to – you know – with you.' Catherine Woodville had the limited vocabulary of the spinster.

'Make me his whore?' Elizabeth had supplied calmly. 'If that is so, then it is one royal wish which will never be gratified.'

'But – but Bess—' her sister's little bird-face had gone scarlet, ''tis said that all such women – I mean ladies – are marvellously wedded afterwards. And – *and that many of their kin are taken care of also.*' This last bit was brought out on a rush of breath.

'Catherine…' Level-eyed, Elizabeth had regarded her sister, 'I have said that I will help with your dowry once you've produced the bridegroom. This promise also holds good for our other four sisters. But let you all be certain of one thing: I will be no man's leman for your advantage – not even the King's if that be his mind. I already have all I ever wanted from His Grace, the reversion of Grey property.'

'You mean you'd refuse him – if he asked? And I believe he *will* ask, from the way he's been looking at you: so strained and sort of hungry—'

'Hungry for intelligent conversation,' Elizabeth had replied tartly. 'He said he wanted to discuss a book with me, "The Romance of the Saint Graal". We are to walk on the lower terrace later for this discussion... And Cath, there's to be no peering through windows. It's distracting.'

Catherine became plaintive. 'One can't see the lower terrace beyond the yew hedge from *any* window. I tried all of them when you were there with Sir Charles de Everingham. And – it's just impossible.'

'What a pity!' Elizabeth smiled. 'You missed his pantomime of how he slew ten Turks – although he's never been out of England.'

∼

For the first time in the three years of his reign, Edward felt no excitement about returning to London. Only Whittlewood Forest and Grafton Castle could stir his emotions now. The brief visit just ended had been joy and torment, elation and despair. Elizabeth had maintained her inscrutable distance. Yet he didn't believe that she was cold by nature. She was merely over-controlled by intelligence. Somehow he must break that control. Next time – *Next time...*

Yet the compulsion to see her again was not, for him, entirely physical. The sharpness of her mind had struck sparks from his own. He'd found himself talking to her not merely about books (she was more widely read than he was) but about all manner of things: ships and buildings and the state of the universities. On all matters she was either well informed or willing to be instructed.

She'd listened attentively to him as they'd walked in the spring garden. That beautiful voice of hers – which so pleased his own keen ear for music – had spoken little but even its occasional comment had shown a mind lively and tasteful, with a total absence of triviality. She felt she must concern herself only with lofty topics.

Himself perhaps, as England's King? But he did not know her mind in regard to himself; she'd kept the conversation impersonal. And those strange eyes of hers had given no sign of physical interest... What colour were her eyes? He felt almost panic-stricken that he might not have noted correctly. Ah yes, they were a silver-grey blue, a most unusual shade. And their lashes were unexpectedly dark in one so fair. That much at least he'd observed without boorishly staring.

He recognised that he must be subtle and civilised with this woman. No easy charm, no bull tactics would serve here. The few hours of her company had matured him by years. And he longed, now, to know the heights of his own potential – heights to which only *she* could point the way. Yet he'd had to separate himself from her; return to Westminster where, he knew, a Castilian delegation was awaiting him to make him a formal offer of royal Isabella's hand.

There'd been tears behind his eyes as he'd ridden off from Grafton in the soft spring twilight – the tears of a young man, hopelessly in love, who was not the master of his own destiny... Even further visits would be dictated by the little time allowed him away from his duties as King.

And by the vigilance of his mother, of Warwick, of all the people who so closely observed him as though he belonged to them, body and soul.

The blaze of anger he'd experienced in York was smouldering still. *He must have independence or he'd suffocate—*

Two days later at Westminster, the Castilian ambassador was shocked by his curt refusal of Isabella's hand.

'Your Grace,' said Alonso Pieres Martel sadly, 'let us pray that, should the Princess Isabella come to power in Castile, she will not remember your refusal of her as a slight, and turn her heart against England.'

'Speak to her fair words from us, señor,' Edward replied restlessly. 'Kings wed among their enemies, not their friends.'

Aye, if Warwick had his way, the King of England would yet wed in France.

5

April, 1464

Richard Neville, Earl of Warwick, warden of the west march and of the cinque ports, captain of Calais, was presiding over the evening meal at his castle of Middleham... Austerely handsome, with his long chiselled face and his dark copper hair just beginning to grey – he was thirty-seven – he sat tall and straight in the dais chair; every now and then sweeping the assembled multitude of his household with the intense scrutiny of a hunting eagle – this likeness to an eagle intensified by the narrow highbridged nose inherited from his great-grandsire, John of Gaunt.

The entire presence of the Earl was awesome and, even in quiescence, somehow dangerous. Pages went about their serving duties stiff with dread of making a mistake. Squires were meticulously well-behaved towards the damsels seated alongside them on the benches. Men-at-arms, and all other household members who ate in the

Great Hall, conducted themselves with extraordinary decorum. Even the dogs under the trestle tables were orderly tonight: they too being fully conscious that the lord of Middleham was at home…

He'd ridden hurriedly north for the peace-talks with Scotland as soon as he'd finished seeing the ambassadors of King Louis in London. The mainstream of the London talks had been about shipping, trade and anti-piracy laws. But the silent undercurrents had borne many other matters along. Subtle French threats against Calais. Subtle promises of a royal French bride for the English King.

Warwick had taken council with no one about these hints. He was aware of their implied flattery to his own power and intelligence: that in the end it was he and he alone who must decide his country's foreign policy.

On the way north he *had* decided. England would ally herself with France. Edward would wed one of Louis' sisters-in-law.

But he himself would not reveal his decision just yet. In the summer, he'd journey to France – ostensibly for more trade talks but in reality to hammer out an Anglo-French marriage treaty with clever Louis. Then, the details of dowry and alliance clear, he'd present Edward with a contract to sign.

It would all be done with the minimum of fuss and the maximum of advantage to England… Warwick knew that, since he'd learned to curb his own temper and impatience, he had become the best negotiator in the realm. He also knew that Louis of France, who had long waited to meet him and cultivate his friendship, would strive to please him in this matter, since there was nothing else Louis could bestow on a guest who already had everything in abundance: wealth, titles, power, fame… The slight muscle-twitch which served Richard Neville for a smile moved now beneath the taut tanned skin of his face. Yes, by the summer's end there'd be a lifetime's peace with France. And the Red Rose of Lancaster – still thrusting here in the north – would die for want of French nurturing.

This feast day of Saint Mark just gone, the Red Rose had lost one of its most vigorous shoots. Ralph Percy, commanding Lancastrian troops, had been slain in a pitched battle on Hedgely Moor by Warwick's brother John, Lord Montagu.

Warwick meditated now on the report of this rebel kinsman's death... It appeared that as Eleanor Neville's son lay dying on the moor, he'd cried out triumphantly: 'I have saved the bird in my bosom!'

What had Percy meant? – that he'd been true to ex-King Henry? Then he'd conveniently forgotten that in Henry's worst extremity he'd abandoned him and sworn allegiance to Edward; turning his coat yet again only after Somerset's rebellion... Still, no matter. He was dead now and his brother Harry was in the Fleet prison. Therefore the great Earldom of Northumberland was unclaimed. So it could be conferred on Lord Montague when the King came north again next month.

Even so, Warwick half wished that Edward would remain in the south. It cost a fortune to put the royal army on the move and he knew that Edward was seriously in debt already. To merchants and staplers of London and Calais. To the Church. To towns innumerable – Edward milked them all and then liberally poured away the proceeds... At the same time though, Warwick conceded, his royal cousin was learning about trade and profit on his own account. Edward had just shipped eight thousand woollen cloths to Italy. For these he should get a good return – as he was getting for most of his exporting ventures now, being lucky in that way. Then the French dowry should put him firmly on his financial feet. Yes, the dowry out of Louis' coffers would be very rich indeed.

Warwick relaxed his shoulder blades against the carved back of his chair. Things were improving slowly he decided after the terrible years of civil war – years which had cost himself a beloved father and brother and which had aged him in the service of the White Rose House. He'd placed the heir of that House upon the throne and had succeeded in holding the throne steady. Now, for the first time in the new reign he could say: 'I will go to France this summer' – and feel reasonably certain that no national crisis would prevent his doing so.

The only danger here in the north was that foxy Somerset still kept the border fortress which the late Ralph Percy had handed over to the Lancastrians. Well, when Edward arrived with the royal army, a major assault could be mounted. Writing from Kent a fortnight ago, Edward had been empathic that he did not intend to be excluded from this campaign; and that, above all else, he wanted his cousin of Somerset's blood.

It was now April thirtieth. The King would have left London two days ago. En route for Northampton and Leicester he'd stay a night at St Albans, a night at Stony Stratford... Calculating the probable date of the royal arrival in Yorkshire, Warwick stared out at the glorious spring-evening sky.

The April sunset light was shafting down from the high narrow windows along the west wall. It shone on the golden vessels and the snowy damask of the High Table where all manner of exotic dishes were being offered, carved, served and removed with the ordered rhythm of a religious service. It picked out the emblem of the earldom on the cloth behind the dais chair: the Bear and Ragged Staff of Warwick. It increased the splendour of the jewels and sumptuous fabrics which adorned the Middleham Nevilles and all their kin.

By the Earl's side sat his Countess; she who was a child-bride more than twenty years ago had brought him his titles and a great inheritance. Anne Beauchamp was a mild, petal-skinned little woman, inclining to plumpness in her mid-thirties. She'd borne her lord two daughters, Isobel and Anne, who were now eleven and eight years old respectively. But her failure to produce a son as heir to this most formidable of all the Nevilles left her in a state of constant vague anxiety. Her lord never blamed her – never spoke of the matter at all – but she always felt it was her fault that Richard Neville had no heir to his greatness... Yet, she sometimes thought wistfully, if only he'd unbend a little; smile occasionally; empty his crowded mind of wars and conferences in order to show interest in her small world, the resulting tenderness and understanding would help her to conceive a son.

But that hope was fading as her husband was increasingly away on the King's business; and so she'd taken to mothering the many boys who served and trained here at Middleham. Particularly she kept an eye on young Dickon, Duke of Gloucester, the King's brother. Dickon seemed silently devoted to Anne, the younger and more fragile of her daughters. And he had many qualities she would have liked in a son of her own: a quiet intelligence, a gentleness which did not lessen his courage.

She knew she herself had little courage. She was easily frightened, and fear left her no pride. Whatever bravery she might have been born with had been taken from her in childhood by her terrible father, the old Earl of Warwick – he who'd been guardian to the boy-King Henry and who'd broken that young spirit also... On her father's death, Anne Beauchamp had gone to live with her brother, the new Earl, whom she'd loved. But he'd died soon after her betrothal to Richard Neville. So she and the Warwick title had come here to Middleham.

The great Earl and Countess of Salisbury were lord and lady of Middleham Castle at that time; strong, dependable people on whose generous love the young heiress had leaned. They'd protected her from all harm, all worry. They'd even protected her from their own riotous brood of four sons and six daughters until the day when she'd had to set up her own household in Warwick Castle for her husband, the eldest of those sons... Richard had returned from France a restless, self-sufficient youth. His abiding passions had been then — as now — war and politics. She'd been bitterly unhappy with him in Warwick Castle and had begged to be brought back to Middleham. Since when, she'd prayed never to have to leave here again.

For she had no ambition to be one of those women — like her husband's godmother and aunt, Cecily Neville — who'd seldom asked anything more than to travel with their lords. Anne Beauchamp wanted only the sentried walls of Middleham; its chapel where she could meditate and listen to the choristers; its Presence Chamber and Great Hall which became almost royal settings when Richard was here.

She turned now to ask him how long he'd be staying but found that he was leaning across to his left, talking about the growing scarcity of coins in the realm with Sir William Hastings, his brother-in-law, who was Master of the Royal Mint... Two years ago, Sir William had married Richard's sister Katherine, the widow of Lord Bonville. They'd been childhood sweethearts here in Middleham, and they seemed very happy here together again now. So the Countess Anne had tried to put out of her mind a scene she'd come upon lately in the South Tower corridor:

Sir William leading a pretty serving-wench into a storeroom for which he had the key... She'd heard the lock turned from the inside; and the girl giggling while Sir William bade her to hush.

She'd had difficulty in looking at the man ever since. So she turned aside now from both him and her lord, and indicated to a hovering page that she'd have a piece of multi-coloured marchpane... While she spooned at the sweet, she tried to excuse again her own inaction that day in the South Tower. She told herself that a handsome man of the world like William Hastings must occasionally succumb to a young girl's charms. Probably Katherine Neville even knew that he did – the thirty-year-old wife had hinted as much and seemed unconcerned. But what really disturbed the Countess was the knowledge that Hastings had become one of the King's closest friends. If Edward were not already degenerate – and many said that he was – then it was men like Hastings who would lead him into greater excesses than he was already reputed to practise...

She'd dreamed last night of the King: that he was racing, heedless and exultant, through a thorny wood which tore the clothes from his back, the flesh from his bones. And when he was naked and all bloodied, he flung himself down under an oak tree in a clearing where thirteen cloaked figures – one with antler horns on its head – gazed upon him without pity.

Trembling, she'd awakened to find a strangely red-hued moon shining in on her bed; its beam spearing the empty place where her lord would lie tonight...

In his room under the eaves, Dickon too was looking at the moon. He was too excited to sleep. For this evening the Earl of Warwick had told him that he'd be travelling to France in the summer as part of the great retinue which was to accompany the Earl when he visited King Louis.

France, Dickon thought – that legendary land! His own father had first journeyed there when he'd been little older than Dickon was now, and the country had claimed half his lifetime... The Duchess Cecily had often told her youngest son about his father's military career in France in the days of Jeanne d'Arc; and about her own marriage to the Duke of York in Rouen and their subsequent life there together. Dickon felt he knew the north of France almost as well as the north of England.

His only present disappointment was that Warwick would not be leading an army there this summer; merely a retinue of about eight hundred people, to show King Louis how wealthy and powerful he was. Still, as an excuse for foreign travel, it would do. And some time would be spent in London en route, so that Dickon would be able to see his mother and other members of his family.

He recalled now how much he used to miss his mother – with a heartsickness which her frequent loving letters made worse rather than better – when he'd first come to Middleham. Just as he'd missed her in Burgundy and cried himself to sleep there many a night! But he'd been a child then, not a young man who'd be twelve this October and who'd already ridden the marches countless times and even been to sea in Uncle William's fleet—

Crossing himself, he offered a brief prayer for the repose of Lord Fauconberg's soul. That valiant little Neville had died in November; leaving one bastard son, Thomas; and a wife who, though mad since childhood, had recently been taken in marriage by another lord, greedy for her inheritance... Poor Aunt Joan Fauconberg, few ever saw her: she was kept permanently locked up in Skelton Castle. But Thomas the Bastard had taken Dickon to visit her once, and she'd kept asking: 'Nephew, have you a girl? And do you love her?' – until Dickon's very toes had curled with embarrassment... But now, looking at the moon, he could admit to himself that he had a girl's name chiselled on his heart: that of his cousin Anne, the second of the Neville daughters. He wondered what she'd say when he told her he was going to France. Nothing, probably. Unlike her sister Isobel, Anne was a very quiet shy child. But Dickon had learned how to be still with her and not frighten her away.

6

May Day, 1464

FULL MOONLIGHT TOUCHED the treetops of Whittlewood Forest but could not penetrate its depths. April leaves were still small and tender; and down in the shadowed places, the shrub roots were already hidden under the thrusting lances of spring: bluebell and anemone and wild garlic. These dark sappy forms speared out of the darker earth between narrow secret paths and gave forth a crushed smell as though they'd been lately trodden by many feet. Yet, people seldom came walking this way – there'd been a nameless fear of the place in the local consciousness since time out of mind.

A denser blackness became apparent only because it moved purposefully towards the heart of the forest – a blackness whose outline was as undefined as that of flowing water until the white lining of a cloak caught on a briar. A woman's slim hand reached out, trying to wrench the lining free.

'I – am – caught – fast.' The words seemed forced between teeth clenched in irritation.

'Oh, do be still,' commanded another, older voice. 'Let me attend to it.' Claw-like fingers darted at the briar. The ensuing struggle with the fabric was accompanied by mutterings in French. These ended with a triumphant 'Voilà' as the silk parted from the thorns.

The older woman straightened up. She was smaller of stature than her companion, who had not bent to help her. 'Let us go on, daughter,' she said. 'We must be there before the moon is at her zenith.'

'I do not wish to go on.' The tone was cold, dispassionate; and its owner stood motionless.

'But you must – *you must*. The Other Ones will be foregathered by now, waiting. It would be lunacy to offend Them. They can be dangerous, Elizabeth.'

Slowly, Elizabeth Woodville turned her face towards her mother. It was a face of finely carved ivory in the filtered light; and the eyes were hidden under waxen lids as they focussed, without lowering of the head, on Jacquetta's shrunken figure. 'Dangerous!' Elizabeth scoffed. 'They who *themselves* quake for fear of discovery and death by fire... Mayhap you too ought to think on these ends, my mother, for you have a wide reputation as a witch.'

'I have had it for most of my life,' Jacquetta snapped, 'and am still unburnt. Now, are you going to accompany me?'

'Oh, I suppose I have come this far. But I tell you it is both useless and unnecessary.' Flinging the points of the black velvet cloak around her slim neck, Elizabeth held them there with her arms crossed over her breasts and began suddenly to walk swiftly onward.

'Daughter—' Jacquetta stumbled after her '—daughter, I beg you not to call what we do *useless*. Especially not here among the sacred trees...' Her gaze, out of oddly slanted eyes, strained upward at the ancient towering deities of Whittlewood. With a curious, reverential gesture – as though to placate them – she touched some of their trunks as she hurried by.

'Very well: unnecessary then,' Elizabeth said over her shoulder.

'B-but no woman can be quite certain of a man, *ever*,' her mother panted. 'So nothing is unnecessary that – that brings him more surely to the point...' She could still remember some of her own more extravagant wiles to attract the royal widower John, Duke of Bedford, long ago...

The point, Elizabeth thought, mercilessly increasing her pace. The point of marriage – God, did any unveiled woman, virgin or widow, ever think of aught else? She was weary of hearing her sisters go on about it. For her own part, she had considered and firmly rejected it. She knew she was cold by nature – or perhaps by self-protective instinct. For the knowledge had been acquired with considerable pain in John Grey's bed before the birth of her first child. After that, the pain had given way to boredom. And it was a boredom she'd had no intention of reliving with any of the suitors who came to Grafton. Until recently, when the King himself had begun to pay frequent visits. Only then had the idea of remarriage become linked in her mind with a dizzying ambition...

The King accounted her frigidity as modesty and virtue. It was this challenge to his wooing which was sending him almost insane from a passion of lust for her body.

She knew the exact degree of that lust. She had assessed it in every quiver of his flesh when he came near her. And, physically detached but with interest sharpened, she'd watched his increasing anguish since the first time he'd visited Grafton this year, in mid-February.

He'd come five times more since then. Always in secret, attended by only one or two close-lipped companions. On all six occasions, Elizabeth had maintained her cool remoteness from his growing ardour. It was easy. She felt nothing. No tiniest spark of his passion penetrated her own body. But her brain had begun to probe the advantages of the unlikely situation: Edward, the irresistible bachelor-King, thwarted in carnal desire! It was said that no woman he wanted had ever refused him. Now, he was obsessed by the notion of possessing one who always sidestepped him...

As Elizabeth moved deeper into the forest, with her mother padding along behind her, she pressed her crossed arms over her breasts and held the cloak ends tight against her throat. Dark velvet against skin of silver whiteness – it seemed that that was what had riveted Edward's gaze two visits ago, when she'd worn a pine-green gown to receive him. He'd muttered something about a childhood dream of 'a fair woman swathed in darkness'. Then – terrifyingly, and without the slightest warning – he was holding a dagger to that slim pale throat which he so admired; swearing to slit it if she did not lie with him, there, at once, in the deserted spring gardens of Grafton.

It was the threat of a madman; a man mad with love. She could still see the leonine muscles of his face and neck; feel his strength, and the iron hardness of his left arm pressing into the curve of her back, bending her over like a sapling – the cold threat of the blade against her stretched neck—

'Lie with me, Elizabeth.'

She'd been already half-lying at the time, along his thigh and against his powerful arm. Her vision had dissolved into the famous blaze of gold that was his hair. Yet still she'd remained uninvolved in his urgent passion except where it touched her life and pride. Her only desire had been to survive and – *to win the royal marriage game.* She'd kept a grip on consciousness to gasp: 'My lord – I know myself unworthy to be a queen – but I value mine honour more than to be a concubine.'

It was her first open statement of intent! She would be Queen of England or die.

Shaken, Edward had pulled her upright. Then he'd sheathed his dagger and gone striding off to where his horse waited. Like one pursued by demons, he'd galloped out of Grafton without a word or a backward glance.

Listening to the wild hooves' pounding, Elizabeth had had a severe loss of confidence. What if she'd overplayed her hand and thrown everything away? Suddenly she was aware of how cold she was. Her teeth were chattering and she'd felt so weak and dizzy that she'd done an unaccustomed thing: she'd gone to her mother for comfort.

Jacquetta's decision, forced upon her that feverish night, had been to call together the Circle of Other Ones, here in Whittlewood, on Elizabeth's behalf...

After twelve nights of rituals in the forest, the King had come back to Grafton today. He was dazed (from lack of sleep, he'd said, because nightmares had awoken him through every hour of darkness). He was also subdued: the deep humility of love's dependence had entered his soul. He vowed never more to assault the chastity of the Lady Elizabeth outside an honourable marriage bed.

He promised to come again – tomorrow morning very early – before setting out with his army for Northampton. Elizabeth was to have a priest and a chorister waiting in Grafton's chapel, with two witnesses who could be relied upon not to speak of the secret marriage until the King himself was ready to announce it. Which might not be for some weeks – months even. It was a delicate business, Elizabeth must understand...

She understood it well enough to know that he might not come at all. Between today and tomorrow, anything could happen to alter his mind. And this mummery in the forest now could have no influence upon a man who slept five miles away at Stony Stratford.

Yet, tonight was to be enacted the thirteenth ritual. And it was the last night of April: May Eve, the most powerful calling-time of the old, almost forgotten gods... The climax of the wishing ceremonies would be reached when the antler crown was donned by the Nameless One, and fresh blood poured by him onto oak roots.

Elizabeth knew that her own presence here tonight was vital, to give physical focus to the concentrated wishing of the Other Ones. She would stand naked in the glade where the moonlight speared down; and the Nameless One would give her the fivefold kiss, on all the parts of her body most desirable to man... No longer could Jacquetta act as proxy for her daughter as she'd done on the previous twelve nights, holding the unwashed garments that had intimately touched Elizabeth's skin – garments sewn with hairs from Edward's head, in a crescent shape, around a fragment of his fingernail.

To be discovered practising this rite of a primeval religion was to die by fire.

～

THE MOON HAD SLID down the sky, leaving a dense darkness in the hour before the early dawn of May Day.

The King's body-squire came from the kitchen of the inn where His Grace always lodged when he was in Stony

Stratford. The squire carried a ewer of hot water for the royal shaving. To his surprise, he found his master already energetically astir in the candlelit chamber.

'Quick, lad,' the King commanded, 'I want to be in the forest by first light. But take care you don't nick me today or I'll have your head.'

When the fair stubble was removed, Edward's squire washed him all over and rubbed him dry; then helped him into a clean shirt and longhose, and brushed his hair for him. For a moment, Edward looked like a burnished archangel. But the swift putting on of old scuffed-leather hunting clothes – doublet and belt, boots and gloves, short mantle and cap – dimmed the celestial quality. In blackish-brown leather, Edward's tall broad-shouldered figure became as inconspicuous as it could ever be. 'Right. Now see that my horse is ready. And tell the groom I want no one with me today.'

When the squire had sped from the room, Edward unlocked a small casket and removed from it a gold ring set with an emerald. This he placed in his gipsire. Then, humming to himself, he went down the yard of the inn. The stable lanterns were still lit there although a pearly gleam was creeping up the eastern sky. This fusion of two lights gave everything an unreal quality. But Edward had had a sense of unreality since yesterday morning. He'd felt lightheaded from the moment he'd made that reckless promise to Elizabeth—

'Tell my lord Herbert to await me in a couple of hours,' he shouted over his shoulder now as he mounted, but even his voice didn't seem to belong to him

The groom and the body-squire stood looking after him admiringly as he rode away with two hounds at his heels. Many great lords were so precious of their persons that they never went anywhere alone. But the King? Well, King Edward was a law unto himself...

The pearly light had intensified to shell pink by the time he neared Grafton Castle. Long clouds that had been grey were now undershot with pale flame. It was a wonderful morning, dewy and fresh. Suddenly, he allowed every fibre of his being to respond to its glory in a way which, he believed, older men forgot how to do... Why, he was young – *young*, and tingling with life and with love. Let the greybeards shake their heads at what he was about to do: marry the woman he adored and defy Warwick, both at one stroke! His life was beginning this May morning. The past was dropping away. Many things in it must be committed to limbo – particular that other, unlucky marriage. But no need even to think of that. No one would talk. Robert Stillington had been promised the comfortable bishopric of Bath and Wells as soon as it became vacant so he'd be the last one to cry 'Bigamy!' And he was the only one with *personal* knowledge of what had taken place at Wigmore except the Lady Eleanor Butler herself, who'd vowed silence...

A screech-owl swished out of a tree to grab some small animal that squeaked despairingly. A hare started up, with an almost human scream, before the dogs. Edward frowned. Even in its splendour, nature was merciless and granted no right of appeal. Life was short, ruled by fear... For an instant, he acknowledged fear within himself. Fear of his mother's censure – of Warwick's rage – of all the discomforts and embarrassments and deprivations which might lie ahead after this day's work... Then he thought of Elizabeth and he smiled with a radiant tenderness. Soul and body, he adored her now. Separated from her – her beauty, her wit, her quick and cultured mind – there could be no life for him. And the gift of life was worth any sacrifice, any gamble...

He reined his horse quietly before the castle gate. There seemed to be no one about – no porter, no sentry. Everywhere looked deserted. Then he espied Elizabeth's elegant brother Anthony, Lord Scales, waiting to do humble groom's service to the King for the sake of secrecy.

Jacquetta appeared at the castle's main door with two of her household women. 'Your Grace,' she whispered, 'these are the witnesses, most silent and trustworthy. So let us straightaway to the chapel.'

Apart from the bride and groom, the bride's mother and the two women witnesses, there was only the priest in the private chapel, and a young man who helped with the brief singing.

The ceremony was soon over. The emerald ring gleamed on Elizabeth's finger. Then bride and groom were quietly mounting the stairs together towards the bedchamber whose door was visible from below.

The door was ajar. Edward saw that the room within was dark, shuttered against the morning light. For a moment he felt trapped by that darkness, as though he were walking towards a dungeon—

Then Elizabeth began to light candles. But he stopped her at the second one – took her ravenously in his arms... The trapped sensation left him. And he felt free, like a god, as her wonderful hair spilt over his hands from the tossed-away hennin and veil.

In an hour, the King was gone from Grafton.

Catherine Woodville, carrying a tray of wine and wafers, tiptoed into her sister's room and stood a moment sniffing the unfamiliar air there: the smell of male sweat—

'Open the shutters,' Elizabeth said.

When Catherine had done so, sunlight flooded in.

Apprehensively she turned to look at her sister, who was lying quietly on the bed with the coverings drawn up to her bare shoulders.

'B-Bess, are you all right?'

Elizabeth seemed not to hear her. She was studying the bed-canopy and winding a strand of her loosened hair around and around her wedding-ring... After a long while, she replied with objective calm:

'Oh yes, I am very well. So too, eventually, shall you be, Cath. And Nan, Meg, Nell, Mary and all our kin.'

'How soon?' Catherine breathed, leaning forward onto the bed.

'As soon as I am acknowledged Queen of England. Though that may not be for some time, I believe. For His Grace will need an extra store of courage to admit that he has taken a wife unapproved by his Council!'

7

Sᴇᴘᴛᴇᴍʙᴇʀ, *1464*

Rᴀʀᴇʟʏ ᴅɪᴅ the Duchess of York lose her temper. But on this September day as she rode from London to Reading, Cecily had been in a simmering rage since the previous night. Now – from the set of her handsome face and the travelling speed she demanded from her horse – her harassed attendants knew that a cataclysmic outburst was inevitable the moment she met the King.

Yesterday, at the meeting of his Council in Reading Abbey, Edward had been forced into an announcement which had stunned all who heard it... The council members had been pressing him to wed the French King's sister-in-law, as Warwick desired him to do – Warwick having returned from Calais in August and being due to re-cross the Narrow Seas in a few days with a definite answer for Louis.

Edward knew that he was cornered at last: even the King of England dared not send his mightiest subject on a wild-goose chase. So, reluctantly, he made his announcement at the council table: that he'd wedded Elizabeth Woodville-Grey five months previously.

While the news was speeded to all corners of the realm – Cecily being the first person in London to hear it – a storm of protest was fairly shaking the King at Reading Abbey for 'this most indiscreet marriage'.

'With a *widow*,' some lords shouted, 'and a Lancastrian widow at that, when Your Grace should have taken a virgin consort!'

'So much older than yourself, Sire, too,' others shook their heads. 'She may not be able to bear healthy children.'

'And sprung of an obscure family—' still others raged '—sired by a commoner. A family with no wealth, no powerful connections! Ah, woe for a foreign alliance thrown away—'

With a gesture of intense impatience, Edward strode from the chamber and went to his private apartments. God knew, he'd need to knit up his nerves before the meeting with his mother which, he surmised, would not be long delayed. Cecily would set out from Baynard's Castle the moment she heard of the announcement. And there'd be a scene to end all scenes between them!

It took place late the following evening. Edward had again retired to the guest apartments when his mother's arrival at the Abbey was announced to him.

'Escort Her Grace of York to us here,' he ordered. 'Then see that all others withdraw from us.'

There was no need for the latter part of the order. Everyone was already putting a discreet distance between themselves and the battle site. Like small animals at the approach of warring lions, servants were fleeing. And even the King's lords-attendant were suddenly remembering urgent business elsewhere. By the time the Lord Abbot had personally escorted Cecily to her royal son's chambers, all the passageways of the huge Benedictine House were deserted, all doors closed. Never had the Great Silence, which the Order maintained from sunset to dawn, seemed so tangible... The last sound any would-be eavesdropper heard was the slamming and locking of the royal apartment doors from the inside, after Cecily had gone through and been curtly greeted by her son.

George of Clarence was one such eavesdropper although he hadn't planned to be – the idea would have terrified him. But he'd been in Edward's closet – having just relieved himself in the adjoining garderobe – when he'd overheard the announcement of his mother's arrival and the scurrying away of feet in all directions. He'd had no desire to meet his formidable mother in the mood he anticipated she'd be in. Nor, suddenly, had he any wish to come out of the closet into a room empty of everyone except Edward. So he'd crouched down between the canvas bath-screen and a row of scented, colourful mantles that were hanging up to have their creases removed by steam. There, his ear was quite close to the doorjamb. Through the crack, he could see the candlelight from the main royal apartment.

A shadow blocked out the light for an instant. Someone had swiftly crossed the room. He heard his mother's voice, sharp, say: 'Edward, I will come straight to the point.'

The King growled in reply something that sounded like: 'So long as you maintain a reasonable tone.' After that, Cecily's voice dropped a little so that George failed to catch all her words although he could detect the vibrancy of her anger throughout... The King was replying in grunts and growls – occasionally a sharp roar to which Cecily would retort on a higher note than the pulsing undertone she'd been using. At those times,

George could hear clearly his mother's utterances. Once, she said:

'Married, indeed! Edward, you know this to be no marriage.' And again,

'If you have children by this woman, *they* will reap a harvest of disaster even if you do not.'

And finally, in great agitation after some reference to 'bigamy' and 'illegitimacy': 'Edward – Edward, you must admit the *real* truth before the present charade goes any further.'

Now the King's answer came like a thunderclap: 'Madame, be silent. My consort is on her way here to Reading. The Duchess of York will do as everyone else will do if they're wise: *acknowledge her as Queen.*'

There was a moment of utter silence. Then, with the ring of steel in her voice, Cecily said: 'The Duchess of York will not even *meet* this latest paramour of the King's. Sire, unlock the doors for me at once that I may depart from hence.'

Edward yelled at her: 'Then you refuse to meet the Queen?'

And Cecily shouted back: 'England *has* no Queen!'

'Except yourself perhaps?' he continued furiously. 'So often the first lady of the realm that now, demoted, you are wild with jealousy?'

In the pause that followed, George could imagine his mother's tall, straight figure freezing into an icicle of contempt. Then he heard her final words to the King – sad rather than angry:

'Edward, may God take pity upon your foolishness.'

It was a prayer which the King's cousin Harry Bourchier, Earl of Essex and Treasurer of England, was to echo in his heart on the following day when he was present at the interview between Warwick and the King.

Warwick's reaction to the royal marriage announcement had been (on the surface at least) much calmer than his Aunt Cecily's. But though more tightly reined, it might well be more sinisterly dangerous.

'My lord,' the Earl of Warwick finally said with restrained reproach to Edward, 'you have made me appear a fool before all the Courts of Europe.'

Edward's response was aggressive. 'If you *do* appear so, cousin,' he replied, 'it is by your own high-handedness. I gave you no leave to treat for Bona of Savoy on my behalf. But then, with equal lack of leave two years ago, you offered me to Mary of Gueldres, did you not? – the Scottish whore for England's King!'

Warwick's lips compressed themselves into a straight colourless line. He could not deny that he'd treated with the widowed Regent of Scotland for a royal English marriage although the morals of young King James' late mother had left much to be desired... Silently turning on his heel now, he quit Edward's presence.

Edward shrugged; then said to Essex who alone had been witness to the interview with Warwick: 'Oh, he'll outlive his anger with me, don't worry. He *must*, for I am his life's work – what else can he do?'

Essex made no reply. He was already turning over in his mind some rumours that had blown lately from France – where English affairs were always so much better known than in England! France had been saying, a whole month ago, that Edward was already wed. And that the overmighty subject who'd made him King might *un*make him as a result, and have himself crowned in his place... 'If this should come about—' French Louis was reported to have murmured on being told of the rumours '—then we might consider *helping* Monsieur de Warwick.'

Still, not even a complaint had come yet from Louis

over the rejection of his sister-in-law. Doubtless he was biding his time to see what would happen – not for nothing was he known as 'the spider' – so Edward best be most careful...

'I know what I will do,' Edward said suddenly. 'Something which will put my Neville cousin in a better mood.'

'What, my lord?' Essex asked.

'Why—' Edward brought his palms down noisily on his thighs '—I'll nominate his clever brother George for the vacant Archbishopric of York! The new Pope will accept my nomination without question. And that will delight *all* the Nevilles – even my lady mother. They've never had an Archbishop within their ranks before; merely a Prince of Durham...'

Speechless, Henry Bourchier stared at the beaming Edward. The King had the air of a man who'd found the solution to a small problem which could now be put out of mind... *Blood of God,* Bourchier thought, *he hasn't the least conception of how much offence he's given to Warwick, or of how deep must be the wound in that unyielding pride!*

It was true that the King's own ability to pardon and forget often blinded him to the very different natures of others. Now it seemed he imagined that the Archbishopric of York for George Neville, and the recently bestowed Earldom of Northumberland on John, were acknowledgements enough to appease their elder brother whom he had publicly spurned...

And it appeared that the King was right. For, on Michaelmas Day, Warwick was in the beautiful Norman chapel of Reading Abbey (where John of Gaunt had wed Blanche of Lancaster in 1359) when Elizabeth Woodville arrived there in great state. Warwick even went out to escort her into the chapel – young George of Clarence being on her other side – and he became the first baron of the realm to do her homage as Queen; his chiselled face betraying no more emotion than did hers... Neither did he flinch during the announcement which Edward made immediately afterwards: that one of the Queen's sisters, Margaret Woodville, was now betrothed to the heir of Earl of Arundel. But Warwick knew, as did everyone else who heard, that this was but one upward step of many which the Woodvilles would make; and that the crowding out of the Nevilles had begun. In future, the Nevilles would have to step back several paces; or *fight*.

Edward rejoiced in the buzz of speculation thus caused: people's attention was being diverted by it from other more controversial matters... For one thing, he'd recently altered the currency; and the new coins, of unfamiliar aspect, had greatly upset everyone. There'd been a flood of complaints, accusations of cheating, demands for recompense, and a vast increase in the illegal export of precious metals... For another, he was fighting to maintain this cherished friendship with Philip of Burgundy in the teeth of Burgundian sanctions against English cloth. All English merchants were incensed at Duke Philip for these new laws, so that Edward had to hide his own affection for the good Duke who had sheltered him – and, later, his brothers – in exile... But the biggest issue which Edward wanted screened from public view was that moneys voted by the Church for a papal crusade against the Turks had (by an Act of God: the death of the crusading Pope) found their way into his own bottomless purse.

Therefore, the more the lords, commons, merchants and clergy gossiped about himself and the Woodvilles, the more cheerful he became. He'd always been lucky. Now his marriage to Elizabeth was turning out to be the luckiest event of his life – quite apart from the fact that he was falling more and more under the spell of her beauty and her intelligence every day... As were the common people, it seemed. *They'd* been perversely pleased when the news of his marriage filtered through to them. For it appeared to them that one of themselves had been chosen as wife by the King whom they loved. Edward had followed his own heart in the matter, they said. And at least he'd wedded an Englishwoman – not some foreigner who might bring as great trouble to the realm as Margaret of Anjou had done!

The royal couple moved to the palace of Eltham for Christmas. There, Edward showered gifts on everyone with a prodigal hand. But particularly on his well-beloved wife to whom he granted lands worth 4,000 marks a year, his manor of pleasance at Greenwich and his manor at Shene. He also gave her a London residence, the great house in Giltspur Street known as Ormonde's Inn.

Afterwards, when the twelve days of Christmas feasting were about to give way to the tedious gloom of January, he ordered the most lavish preparations to be put in hand for Elizabeth's crowning early in the summer. There was nothing like a forthcoming coronation, he believed, for keeping people in good humour. And happy subjects were the easiest governed.

But the King's mother was far from happy... Since September, Cecily had lived through a nightmare of indecision: whether to maintain her silence, or to denounce Edward's marriage as invalid before any child was conceived of it.

She felt that events had outpaced her. For all she knew – cut off as she was now from all but the most formal intercourse with her son – Elizabeth might be already pregnant although there was no sign in that willow-slim figure.

Then, always, the royal pair seemed so merry together: would Edward ever find such contentment again? Cecily shrank from rending the rich happiness which was so evident to all. And things were settling down now after the uproar: the commons were delighted by their Queen's beauty, the lords reluctantly charmed by her aloof dignity. Also, more important embassies were being sent into England these days than ever before – clearly, foreign rulers were not only unperturbed by what had happened, but were pleased that no marriage alliance had been formed between England and their own enemies.

For Cecily to state publicly at this late date that the royal union was invalid and bigamous would be tantamount to toppling the throne – to destroying Edward and the possibility of his returning friendship for herself... No, she'd seen enough destruction in fifty years of her life; she'd suffered enough loss. So she'd remain silent, and pray that no child be born to Elizabeth. That way, George of Clarence would continue to be regarded as heir apparent to Edward.

Cecily had ascertained that the real heir – Eleanor Butler's son, born prematurely in the August of 1461 – was now being fostered by humble parents near Wigmore, the place where he'd been conceived; and that his heartbroken mother had retired to the Carmelite House at Norwich as soon as news had reached her of Edward's union with Elizabeth Woodville – until then, she'd gone on hoping that he'd acknowledge her and the boy... Cecily's informant further reported that the Lady Eleanor was in fragile health and had fallen into a melancholy; that nothing now remained of the vital Talbot spirit which had made her the benefactress of Corpus Christi College, Cambridge, where she'd been well known for her learning.

Yet, however soon great Talbot's daughter might quit this world entirely, the fact was unalterable that she'd been alive, and still legally Edward's wife, when the May Day marriage service had been performed at Grafton. Therefore that marriage was null and void; and no child born of it could legitimately inherit the crown from its sire.

Wearily, Cecily went over and over the whole wretched business but could see no solution for Edward. Heedless and reckless, he'd done what he'd wanted to do, and only mature years would show him the folly of it.

She was relieved to think that she herself was unlikely to be alive when the issue finally had to be faced. Edward was only in his early twenties yet. A young King of such robust constitution as his must be able to look forward to a very long reign, with little danger even of being called to arms in a country where peace was becoming more stabilised from month to month... The battle of Hexham last year had weeded out several other Lancastrian rebels besides Somerset. All had been executed. Now remained at large only Henry of Lancaster himself.

No one knew exactly where Henry was except that the north-country must be harbouring him because the Scots no longer dared do so.

Saint Edward's Crown would never be securely Yorkist while Henry of Lancaster was free. Therefore, there were armed riders out seeking him at all times – Yorkist gold in their saddlebags with which to tempt would-be informers.

8

July, 1465

THERE WAS nothing to distinguish the robed figure, walking in the cloisters of Furness Abbey, from any of the other monks except that this one seemed to be so much less of the world than they... They gossiped: he kept apart and was silent. His gaze was fixed abstractedly upon the worn flagstones. His shoulders were hunched so that the black cowl shuttered off any roundness of vision he might have enjoyed: the marvellous stonework of the arches carved three centuries ago in Stephen's reign or the lift of the summer sky beyond, over the Abbey's hill pastures and forest lands which extended from Lake Windermere to Coniston Water.

Henry of Lancaster, the deposed King of England, felt no desire to raise his gaze from the safe smooth flagstones, nor even to glance beyond the walls which now sheltered him. Sometimes, when his mind was more than usually clouded, he thought he'd always been a monk in this

Abbey; that nearly forty years of kingship had been but a dream – a dream turning into a nightmare of being the quarry in a relentless hunt... Then his memory would clear and it was the tranquil present that became unreal, utterly without sensation; his feelings responding only to those events whose memory tormented him.

How often had he started from sleep, to stumble panic-stricken through darkness – cold – days without food – until some other temporary refuge was offered? How many times had the skin of his feet healed and split again, lacerated by ice or stones or the harsh heathers of moor or fell? And, oh sweet Jesu, how far had he travelled in all, to and fro and around and around? Scotland. Northumberland. Durham. Yorkshire. Westmorland...

Left to himself, he'd have given up long ago. The constant terror which he suffered was an overwhelming agony, making his heart beat as though to burst, even in a peaceful place like this. So that sometimes he prayed for capture, an end to the pain of fear... It was a pain he'd known intimately since boyhood when the old Earl of Warwick – long since dead – had been his guardian and used to beat him with a birch-rod. He still prayed for the repose of the Earl's soul.

Henry had never been a brave man. Never a robust one. Nor even a good traveller – in all the years of his reign he'd rarely moved outside the Home Counties. The longing for quiet and immobility had always been with him: a monk's cell, some holy books and his beads, with long periods of sleep that was more than a sleep – he'd have asked nothing else of life if God had not called him to the turmoil of sovereignty.

But God *had* called him. Almost before he was out of his cradle, his mighty sire, King Henry the Fifth, had died in France. And that same inscrutable God who eventually cast him forth into the wilderness was now lending him brave friends who daily risked their lives to save his, so that Margaret's son might succeed to a crown which Lancaster had never relinquished.

Margaret; his heart ached for her every day of her absence. How long now since she'd last gone away, taking the young Prince with her? Henry could not remember. Except that he'd been in Scotland at the time. And that he'd wept on her breast when she'd bidden him farewell — as though he were a small child again being torn from his mother, Queen Catherine, not a middle-aged man saying goodbye to a wife who promised to return in the springtime.

Margaret hadn't come back. He'd waited and hoped and prayed but she hadn't come... Kind people had explained to him, very patiently, that she was gathering another army abroad; that she was seeking aid from Burgundy, Brittany, France — from anyone who'd help her and the band of English exiles with her in her father's lands. But these negotiations took time, Henry must try to understand... Meanwhile, he himself must cooperate with those who strove to keep him out of Yorkist hands, because his capture would be the doom of Margaret's hopes.

So he'd done as he was told by the few faithful friends who still remained with him: old Doctor Thomas Mannyng, once Dean of Windsor; garrulous John Bedon, a Doctor of Divinity; Isiah Ellerton, a former groom of the royal stables. The circle of friends was very small now, since last year's disasters at Hedgely Moor and at Hexham, with the many executions which had followed the latter battle. Yet there were still lords and abbots of great houses in the north-country who'd lodge the ex-King for a while if he could be smuggled inside their gates—

Henry's heart gave a painful leap. He'd been a goodly

time here now at Furness Abbey. Very soon, he felt, it would be suggested – as it always *was* suggested, either by his own friends or by his hosts – that he move on again.

His very soul cried out in anguish at the idea of another uprooting – another journey with all its pains and terrors. Yet it was he himself who'd asked to leave the comparative safety of Scotland... For some reason, he'd grown anxious and fearful there; homesick to the point of being physically ill. So he'd begged the Scots to let him return across the border. And they'd let him go with such alacrity that he'd realised what an embarrassment he'd been to them.

Long periods of hiding had followed in various fortresses held by the Lancastrians. He'd been treated with great reverence by all the commanders; had been asked to receive back men like Somerset and Percy who'd broken their oaths of fealty to him but were then repentant. And he'd presided over the war-councils whose proceedings he had not understood – often with the noise of the besiegers from without confusing him still further... It was at one of those meetings – in Bywell Castle – that he was so nearly caught, he'd left his jewelled cap of estate behind when he'd fled. That cap (garnished with two crowns of gold, and fret with pearls and rich stones) had been the last item of his kingly regalia. And he'd heard, much later, what had become of it...

Lord Montagu had taken it to Edward of York, who was then in the hilly town of Pontefract. Edward, looking at it, had said with a burst of passion:

'Would that Henry's head were inside of it!'

From that day, more than a year ago now, there had been no respite in the Yorkist hunt for the ex-King. His capture had become a contest for those seeking Edward's favour—

Henry halted in his progress around the cloisters. The developed instinct of the fugitive warned him that something had just altered; perhaps only the tone of the brethren's conversation... Yes, the other monks were gathering now around a newcomer who was being introduced to them by the Infirmarian.

'This is my kinsman Matthew, come all the way from Abingdon. And before that he was at Westminster, no less, for the Queen's coronation on Whit Sunday!'

The Queen— Thinking it was Margaret who was being referred to, Henry rushed forward to join the group. *Oh, holy Virgin, let me have news of her...* He pushed his cowl back lest it impede his hearing.

The young monk from Abingdon was tall and so could see over the heads of the others. His casual glance became an intense scrutiny as Henry approached. Henry, feeling the sharpness of the look, pulled the cowl forward again over his limp hair and white face; and then stood slightly sideways to listen to the young man's words – which had not faltered at all in their lively report of Elizabeth Woodville's appearance even when the speaker's attention had darted elsewhere for the moment...

Elizabeth? – Henry thought dully. The monk's tale was about some lady called Elizabeth. Not Margaret... Heartsick, he turned away. And felt the young man's eyes boring into his back while the loud, confident voice followed him with a story in which he had no interest:

'Aye brothers, she rode to Westminster in a chair drawn by three coursers, two bays and a white – cost fifty marks the three! And the chair and pillion cushions alone were worth £27, I heard. That was without the £280 for the cloths of gold which the King had of John de Bardi the Florentine...'

So, Henry thought, there was a new Queen now as well

as a new king. And clearly her coronation had lived up to the lavish standards of the House of York. But what a memory for sums of money that young Brother Matthew of Abingdon had! It was almost as if he loved the very sound of the figures. Ah, how hard must he find it to keep his vow of poverty... Shaking his head over such foolishness, Henry shuffled off to his cell; prayed there for an hour; then fell asleep.

It was dark when Dr Mannyng came to arouse him. 'Your Grace – my sweet lord – we must go from hence!' The message was all too familiar.

Without protest, Henry got up and allowed the old doctor (whose hands were awkward from the white leprosy) to help him into some travelling clothes.

'Thomas, where are we going?' Henry asked then; weariness and despair giving his voice a sighing quality.

'Back to Yorkshire, my lord—' Mannyng tried to sound very cheerful. 'The good Father Abbot here has arranged for you to be received by Sir Richard Tempest at Waddington Hall.'

It was July 9th when the travellers reached the home of the Tempest family. Sir Richard made them welcome. He then assured them that it would be safe for them to sit with him – and several other Lancastrian gentlemen who'd come to pay homage to Henry – at the High Table; there to eat the evening meal with all his loyal household.

But the supper had barely begun when the doors burst open and a group of armed men rushed in, led by Sir Richard's brother, John Tempest—

Throughout the ensuing melee, the host made no attempt to defend his royal guest – it was clear that he'd planned the entire attack with his brother. But there were some who *did* defend Henry; and so valiantly that he was carried – physically unharmed but deeply shocked – out through a secret door, and from thence to a wood that gave onto the wilderness of the Pennine foothills.

Yet the pursuers were only temporarily shaken off. Four days later, as the exhausted fugitives tried to cross the Ribble at the ford of Bungerly Hippingstones, Henry was captured – one William Cantelowe, a mercer, being the first to lay hands upon the anointed person of the ex-King... Then Sir John Tempest closed in with his other armed followers.

With leather thongs, they bound Henry's feet to the stirrups of the saddle in which they propped him. 'Lest he escape again,' they said. Though it was obvious to anyone (even to Brother Matthew who'd guided the hunters and was now waiting, a little way off, for his payment) that Henry of Lancaster was beyond all personal effort; and that his friends Mannyng, Bedon and Ellerton were incapable of aiding him further because they were bound together like felons...

On July 24th the prisoners reached London. The Earl of Warwick went out to Islington to meet them and, there, he formally arrested Henry of Lancaster in King Edward's name. Then, the man who'd ruled England for thirty-nine years was led captive through Cheapside, and so through all London to the Tower.

Recognising his prison, Henry recalled what his friends had once told him: *that his capture would be the doom of all Margaret's hopes.*

It was for failing his valiant consort that he wept as the keys were withdrawn from the locked doors of his apartments.

9

July, 1465

FOR NEARLY TWO YEARS NOW, the castle of St Mighel had been the headquarters in France of the exiled Lancastrians and their Queen... There, from the small allowance paid to her by her father, René of Anjou, the indomitable Margaret was rearing her son, feeding her friends and continuing her efforts for the restoration of Henry's sovereignty in England.

The decades of dangerous turmoil had dealt harshly with Margaret's appearance. Twenty years ago she'd been the most beautiful young bride in Europe. Now, at thirty-five, she was haggard, grey; and the all-embracing radiance of her former vitality had narrowed to one intense fanatic flame which seemed to sear the flesh off her bones. She was blade-thin. Even the once shapely bosom was flattened under the shabby robes that hung loose on the ex-Queen's figure.

Yet she still had an extraordinary dignity and presence.

Poverty and hardship had not lessened her imperiousness. Her well-known gesture of tilting her head back to regard people – through those green eyes of hers – down the length of her straight nose, yet had power to overawe – to remind everyone that, even recently, she'd been received as lawful Queen of England in Rouen and in Bruges... Nor had her courage been eroded by several close contacts with death. Once, she'd been attacked by a murderous band of robbers. Twice shipwrecked. Many times besieged and pursued by Yorkists. Yet, contemptuous of danger, she'd passed close to the English forces at Calais two years ago in her determination to talk with Duke Philip of Burgundy.

The main effect of these adventures was that Margaret had gradually lost, or given away in travel payments, almost all her jewellery. These days she went starkly unadorned except for her wedding ring: the gold band set with a ruby which had once belonged to the late Cardinal Beaufort...

She looked broodingly now from the red-rose glow of the ring on her thin hand, clenched over the council table, to the empty places of the Cardinal's grand-nephews. These brothers of the executed Somerset had escaped from England to join her. But they'd grown restless of the inactivity here, the waiting, the dashed hopes. Eventually they'd gone off to fight in the War of the Public Weal which the heir of Burgundy and the Duke of Brittany were waging against Louis of France – a war in whose recent battle, at Montlhéry, on the Orléans road, Margaret had lost her greatest friend and champion, Pierre de Brézé.

Brézé's death was still a throbbing wound in her scarred soul. But she had not wept for him any more than she'd wept for William de la Pole long ago, or for either of the two dead Dukes of Somerset whom she'd loved.

Dry-eyed still she looked around the council table. At

Sir John Fortescue, her chief adviser and tutor to her son. At Henry Holland, the Duke of Exeter who'd wedded a daughter of York and been divorced by her for his adherence to Lancaster. At Dr Morton, once Bishop of St Asaph, deprived of his See two and a half years ago. And at all the others—

'How many will leave me—' Margaret wondered '—now that Henry is a prisoner of the Yorkists?' That news, received an hour ago, had hit her like a blow between the eyes. Henry captured – locked up in the Tower with only leprous old Mannyng for company... Edward of York and his so-called Queen (whom Margaret remembered as one of her own ladies-in-waiting) could, from this month of July 1465, conveniently forget Henry of Lancaster. But Margaret would never forget the exasperating and pathetic man who was her husband and her life's cross. She'd keep his cause alive for the sake of her twelve-year-old son.

'Gentlemen,' she said now, 'let us review our position at this present time and then decide how to proceed... We have sent many letters to the Kings of Portugal and Castile, promising them our friendship when Lancaster is restored to England's throne by their aid. We believe that Castile, in particular, will not quickly forget the recent insult to her royal Isabella, whom Edward of York rejected for his present widow-wife. Ah, what foolishness was that marriage! But how gloriously to *our* advantage because it has created a rift between Edward and the Earl of Warwick. And Edward cannot survive without his mighty Neville cousin.

'Next, there is the question of Burgundy. As you all know, Duke Philip is sick again and likely to die this time. Charles of Charolais lacks his father's love for York! When Charles comes to full power in Burgundy, I believe that Lancaster may expect his friendship.

'Gentleman, I believe we yet have much hope of aid. And I have said as much to King Louis in my letters to *him* – that, if he will not help us, there be many other rulers who will!'

Sir John Fortescue, at the Queen's right hand, sighed soundlessly. Margaret's arrogance in her dealings with Louis had done much harm to the cause of Lancaster. Sir John had begged her to be more tactful although he'd always realised that tact was not in the Queen's headlong nature. Often, he prayed God that her son would grow up to be more diplomatic—

'So I command you all now,' Margaret was continuing passionately, 'not to be cast down by setbacks and delays. Because the passage of time leads but to our noble Prince's maturity!'

Her gaze became incandescent as she turned it upon the boy by her side. He was an Angevin: dark, handsome, green-eyed, strongly resembling herself and also his Uncle John, Duke of Calabria, who was sitting next to him.

Margaret put her hand on her son's slim shoulder – the hand wearing the blood-red stone. One day, this Prince would be King of England, even though she might have to battle to her own last breath for his rights! She caught her brother, John of Calabria, watching her; an unfathomable expression on his dark sardonic face. 'What is it?' she asked sharply across the Prince's head.

'Oh, merely the ghost of an idea, madame. And one which only I and Louis of France might find amusing.'

'If you can amuse Louis just now, John,' Margaret snapped, 'then you are a talented jester indeed.' The armies of the League had chased Louis into Paris. There he yet remained, admitting defeat at the hands of Burgundy, Brittany, Armagnac... John of Calabria had also been with the League's forces but was now bored with victory over the King and was on his way home. En route, he was visiting his sister Margaret here in St Mighel.

A bizarre notion had crossed John's mind a moment ago (son of a poet, he was given to toying with abstractions). It was this: if Margaret were bent on cultivating Edward of York's enemies, why did she not ally herself with the disgruntled Earl of Warwick?

Of course it would be an outrageous suggestion at first – one which would knock Margaret prostrate with one of her headaches, for she and Warwick were sworn foes. Yet it seemed to John's objective mind that the ex-Queen and the ex-ruler of England had much in common, and that they'd obtain their separate aims by uniting. Warwick could take the boy-Prince and mould him for kingship as he'd moulded Edward of York... Yes, the plan was worth putting to Louis of France some day, if only to relieve the tedium of Court life. Louis would pick his yellow teeth; then would lope crookedly away, to examine the scheme for possible advantages to France... John of Calabria smiled.

His sister had now begun to question again the courier, William Joseph, who'd brought news of Henry's capture. Margaret had an obsessive interest in everything to do with the House of York.

'This widow—' she was asking harshly '—who calls herself Queen of England, does she give any sign of presenting the usurper with a child?'

'There is no outward sign, Your Grace,' the courier replied. 'Yet gossip has it that an infant will be born in the spring.'

On February 11th, 1466, the first royal child was born. Disappointingly, a girl. But so gold-fair and perfectly formed that she was a joy to look upon.

George Neville, the new Archbishop of York, baptised

her and gave her her mother's name, Elizabeth, according to the wish of the proud and delighted King. Edward was so overjoyed at his daughter's birth that he'd lavished gifts everywhere; and had even ordered his steward to 'send some wine to Henry in the Tower; also let him have a new bright-coloured gown and mantle – his last one must be well-worn now, these seven months.'

The sponsors at the front, too, proclaimed the mood of expansive joy, if only by their reconciliation to one another's company. Cecily, Duchess of York, was standing as one godmother; Jacquetta Woodville the other; and the Earl of Warwick as godfather.

But it was not until Cecily had held her new grandchild in her arms for the first time that she'd become resigned to Edward's irregular union with a woman whom she herself would never like, never trust... Now, handing Elizabeth's child to the Archbishop, she thought: *But no one need ever know that this beautiful infant has not the right to be called Princess.* It was only in that moment that she entered wholeheartedly into the conspiracy of silence with the three who knew the truth at first-hand: Robert Stillington, lately consecrated Bishop of Bath and Wells; Eleanor Butler, slowly dying in a Norwich convent; and Edward himself – happily making plans for next month's churching of his daughter's mother whom he still adored.

'Aye,' Cecily admitted to herself, 'babes have always twisted me around their little fingers. And for this one, now, I can forget the embarrassments and the humiliations which the Woodvilles have already brought upon my House.'

Elizabeth's churching in Westminster Abbey was an event almost as magnificent as her coronation there had been. Priests, scholars, minstrels, barons and knights, heralds and pursuivants, all walked in candlelit procession, singing as they went, before the golden canopy of the Queen. This was borne by four of the highest nobles in the land. Behind followed the Queen's mother with fifty-nine other ladies, all gorgeously attired.

When the Abbey service was over, there was a banquet in the Palace of Westminster. So great was the throng attending (even the King of Bohemia was represented) that four huge rooms were needed to seat everyone, and fifty different courses to satisfy their varying tastes. Then there had to be gifts for each one of the scores of minstrels throughout the meal and during the dancing that followed. These gifts were handed out by Warwick who, seated in the royal palace, was acting for Edward: because a King might not attend his consort's churching feast.

However, the Queen made up in formal dignity for the lack of her lord's splendour. In a separate chamber that was dazzlingly decorated, Elizabeth was enthroned upon a golden chair surrounded by ladies kneeling at a deferential distance. Even her own mother had to kneel to her until the first course was served on the solitary gold table...

From their crowded board in the next room, the Bohemian guests craned their necks. They were Leo, the Lord of Rozmital and his companion, Gabriel Tetzel... Of all the marvels they'd seen in England during their ambassadorial visit, the almost eastern grandeur of England's Queen was the most amazing. Except perhaps for her silvery beauty, famed throughout Europe. In their hearts, the Bohemians doubted the story that this Queen was common-born.

'How could any commoner—' murmured Leo '— maintain such disciplined formality, such *impassivity*, without a lifetime's training in it?'

'Perhaps we should remember, my lord,' replied Tetzel, 'that *this* Queen was raised in the Court of the *former*

Queen. Possibly she learnt her royal bearing there...' But he'd never heard that Margaret of Anjou had shown such total lack of mercy for her ladies: Elizabeth had now kept hers kneeling for close on three hours!

The Woodville family then came under discussion between the two foreigners – discreetly, in their own language, so that no one might follow what they said even if they could hear above the surrounding din... Tetzel enumerated what great things had been done for the Queen's sisters, all either brilliantly wed or betrothed now. Anne Woodville had married William Bourchier, son of the Earl of Essex. Eleanor had become wife to Anthony Grey of Ruthyn, son of the new Earl of Kent. Mary was betrothed to Lord Herbert's son, Lord Dunster; Margaret, to the heir of the Earl of Arundel. And Catherine – a plain girl, it was said, and the least clever of all –Catherine had been given the greatest prize; for *she* had just been betrothed to a most noble youth residing in the Queen's own household: Henry Stafford, the boy-Duke of Buckingham!

Nor were these all of the Queen's kin to have benefited so far. Her sire, Richard Woodville, Lord Rivers, had just been made Treasurer of England and her priest-brother Lionel, Dean of Exeter. While her youngest brother, John, had quite overstepped himself in the rush of family ambition: becoming at twenty years of age, the husband of the wealthy, elderly Katherine, Dowager-Duchess of Norfolk, the King's aunt – a thrice-wed woman nearing seventy! 'The diabolical marriage' this was being called; and it had caused great scandal, remembered the Lord of Rozmital with a pained expression...

But there was one *worse* scandal, Gabriel Tetzel whispered.

'What is that?' Rozmital asked. 'I have not heard of it.'

'It concerns the sum of 4,000 marks, my lord. Said to have been paid recently by the Queen to Anne, Duchess of Exeter, the King's sister — she who took another husband when her first went into exile with the Lancastrians.'

'That poor wretch we saw in Burgundy? — the man walking barefoot, begging his bread?'

'The same, my lord: Duke of Exeter and brother-in-law of England's King... But about the Woodville affair. This poor Duke had one daughter by his Yorkist wife. The child-heiress has been betrothed since infancy to a nephew of the Earl of Warwick. Not any more, however! *Now* the little Holland girl is fiancée of one of the Queen's own sons by her first marriage.'

Rozmital stared at Tetzel. If this story of grasping indiscretion by the Woodvilles were true, then the breach of faith with the great Earl of Warwick's family might be very serious indeed. Furthermore, it would drag the wretched Exeter divorce business into public view again and *that* would not enhance King Edward's family reputation... 'The merciless Duchess' people had called his sister Anne, ever since she'd put her young husband from her and deprived her child of its father. Now she was proving as bad a mother as she'd been a wife: selling the little Holland girl to the Queen's son for 4,000 marks—

Rozmital shook his head. It was a sorry business, this unsubtle advancement of all the Woodville kin. The King must be under a spell, not to see what great offence was being given to old supporters of his House. Especially to the dangerous Earl of Warwick who, for all that he was presiding here today at the Queen's churching feast, was looking grim and abstracted... Was the Queen's present display of haughty magnificence a calculated blow to Richard and George Neville? — the Earl and the Archbishop who'd enjoyed a monopoly of magnificence until now. *Their* banquets had been notorious; their hospitality limitless; their ability to lavish gifts greater even than the crown's.

Now one would have to watch if the Woodvilles could attract as great a following as that of the Nevilles. The Lord of Rozmital did not believe that they would. For all their handsomeness and brilliance, the newcomers lacked a certain quality. Could it be passion? – that explosive force of love and hate and outrage which only great souls might know—

His musings were cut short by a glimpse of a truly beautiful young woman curtseying to the Queen before taking part in the dancing just begun.

'Who is she?' he asked of Gabriel Tetzel.

'*That*—' Tetzel replied '—is the Lady Margaret of York, youngest sister to King Edward. There was talk last year, you remember, of wedding her to Dom Pedro of Portugal? But now, well, it is a rumour of Burgundian interest.'

'Burgundy, huh?' said Leo. 'Surely such an alliance would further discontent the Earl of Warwick who mislikes the Duchy?' But he wasn't looking at Warwick. His gaze was fastened on the dark and vivid beauty of the Lady Margaret Plantagenet.

'Maybe it would,' Tetzel agreed, 'though how convenient for the new Duke of Burgundy himself, that he should happen to be a widower! I think he should be known as Charles the Lucky instead of Charles the Bold if he gets the Lady Margaret for his second wife…'

10

June, 1468

THE LADY MARGARET Plantagenet of York was sitting in her mother's solar at Baynard's Castle, by the window which overlooked the busy Thames. It was June 17th, 1468.

Margaret still had difficulty in realising that this was the last evening she'd spend in her mother's home; that all her intimate belongings were packed in chests and baskets, ready for the long wedding journey which would begin tomorrow... Many a time over the past two and a half years, she'd been impatient to set out on this journey, and had often felt like screaming at the difficulties and delays which had been put in the way of her marriage to Charles, Duke of Burgundy. But now that everything was finally in order – from the papal dispensation to the first payment of her huge dowry – she was infinitely sad.

She looked around her mother's beautiful tranquil room. Every object here was part of her own growing up. Everything had a place in her family's history – souvenirs from France and from Ireland, mementoes of her dead father and of her brother killed alongside him at Wakefield. But, above all, the solar had the stamp of her mother's presence.

Tears tightened her throat. Among all the children of York, she, the youngest daughter, was closest to the widowed Duchess Cecily. They'd lived here together in the old Gloucester residence of Baynard's Castle for almost nine years. Margaret was now a mature twenty-two, and she understood her mother's well-hidden desolation at the prospect of her leaving England. For the first time in her family-filled life, Cecily would be utterly without close kin under her own roof. And it would go hard with her, Margaret knew – much harder than with herself who must soon become absorbed into another environment, whether she liked it or not.

She was ashamed of certain fears she had for the future: its foreignness, its demands upon her who would be Duchess of Burgundy and, above all, marriage to a man whom she'd never seen – a thirty-five-year-old widower with a daughter aged eleven.

Margaret had gone to great lengths to conceal her worries about all these things. She'd worn a confident mask, and had given even freer rein than usual to her vital, outward-going personality. She was merry, overwhelming and positive; tireless in her enjoyment at ball and tournament, hunt and reception. Even her energetic brother, the King, had to plead laughingly sometimes:

'Mercy, Meg – we cannot keep up with you!'

Even to Edward, she had not admitted the truth, that she dare not take time to think of what lay before her: a political marriage in the interests of the House of York, with a mighty Duke who was a Lancastrian sympathiser! Charles of Burgundy would wed her solely to spite his hated overlord, Louis of France. And Margaret would have to work very hard indeed to gain any advantage for England from this alliance. But she was determined to try and to go on trying for the rest of her life. England and the House of York would always be her priorities.

For his own part, Louis of France had already done everything in his power to prevent the Burgundian marriage – his latest weapon being that of slander when he'd put it about that Margaret was 'light and free' in her ways, and would not go a virgin to any husband foolish enough to wed her... Margaret had wept in her royal brother's arms when this arrow had reached home; but was consoled by Edward's cheerful remark that, well, she *was* leaving several broken male hearts behind her at his Court – and was not that better than to go unmourned?

How I'll miss Edward's odd philosophy, she thought now. For all his faults (and she was not blind to these) he'd been a wonderful brother to her, and the tune of their temperaments had chimed in a wild harmony. Yes, she'd miss him. She was prepared to do anything in the future to repay his many kindnesses.

She'd known for a long while that Edward must run himself into serious debt to provide her dowry and the lavish requirements of her new household. But what had he done? Roared with laughter at the bills for gold plate and tapestries, jewels and fabrics – and drawn up an opposite list of potential creditors!

Margaret had to smile at her brother's phenomenal ability to raise, and spend, money. But there were occasions – particularly now – when his methods disturbed her; for they showed an almost animal indifference to a victim's suffering – inflicted, without sensitivity, so that Edward himself might continue to survive and prosper... Within the past week, Margaret had had to fling herself to the defence of Sir Thomas Cook, who'd been imprisoned on a treason charge utterly unproven so far. Yet his two fine houses had been ransacked, and all his goods carried off by servants of the Queen's father – who had now been made an Earl as well as Treasurer of England! People in the streets were saying these days while the trial was pending that 'Tom Cook's only crime is to be wealthy when the King needs money'. And all that Margaret's pleas on the unfortunate man's behalf had achieved to date was that he'd been admitted to bail. Yet she knew in her heart that he (and many another lately arrested in connection with a new Lancastrian invasion plot) was already ruined: not so much for alleged correspondence with rebels abroad as for the fact that King Edward was hard pushed to find the Burgundian marriage moneys.

Margaret had told her brother what was being said in the streets. And had told him furthermore that she herself would study the reports of Sir Thomas Cook's trial.

'Sis, you'll be too busy a-wedding,' Edward had shrugged. Yet he'd met her eye warily, recognising there a sharpness that matched his own under the easy, affable exterior...

In moments like these, Margaret could almost dislike the King for his natural cunning, his ruthlessness and his Woodville-intensified greed. At such times, she'd find herself contrasting him with the simple George of Clarence, who was really her favourite brother although she could never decide why; perhaps only because they'd shared nursery and schoolroom... George was eighteen and a half now; a tall, handsome young man outwardly very like Edward but not so broadly built. And he was still heir to the throne – although the Queen's second confinement, due in July, might well put an end to that privileged position for him... Poor George! He was so vulnerable, both from without and from within himself. Margaret suspected that her love for him was partly a desire to protect him with her own strength. Though to protect him from what, exactly, she did not know...

Maybe from their cousin of Warwick, in whose company he was spending much time lately. There'd even been a rumour that George wanted to marry Isobel, Warwick's eldest daughter. But the King had soon quashed that ambition, if it had ever existed, because he wanted no further close ties between his own family and the northern Nevilles. A state of tension had existed between himself and them ever since the Woodville marriage. And at one point last year (when Edward took the Great Seal away from George Neville of York and gave it to Stillington of Bath and Wells) Warwick had retired to Middleham Castle and there maintained a state of ominous silence and inactivity – refusing even to come to Court when summoned! Finally however, on being told that there were charges against him of being in correspondence with Margaret of Anjou, and of being the inspiration behind a band of north-country rebels under one mysterious Robin of Redesdale, the Earl had issued forth from his eyrie and resoundingly proved his innocence... So, once again, the widening chasm between him and Edward had been bridged. And Warwick was to be in Margaret's retinue tomorrow when she left London and set her face towards her new country—

Her mother came bustling into the solar, exuding a determined cheerfulness. 'Now, Meg, everything's done and well done!' Cecily was a little out of breath from the steep climb up the stairs. 'So at last we may sit for an hour.'

An hour, Margaret thought. *The last we may ever spend together.*

She was glad when her mother walked round behind

her, to caress her neck and shoulders with firm, familiar hands. That way she wouldn't see the foolish tears that had gathered in her daughter's eyes.

But Cecily felt the tears in her own eyes; felt the wrench of the heart that had been a recurring anguish in her life, now as well-known as the ache of an old wound. Suddenly it seemed to her that the circle of experience was complete. Because now she was in her own mother's position of more than thirty years before – a heartbroken widow bidding farewell to a youngest daughter who'd been her sole companion. Now she knew how the Countess Joan of Westmoreland had felt when the young Cecily Neville had gone off to France to wed Richard Plantagenet.

Truly, all women travelled the same road; passed by the same milestones.

Compulsively, she kissed the top of Margaret's head; and visualised that head, in babyhood, lying against her own full breast, in a room at Fotheringhay Castle.

'God bless you, Meg,' she said. 'You have given me much happiness.'

A happiness that would have to be paid for now, from henceforth until death, by loneliness and a sense of irretrievable loss: by listening for a voice that would never again, in her hearing, laugh and sing and chatter about this young man and that. There would only be the beautiful room, silent and memory filled. Meg would never come back to it. Although the great Duchess of Burgundy *might* come, a stranger—

For a moment, Cecily hoped that her daughter would not have any children – would never know this pain.

On the morning of June 18th, Margaret, escorted by Warwick and many other earls and barons besides those who were to go with her to her journey's end, set out from the King's Wardrobe at the Blackfriars. After offerings had been made at St Paul's, and the mayor and aldermen had presented a wedding gift of one hundred pounds in gold, the titled throng headed for the monastery of Stratford Langthorne, where the King and Queen were staying...

Having spent a few days there to enjoy some farewell feastings, Margaret proceeded to Canterbury. Her retinue now included her three brothers: King Edward, George of Clarence and Richard of Gloucester, with all their badged attendants and their banners. It was a spectacular procession which reached Margate on June 23rd, where the *New Ellen* of London lay with thirteen other ships, ready to take the bridal company to Flanders. All the vessels were well armed to defend them against the marauding French who might try, even at this late date, to prevent the Burgundian marriage by a simple act of piracy...

With Clarence beside him, Warwick stood a long time on the quayside, watching the vessels sail away. Then he stared through the shimmering heat haze towards the coast of France. What would Louis do, he wondered, if England and Burgundy were to unite with Brittany to attack him? He could not defend himself on three fronts. So the wisest course – now, without delay – would be to use attack as the best means of defence – *attack Brittany*, before England and her new ally were ready to aid the western Duchy.

Aye, that's what Louis would do. Warwick understood the mind of the French King and intended to talk with him again one day. But he must first repair his own position at home...

Turning, he grasped Clarence's arm and – talking amiably to him – led the young heir apparent towards an inn.

11

July, 1469

HEEDLESS of the spray pluming over the bows of his great ship, the *Trinity*, Warwick stood by the fo'castle rail and stared through the darkness towards Calais.

He'd lost count of the number of times he'd made this voyage since boyhood; and of ships he'd commanded these twenty years past, to beat menacingly up and down the Channel or around the French and Irish coasts. The rhythm of the sea had always been in his body. Now, at the age of forty-one, he knew that its ferocity was a component of his soul.

Yet, for four years he'd stilled his own storms, hardly allowing a ripple to show on the millpond surface of his loyalty to the King. The effects of Edward's ingratitude and indifference he'd allowed to sink quietly out of sight. The vultures that were, to him, the Woodville family, he'd banished to an unfrequented shore of his mind.

But he thought obsessively now of the many men torn

apart by those vultures. Particularly of Sir Thomas Cook, imprisoned just before Margaret of York had gone to Burgundy thirteen months ago. The innocent alderman-mercer had finally been allowed to buy his freedom for £8,000. Then Elizabeth Woodville had come forward with a demand, based on the ancient right of 'queen's gold', that for every thousand pounds he paid to the King by way of fine, he must pay her a hundred marks. Ruined, Cook had crept off to his pillaged house, in which not one item had escaped the greedy fingers of Richard and Jacquetta Woodville, the Queen's parents, who had long cherished a spite against Sir Thomas: woe to anyone whom the Woodvilles misliked!

Yet at least Cook's life had been spared. There was another man who had lost his because he'd once spoken tactlessly to the King about Elizabeth... That man was the valiant and learned Irish Earl of Desmond: he who'd been good friend to the House of York since 1449 when Richard Plantagenet was King's Lieutenant in Dublin... As deputy-governor afterwards, Desmond had continued to render faithful service to the English crown; and, four years ago, he'd visited King Edward – who, as a small boy, had loved his daughter Mary! The Earl and the King had laughed about this as they'd ridden together in the easy familiarity of long friendship. Then Edward had asked the Earl what he thought about his recent marriage.

Desmond's reply was that, in his opinion, Edward would have been wiser to wed some great foreign princess whose connections would have helped to stabilise his throne; and that even now it was not too late to divorce Elizabeth Woodville for the country's good.

Unluckily, the Queen heard of this conversation and, at once, began to plot Desmond's destruction. She had her merciless friend John Tiptoft, Earl of Worcester, appointed deputy in Desmond's place. Then Worcester had the Irish Earl attainted on a wholly false charge of treason.

With his two small sons, the accused nobleman came bravely to Drogheda to prove his innocence. But Worcester had had the children killed; and, on February 14th of last year, their father was executed – his death warrant sealed with the King's own signet ring which Queen Elizabeth had purloined.

It was reported that the King was exceedingly wroth with his wife for this deed; and that he'd shouted at her—

'You have given me one girl. If the infant in your belly now is another, it will be long before I come to your chamber again. And may God punish you for the deaths of noble Desmond and his sons!'

But Edward had not kept his threat to stay away from his wife although her second child also had been a girl... The Queen's beauty was like a honey trap which drew and held him. Only eight months after the second Princess's birth, she had a premature infant – another girl; born on March 20th of this year and christened Cecily for her fairness which reminded everyone of the 'Rose of Raby', her paternal grandmother.

Warwick gritted now into the salty wind: 'Edward cannot get a son any more than I myself can!'

Which meant that George of Clarence was still heir to the throne. And at this moment George was aboard the *Trinity* with Isobel Neville, Warwick's eldest daughter. The couple would be married tomorrow in Calais despite the King's express order that such a marriage should never take place because it would bring the sixteen-year-old Neville heiress to the steps of the throne.

'So let Edward take care,' Warwick muttered. 'And let him return to good Neville council – without which he's come so close to disaster of late!'

The King's Burgundian alliance had done him little good in terms of trade: English cloth was still not allowed into the Duchy, and he was virtually at war with the Hanse towns. Beleaguered Brittany had cost him a fortune in arms-aid and shipping before suddenly making her peace with France. He'd also lost the Castilian alliance – so his sacrifice in renouncing his claim to the throne of Castile had been useless. And France, his perennial adversary, was now talking loudly about helping Margaret of Anjou... All these troubles might have been avoided, Warwick reflected, if only Edward had listened to him, the head of the Neville family.

Well, Edward would *have* to listen when the Neville heiress was wedded to his own heir apparent. There was little love lost these times between Edward and George of Clarence. So he'd be as nervous of George's future intentions as he'd always been of Margaret of Anjou's. He'd feel threatened; insecure among his present foolish friends. So he'd come running to his former councillor. And that was *all* Warwick wanted: a renewal of his own power and status before the world, after an acknowledgement from Edward that he was indispensable. There had been no truth whatever in the charge that his sympathies were swinging towards Lancaster: of all the women in Christendom, Warwick disliked Margaret of Anjou the most.

His hand clenched now around the wet deck-rail. Ah, to be able to grasp like this once more the government of England! To feel the ship of state moving confidently under his own command while the princes of Europe, before whom he'd been humiliated, looking admiringly on! Dear God, for *that* he'd bribe a dozen Papal Legates to grant marriage dispensations, not just the one he'd had to sweeten for the paper now in his sleeve – a paper making legal the marriage of second-cousins George and Isobel.

Even the remotest preparations for the act of defiance had cost him dear; and one wholly unforeseen incident had menaced the final arrangements.

Three weeks ago, the *Trinity* had been lying in Sandwich harbour where she'd spent the winter undergoing so total a refit that it was felt necessary to have her blessed again. So the Archbishop of York had been invited down to Sandwich from his great new house, 'The Moor' in Hertfordshire (where the King had visited him recently but had learnt nothing of what was afoot) and he'd duly arrived with a multitude of attendants, including the Bishop of London and the Prior of Christ Church. On June 12th, the blessing of the *Trinity* took place.

'We dedicate to Almighty God this great vessel, which has been restored with all human skill for the good service of our liege lord, King Edward, that his enemies may be defeated upon the seas and his realm kept in perpetual peace.'

Thus had intoned the sonorous voice of the Archbishop. But his shrewd eyes had rested on the vessel's owner, who was standing with George of Clarence. After the ceremony, His Grace had separated Warwick from the younger man to whisper warningly:

'Brother, take care. Our formidable Aunt Cecily is on her way here – you know the instinct she has for trouble among her brood! Well, I believe she will try to talk to Clarence on the subject of obedience to his King. You must prevent that. Her influence is still great with all her children, and she may dissuade this one from the course we have agreed.'

Warwick had nodded. And had then hurried off to prevent communication between mother and son by the simple expedient of making Clarence senseless with drink. After that, he'd taken the head-sore young Duke to Queenborough until Cecily had returned, apprehensive and defeated, to Baynard's Castle... Warwick had even been temporarily sorry for his godmother-aunt when he'd heard of how distressed she'd been—

The quay lights of Calais were showing now through the dark, and the *Trinity* beginning to tread her way into harbour, where she was expected and elaborately prepared for. The port town of Calais was always sensitive to the movements of the Earl of Warwick, its most respected warden and captain.

Looking over his shoulder, the captain of Calais watched the emergence of voyagers from below deck of the *Trinity*.

First came the Archbishop of York; weighty, smooth-faced; fashionably attired as usual in the clothes of a Court noble. For York found the traditional garb of the Church as outmoded as its teachings about clerical poverty.

Following him was the other George, royal Duke of Clarence: handsome, decorative, charming when he chose to be; a good talker although prone to indiscretion, and easily diverted from the main theme of an argument.

Clarence was turning now to assist his fiancée Isobel on deck... Laughing, she hid in his arms as the wind snatched at her bright hair which was inadequately pinned under a tiny veil. She looked young and slight and utterly unprepared for what she was about to do—

'Isobel,' her father called harshly, 'button your cloak!'

It was the last thing he'd promised his tearful Countess at Middleham, that he'd make Isobel take care for her fragile chest.

The wedding was solemnised in a church at Calais on July 11th by the Archbishop of York, in the presence of the bride's father, five other Knights of the Garter, and many lords and ladies with their attendants.

When he walked from the altar with his young Neville wife by his side, George of Clarence became the inheritor of half that great dower which Anne Beauchamp had brought to her lord, Richard Neville. The other half was to go to Anne, their younger daughter, whenever she should wed.

It was this potential wealth and power – along with the acquisition of a father-in-law who would ensure that he always remained heir to the throne – which had overcome Clarence's very real fear of the King. That, and lively, pretty Isobel herself, whose nearness had lately begun to excite him although he'd never been much interested in girls before…

But now, the question crowded into his mind again – 'What will Edward say? What will he *do*, when this deed of ours is made known to him?' Men had been called traitors for less. Clarence had seen such men executed, by a refinement of barbarity which had turned his stomach.

~

EDWARD WAS SPENDING a pleasant week at his castle of Fotheringhay in Northamptonshire. Elizabeth was there with him, and she'd had the three little Princesses brought up from Shene by their governess, Lady Berners. The children now occupied the old nurseries of Fotheringhay where all the Yorks had spent a part of their own childhood.

Nothing had been altered in those sunny rooms (Edward could still find the place where he'd carved his name under the window ledge along with that of his dead brother Edmund) and the views of the tranquil River Nene beyond – and the bridge – and the church – all seemed changeless as time itself. This was a serene old castle, whose fetterlock-shaped courtyard had embraced generations of Plantagenets.

Yet Edward had known a vague sense of unease ever since his arrival on this occasion... In the windless July sunshine he'd travelled by water from Croyland Abbey where he'd been making a pilgrimage in the company of his solemn young brother, Richard of Gloucester. Richard had then boarded the royal barge with him for Fotheringhay – although it had been clear from the outset that the barge's mostly-Woodville passengers were not to Dickon's taste. He was barely civil to them. Heaven knew what Warwick had been teaching him all these years at Middleham – certainly not manners!

Still, it wasn't a sixteen-year-old's northern boorishness which disturbed Edward. The lad was polite enough to the Queen and was positively charming with the little Princesses. No, it was something else entirely which agitated the royal consciousness: some deep instinct – inherited, doubtless, from his mother – which warned of impending trouble, and which had first begun to stir about a month ago. That was when he'd visited the great new house, 'The Moor' which George Neville had had built for his ample self in Hertfordshire...

A splendid house. Designed to uphold the usual Neville statement of permanence: 'Here I am and here I mean to stay.' No expense had been spared on its construction or decoration: 'The Moor' was an opulent palace, created for great banquets, great hunting parties—

And great intrigues? The antennae of the King's mind had quivered throughout each hour spent there. Yet everything had been so smooth and well-ordered. Nothing hidden. No questions unanswered. And the princely radiance of His Neville Grace had illuminated every chamber, every cupboard and chest, every piece of paper upon which Edward's suspicious eye had alighted.

Nothing. Not a shred of evidence which might add George Neville's to the growing list of traitor's names.

Relieved, Edward had bidden his host a gracious farewell. He was weary of plots and tortured confessions and executions. The deaths of Hungerford and Courtenay in his presence at Salisbury last January had especially sickened him – not by their details but by their necessities. So he was glad that there was nothing wrong at 'The Moor'; no new treachery hatching there behind the broad, smooth forehead of the Archbishop... If there had been, he'd have coaxed it out during the hours of conversation he'd had with George Neville. For George was proud of his own wit, his cleverness with words. And never had he had a more attentive listener than Edward, waiting to trap him. But George of York had committed no indiscretions. Even over the thin-ice subject of whom Clarence ought to marry, he'd skated with swift safety, and had arrived on the firm ground of his brother John's latest military victory against rebels.

On the banks of the Nene now, Edward brooded about rebels in general. He wondered if his own apprehensions had their roots in recent reports about risings in the northeast and northwest under two leaders, each confusingly called 'Robin'.

The King had convinced himself all along that these revolts were trivial – local agitations over small grievances like the peppercorn tax at York which had lately cost one of the 'Robins' – he of Holderness – his head. Energetic John Neville had seen to *that* execution as soon as the rebels' demands had included the release from prison of the Percy heir. For how could Neville enjoy his hard-won Earldom of Northumberland if the real heir to that title was free?

But the other leader, known as Robin of Redesdale, was still alive, at large and causing much trouble around Lancashire. Eventually, Edward supposed, he himself would have to deal with him. Still, he wouldn't hurry over to Lancashire this hot summer weather. Instead, he'd wait to see if Lord Montagu would dash across the Pennines in his place, as he'd dashed to so many other emergencies in the past.

Likely, this time, John would not; for he was not warden of the west march, only of the east. It was Warwick who held responsibility for the west, and Warwick was either in Kent or gone over to Calais to try out the new fittings of his ship, the *Trinity*.

Well, the matter could wait until he returned north. Then it would be interesting to see what *he'd* do about this so-called Robin of Redesdale.

Edward's spies had discovered for him the true identity of the rebel leader. He was Sir John Conyers of Hornby; who was married to Alice, daughter of the late Lord William Fauconberg, Earl of Kent, royal and Neville uncle... Edward now believed that Warwick might hesitate to attack kinsman Conyers; especially as 'Robin' had once offered him armed aid at Middleham, it was said.

From the length of the inscrutable Earl's hesitation, conclusions might well be drawn about his loyalty to the crown. Edward intended to test Warwick's loyalty once and for all – he'd been suspicious of it long enough.

With that intention arrived at, he'd discovered the cause of his own unease.

12

August, 1469

ELIZABETH'S ATTENDANTS were preparing her for bed on this last night of King Edward's stay at Fotheringhay Castle. They'd brushed out her wonderful hair and rebound it into a gilt-mesh snood. They'd bathed her white body in rosewater and afterwards massaged it all over with perfumed creams. Now, while she lay on the closet-couch, wrapped in warm towels and with pads soaked in witch-hazel over her eyes, two women polished her finger and toe nails; another smoothed the loose robe she'd wear to receive the King and a third made final adjustments to the new black silk sheets on the royal bed.

Behind the cool darkness of the eye pads, Elizabeth's brain was busily checking the armaments of seduction. Tonight, nothing that would stimulate Edward's flagging interest must be omitted. The times were over when she could have afforded to be casual with him. Now at thirty-three, she was having to fight for his attentions with every weapon at her command. If she did not become pregnant soon of an heir to the throne, her already-precarious position might worsen. Because Edward – encouraged by those close companions of his, Hastings and Herbert – was beginning to find his bed-sport elsewhere... Sometimes lately, especially in London when he'd come to her of a night, he'd kissed her rather absent-mindedly, made some jesting excuse about his limpness and fallen promptly into a snoring sleep.

Things had been better here at Fotheringhay. There were few chaseable wenches in the village and, also, Edward was feeling sanctified by his recent pilgrimage to Croyland Abbey. So he'd made love to her for the past six nights. And now, if the old wives' tales had any truth in them, all that was necessary for the conception of a boy-child was a seventh intercourse at this precise time of Elizabeth's personal month.

She'd been calculating and manipulating towards this end since March when the new baby had been born – dismayingly, a third girl; and Elizabeth had known a recurrence then of that sharp anxiety she'd first felt, when Edward had threatened to come to her no more if she did not bear him a Prince.

Never at any time had she allowed the anxiety to show. Yet her shrewd mother-in-law, the Duchess of York, had seen through the mask of calm confidence when the last infant had been christened Cecily after herself at Elizabeth's request... Elizabeth was making the gesture in an effort to win her friendship at last. She was admitting that she needed the older woman's help. And Cecily had been sympathetic. But *un*helpful—

Anyone would imagine she didn't want the King to have a son, Elizabeth thought furiously for the hundredth time. Yet what could Cecily's motive be for that? Her dislike of her royal daughter-in-law? Or her wish that her own son, George of Clarence, should remain heir-presumptive?

Elizabeth did not know. Though sometimes in the Duchess's company, she was aware of a strange unease when Cecily looked at her and Edward together. Because there was an expression then in the eyes of the King's mother that was neither dislike, jealousy nor personal ambition, but merely an unfathomable harassment as of great worry – great pain.

Well, her ageing Grace of York would have to take care of her own troubles, whatever they might be. Elizabeth had made the grand gesture of friendship towards her and had been firmly rejected. So let Cecily see as little of her own namesake grandchild as she did of the other two Princesses! Let her continue to fuss instead over the de la Pole boys at Wingfield Castle – of whom the eldest, John, now aged five, had been created Earl of Lincoln three years ago by his doting uncle, the King.

The Queen's mouth tightened as she thought of these three sons born to her sister-in-law, the stuttering young Duchess of Suffolk. Everyone had concluded that John de la Pole's wife was barren: several years wed and no loosened girdle! But then, like some sainted biblical wife, she'd suddenly begun to breed; and now had three fine boys to console her for a lamentable husband and a shrewish mother-in-law, old Alice Chaucer who was perpetually at war with her own tenants in East Suffolk—

The Queen snatched the pads from her eyes and, tossing the towels aside, stood up naked. She looked at her breasts: they were firm still. And her legs were as beautiful as ever. But she noted with dismay that the stretch-marks scattered across her stomach by repeated pregnancies were not responding any more to creams and massages. Deeply etched, they were like the wrinkles of old age.

'My robe,' she ordered; and the beautiful white silk of the loose gown, tied with ribbons at the open sides, immediately covered her; while her feet were guided into gold slippers by a kneeling servant.

'Now close the shutters.' The summer evening sky was still translucent but she wanted no natural light in the bedchamber, only scented wax tapers here and there... Nor did she want Edward to be distracted by sounds from the castle meadows all about where his troops were encamped ready for tomorrow's march north. Tonight, he must be made to concentrate only on loving his Queen, and leaving her with a Prince in her womb...

As she lay back on the black silk bed and heard Edward's footsteps approaching her door, she felt confident of success. She would be urgently physical, for once, with her husband. She would conceive his child and it would be a boy.

She looked at the ring on her hand which Edward had sent her today as a gift... Suddenly, she remembered the Irish Earl of Desmond and his sons – all dead these four years past by her own theft of a ring to seal their death warrant.

'I never meant the children to be killed,' she whispered now. 'Oh God, protect the son I hope to get—'

Edward strode, whistling, into the bedchamber and stood to sniff appreciatively at the many perfumes. Then, before slamming the door behind him, he shouted to his attendant in the corridor:

'Be off, all of you. But call me at first cock-crow; I want to be on the Grantham road by dawn.'

So truly, there's only tonight, Elizabeth thought with an edge of desperation. *heaven knows when I shall see him again.*

For the first time in their married life, she kissed him hungrily; and asked no favours of him except his love.

Very early in the morning, the King set off for Grantham and Newark with his army. The infantrymen looked resplendent in their new jackets of blue and murrey, emblazoned with white roses. The tents and artillery, piled onto carts, had a comforting appearance. The banners waved bravely. Yet Edward had felt a great reluctance to set forth today. The apprehensions which had plagued him all week were now sharpened to a conviction of imminent catastrophe.

He'd taken extraordinary measures to protect himself and his family against he knew not what. He'd doubled his personal bodyguard and the garrison of Fotheringhay. He'd sent scouts out all over the country with orders to report to him the most trivial rumour of unrest.

This morning, he'd knelt through three Masses before setting his face northwards, with his friends, his doctors, his astrologers and his men-at-arms close about him – the pressure of Elizabeth's farewell kiss still hot on his mouth, and the scent of his children's skin sweet in his nostrils...

A royal scout came galloping into Newark. He had a document which the King must see at once.

Edward had just reached his lodging there. He read swiftly through the manifesto which was signed 'Robin of Redesdale'. Then he flung it at Richard of Gloucester with the terse question:

'Whose style of writing is this, brother?'

Quite clearly, it was Warwick's. Its formality, the scope of its content and its uncompromising censure of the King since his Woodville marriage – none of these points of authorship were lost upon the frowning young Dickon nor upon any of the Woodville menfolk crowding around, reading the manifesto over his shoulder.

'Well—' Edward barked '—what say you all? Did some rustic knight compose the list of complaints against his

King? Or was it carefully drafted for "Robin" by some lord so highly placed that he knows every aspect of Court life, foreign policy, church and army and *naval affairs*?'

Without waiting for a reply he spun on his heel and went charging and shouting out into the courtyard of the Newark inn:

'We leave in half an hour. For Nottingham.'

They'd come too far north now from Fotheringhay to return quickly there: Nottingham was the nearest strong fortress. Besides, it was the most strategically placed in the midlands. There, a threatened monarch could either withstand a siege or thunder out to meet his enemies advancing from whatever point...

As he swung himself to horse and raked an eye over his hastily-reknit army, Edward had little doubt but that his real enemy would come up from Kent – the reported forces of Robin of Redesdale to the northward were but a lure placed by Warwick. Accursed Warwick! He could always whistle up an army in Kent as soon as he landed there from Calais – he was, after all, warden of the cinque ports.

Warwick – Warwick – drummed the hoofbeats of the King's horse galloping out of Newark. *Traitor – traitor –* to have been the spirit behind the northern rebels all along.

The threats and demands of the 'Robin' document still formed a seething confusion in Edward's brain but he'd isolated a few points by now. Its ominous opening lines for instance: they classed himself with the three deposed monarchs of England's history – Edward the Second, Richard the Second and Henry the Sixth – because all three had 'excluded the lords of his blood from his council chamber, and had listened only to grasping favourites.' There followed the names of the Woodvilles, the Herberts, 'and others of mischievous assent and opinion whose greed has been satisfied by the impoverishment of this realm.'

The King was then accused of taxing his subject for wars against Scotland and France which he had never waged; and of robbing his clergy for a crusade which he had never undertaken.

Aha, there indeed was the long memory of cousin Warwick! All the way back to the synod of Doncaster five years ago, after which the Pope had obligingly died... Edward could not recall one single item on which he'd spent the crusade moneys there collected.

But he was presently beginning to recollect other lines from the manifesto. That 'the King hath accused of treason those whom his favourites misliked; so that no man of worship or riches, either spiritual or temporal, can be sure of his life or property'. Also that 'he hath broken his promises, freely given before Parliament, to live upon his own profits and not tax his subjects except for urgent causes. He hath also diverted to his own purposes those moneys meant for the keeping of the seas.'

Again, this was unmistakably the voice of Warwick the admiral: as solicitous for his ships as a mother for her infant! May he and the *Trinity* feel the bottom of the Channel—

But for all his rage, Edward was frightened. His mind kept returning to the first lines of the manifesto where his own name was listed with those kings who had been deposed. Warwick had made him. *Warwick could break him.*

When, inside gloomy Nottingham Castle, he was given the news of Clarence's marriage to Isobel Neville, an icy finger touched the back of his neck. He thought of Edward the Second, hideously murdered at the Castle of Berkeley; of Richard the Second, starved to death at Pontefract; and of Henry – still wearily restating his right to kingship – shut away in the Tower these four years past...

All at once, Edward found stone walls unbearable. However safe this fortress of Nottingham might be, he could not stay here. He would march south; challenge the army which Warwick and Clarence was now reported to be leading out of London towards Northampton.

Edward had some hopes of reinforcements from Wales. He'd sent his father-in-law, Earl Rivers, posting westward some days ago to hasten the march of Herbert's troops. Rivers had taken his youngest son, John Woodville, with him – he who had the distinction of being both the King's brother-in-law and the King's uncle, by reason of having wedded old Katherine Neville!

With a feeling of having escaped suffocation, Edward rode out of Nottingham Castle. People lining the city's streets cheered him as he passed with his troops. He was still very popular, it seemed – still the 'golden monarch' of the common folk. Yet, the citizens of London had allowed Warwick and Clarence to march through the capital from Kent, knowing full well that *their* army was on a collision course with the King's.

Through the sultry summer days, the two forces approached closer and closer to one another. Edward was aware that Robin of Redesdale's band was pressing down behind him from the north, but he remained confident that the Welsh reinforcements would reach him before either Robin or Warwick did. So he moved toward the town of Olney in North Buckinghamshire – a town for which he had a certain affection because he'd sometimes stayed there during his secret courtship of Elizabeth.

Stooping under the familiar inn-sign now, Edward tried to be the same man he'd been then: confident, cheerful, relaxed – the amiable giant who always remembered the name of the meanest servant and made that servant feel like a king. But, this August day of 1469, the King himself was grey-faced – hollow in his stomach from news just received:

The Welsh reinforcements had been cut to pieces at Edgecott by Robin of Redesdale's men and a small advance party of Warwicks' army. The Welsh leader Lord Herbert, Earl of Pembroke, and his brother Sir Richard Herbert (both of them close friends of Edward's) had been beheaded in Northampton by the orders of Warwick himself. And, in the Forest of Dean, the two Woodvilles – the Queen's father and her brother John – had been captured; hurried to Gosford Green near Coventry and there executed.

As these tidings had spread through the royal army, the main body of it had turned and fled, deserting its King and leaving him only a few servants.

He entered the dark inn now from the bright sunshine of the yard and thought for a moment that the place was quite empty. By contrast with the cheerful bustle that there used to be here, all was eerily quiet... Where was lame Rob and little Kate? Where was bosomy Marge and her big husband?

Then he saw them: standing with their backs against the furthest wall and staring stonily towards the scarred keg-bench under the window.

At the bench sat the opulent figure of His Grace of York. Behind him, the Earl of Oxford, who was married to Warwick's sister, Margaret Neville.

The Archbishop arose ponderously; nodding, as he did so, to two men-at-arms near the inn door. They slammed and bolted the door behind Edward. The other armed men poured out of the kitchen and down from the loft bedrooms.

'My lord King,' George Neville said in his beautiful

voice, 'it is my sad duty to arrest Your Grace and to take you to my brother's castle of Warwick for a little time.'

A little time, Edward thought wildly. *What then* – what afterwards? Subjects cannot condemn their King to public death. But what may not be done in private—?

His mouth was too dry to form words. As in a silent nightmare, he watched the men-at-arms group themselves around him – not jostling or touching him in any way but forming a solid leather-coated wall between him and freedom. On their sleeves they wore the Star badge of Oxford. He could hope for no pity from that House, two of whose members he had executed; and the present Earl, standing quietly nearby now, had been lately tortured by his orders in the Tower, during the Cook trial... Oxford, he noted remotely, was wearing white silk gloves over his mutilated hands—

'Sire,' the Archbishop was saying, 'let us set out for Warwick Castle. Then, when we have rested there and taken council, we shall go on to Middleham where Your Grace is to be kept.'

'As prisoner?' Edward shouted as he was led outside. 'And for how long?'

'Aye, Sire—' Oxford spoke for the first time '—as prisoner of the Earl of Warwick. And for as long as may be necessary to right this land's wrongs.'

Edward glared from Oxford to the Archbishop who had now emerged from the inn. For Oxford, he felt nothing except contempt: the Earl had poured out a sobbing confession in the torture-chamber which had led to the arrests of many other men while securing his own release. But, for the Neville Archbishop who had so lately been his smiling host at 'The Moor' (and who had then darted off, quick as a water-rat, to read the marriage service over foolish young George and

Isobel) the King had suddenly conceived a searing hatred. Irrationally, it was a hatred far more intense than he felt for either Warwick or Clarence... For as long as Edward might live, his lust for vengeance would pursue George of York—

'I never wronged you,' he said bitterly now to the Archbishop, 'except maybe when I took the Great Seal from you and gave it to Robert Stillington. Is *that* why you treat me thus?'

The fair Neville eyebrows lifted a fraction. A plump white hand fastidiously brushed a cobweb from a gold-eyeleted sleeve.

'My lord King may bestow the Great Seal where he wishes,' York said then, 'and mayhap the good Bishop of Bath and Wells is a better keeper of it than I... No, my liege, that was not what stung me.'

'What then?'

'A little jest of Your Grace's at my expense. It was when I had an innocent ambition to become a Prince-Cardinal of the Church. You Sire, by your influence with the Holy Father, blocked my advancement. And when Canterbury was given the Cardinal's hat in my stead, you mockingly sent me the Pope's letter... Such sharp-edged jests, Sire, may be weapons that turn upon the sender.'

'I see. Thank you for this lesson, Archbishop. I will remember it, and be more adult in my behaviour in the future.'

Thoughtfully, Edward mounted his horse which was surrounded by Oxford's men-at-arms. So, he had always been brash and tactless; a boy among grown men who were dangerously jealous of one another. Well, from this day forward, his would be one of the most discreet and cunning brains in Europe. *And he would use that sharpened brain to regain his freedom—*

A woman was thrusting her way through the armed men.

'Let me pass, you scum,' Margery of the big breasts was shouting. 'I'll kiss my King farewell or die for it!'

As she stumbled against his horse's flank, Edward could see that her plump red face was nauseatingly awash with tears; yet it seemed to him that he had never beheld a more beautiful human face, loyal and loving... Almost with humility, he bent down and kissed it – tasting the salt; smelling the sweat and grime that was the composite odour of all his lower subjects. And suddenly it came to him that *this* was how he would obtain release: by the passionate objection of the commons to his imprisonment, and by their stubborn refusal to be governed by any other man while he lived.

A surge of ridiculous optimism flooded through him as he was led captive out of the inn yard. The wheel of fate would swing him up again! And who might predict to what desperate straits his enemies could be reduced, in the course of time?

13

April, 1470

THE APRIL NIGHT had settled to a steady drizzle as the fugitives approached the quayside at Exeter. Warwick had paid the masters of six small ships to carry himself, his family and a few score attendants to Calais. Flight from England was the only safeguard from the King's fury. Impatiently, he motioned his wife aboard...

The Countess of Warwick was too numbed from terror and fatigue even to notice the narrow sloping gangplank, spanning dark water, up which she was being hustled. She was aware only of England's length between herself and Middleham Castle; where the King, who now pursued her husband and her son-in-law, had been so lately a prisoner... Slipping and stumbling on the wet wood, the Countess moaned softly to herself.

'It's all right, Mother, we're safe now.' Her younger daughter, Anne, placed a comforting arm around her waist and drew her across the rocking deck of the *Mary*

Exeter towards an awning that offered some shelter from the rain.

'We shall never be all right again, child. Never, *never*. Oh, where is my poor Isobel?'

'She's coming, with George...'

The figures of the young Duke and Duchess of Clarence swayed into the light of the deck lanterns, George supporting his nine-month-pregnant wife. Both their faces were so white and strained that Anne started towards them with a gasped 'George, what's wrong?' There seemed no point in addressing Isobel who appeared to be almost unconscious.

George said distractedly: 'Her labour has begun. Jesus, at such a time! What shall we do – *what shall we do?*'

Before Anne could reply, her father's voice came harshly from the top of the gangplank: 'Take her below, of course. See to the servants and the baggage. We cast off at once – the King is near.'

'The King.' Clarence froze to paralysis for a moment. Then, pushing Isobel into Anne's outstretched arms, he fumbled for the flask at his belt. With his head tipped back and his throat stretched, he staggered towards the rail.

The Earl of Warwick was striding on deck at that instant with the few friends who remained to him (he'd lost several at the 'battle of loose-coat field' – so called because many had fled from it before the King's onslaught, leaving their weapons and mantles behind). He paused briefly now to stare at his son-in-law. But Clarence remained oblivious of the look in which anger was mixed with a contemptuous disgust: Clarence had grown used to the idea that his wife's sire did not care much for his company any longer.

In the teeth of a gale, the *Mary Exeter* and her five attendant vessels battled eastward, past Portland Bill and St Albans Head. Then, swinging into the Solent where the

Isle of Wight gave some shelter, she made for Southampton.

In Southampton Water, Warwick knew, his own great ship the *Trinity* was riding at anchor among other vessels of the royal fleet. He intended to take her from under the very nose of the absurd new admiral, Anthony Woodville – that most elegant of the Queen's brothers, who had lately inherited his dead sire's title of Earl Rivers... That the King had given Rivers charge of his entire fleet was a measure of how limited was the royal choice these days, Warwick thought; and he savoured again for a moment the satisfaction of executing favourites. Ah, it had been worthwhile, the seizing and imprisoning of the King! – those few weeks of total power until the people's agitations for Edward's release had had to be met.

As Warwick strained now for a sight of the *Trinity*, he remembered how changed Edward had been for a while afterwards. The King had seemed uncharacteristically quiet and self-restrained. All the old boisterous exuberance had gone out of him: he'd been thoughtful – watchful – extremely civil in his language to everyone, even to the Archbishop of York and the Earl of Oxford. But Oxford had fled abroad now. And George Neville was under armed guard at 'The Moor'.

Still, all winter, Edward had shown no malice or resentment for the humiliations he'd suffered – no passion or craving for revenge. A kind of sad maturity had come over him; but, with it, an even more inflexible will than formerly to do exactly as he deemed fit, without advice from anyone.

It was this determination of the King's to go his own way – to wear the Burgundian Order of the Golden Fleece; to remain at enmity with France; and to keep the surviving Woodvilles safe about him, even to the point of freeing that old harridan, Jacquetta from a witchcraft charge – it was all of these royal attitudes combined which finally convinced Warwick that he could never re-assert his former influence. Edward was not afraid of him, his ex-jailer. In fact, imprisonment had shown Edward his own strength: that the greater part of the country was behind him.

Most parts in fact, except Lincolnshire. There, at the turn of the year, a Lancastrian revival had begun to stir...

Warwick had planned to lead the King into dangerous Lincolnshire; isolate and surround him there; and hope that Edward would be killed in the ensuing battle or driven into exile. In either case, Clarence was to have been crowned at once in his stead, with Isobel Neville as his Queen.

Isobel's father sighed heavily now for the recollection of so many plans that had gone astray, and for his own fast-diminishing affection for Clarence. It was Clarence's carelessness and stupidity which had allowed certain letters to fall into the King's hands – letters detailing the intent to have himself made King, even while he was still dissembling to convince his brother of his love!

That had been the end of Edward's clemency and tolerance. He'd added up the evidence – of riots stirred, of seditious writings circulated – and had arrived at a verdict upon both Warwick and Clarence: that, not content with depriving him of his chosen friends, they were determined to deprive him of his crown also: *they were self-damned traitors*. Like a thunderbolt, the King had issued out of York with a huge army and had pursued the rebels though all his realm, executing their adherents as he went, at Pontefract, Doncaster, Newark, Nottingham – and keeping by his side the fearful John Tiptoft, Earl of Worcester, who had executed the Desmond family... Worcester had been made Constable of England after the 'battle of loose-coat field' so that rebels might know they could expect no mercy... At Nottingham, the King put a price on the traitors' heads. At Coventry and Salisbury he called men to arms to help him pursue his 'most treacherous kin' who were reported to be in the west country. Then he thundered down into Devon, hoping to fall upon them before they could quit the realm.

But the *Mary Exeter* had come to the rescue in the nick of time. Now she would be assumed to be on her way to Calais, not beating up the Solent with a piratical plan in her commander's mind: to spirit away the *Trinity* and any other vessel available of the royal fleet. Ships were more negotiable abroad than gold.

Warwick's raid on Southampton was a disastrous failure. Not only did Admiral Rivers beat off his attack, he took from him two of the *Mary Exeter's* convoy vessels as well, with the crews and passengers. The other three vessels, led by the *Mary*, fled southeast past Spithead and made all speed for Calais.

It was the first time in his career that Warwick had ever been beaten at sea. Angry and humiliated, he retired below deck to snatch a brief sleep after Beachy Head had been safely rounded. But Isobel's constant moanings from beyond the partition kept him in a state of half-waking. Yet he dreamed – a strange and disturbing dream...

In it, he was back in his own Castle of Warwick; and he was examining (as he'd done last September while the King was a prisoner there) an image of a man-at-arms which had been brought to him by one Thomas Wake. This image was made of lead. It was about a finger's length and had been broken across the middle, the breach joined with pieces of wire.

'My lord,' Wake had told him at the time, 'this witchcraft figure has been found in possession of the Queen's mother, Jacquetta Woodville. It represents yourself, and it has been used to compass your destruction by means of spells and incantations… Two other figures also the Dowager-Duchess had: one representing the King and the other the Queen. And they have been bound to one another with silver wire from the head to the feet, since a full year before the royal marriage. To this I have a witness.'

Warwick had thrown the leaden image down upon a table. Much as he'd have liked to see Jacquetta burnt for a witch, he wasn't going to waste his time on such unproveable nonsense as this… He'd dismissed Wake, advising him to take the image with him and make his allegations elsewhere; and he'd never seen either the man or the leaden statue again. But he *had* seen Jacquetta in connection with the charge. In February, she'd come before a meeting of the Great Council; at which the King was once more presiding and both Warwick and Clarence were present – their plans to depose Edward still being secret at that time.

To this Council, Jacquetta made a pious declaration that she had 'always believed in God according to the truth of Holy Church' and had never practised any form of witchcraft in her life.

At the insistence of the King, the Council freed her…

Now, in his dream, Warwick was reaching again for the leaden figure which Thomas Wake was holding out to him. But when he took it in his hand, he saw that it was a perfect miniature of himself, not the rough and unrecognisable image that had been shown to him last September… This figure had been stripped of its armour; it wore only a loin cloth. And it was wounded all over in its leaden flesh – blood spurting from the deep gashes… As he tried to wipe the sticky redness from his hand, he heard Jacquetta's voice screaming:

'I believe in the Devil according to the truth of the Other Ones. I have practised witchcraft all my life; and have used it to secure two husbands for myself and two for my daughter Elizabeth. Also I have called upon the Power to protect Edward. Know ye, his enemies, that he is invincible from without. *Only the King can destroy the King—*'

Sweating, and wiping his hands feverishly on his shirt, Warwick started up. He imagined he could still hear Jacquetta screaming – just as he'd heard her in Calais long ago, across the bonfires, after he'd kidnapped herself and her family. God, how she'd cursed him then—

But no, this voice was full of pain and terror, not malediction. *This voice was Isobel's.*

Heedless of the tradition which kept all men outside a child-birth room, he rushed into the women's quarters. He took his daughter in his arms and rocked her back and forth against his chest... He was only dimly aware of the other people in the pitching, candlelit space. His wife. His younger daughter Anne. A few female servants.

He asked a woman who seemed to be acting as midwife:

'How long must this go on?'

But the anxious woman did not know how long Isobel's labour might continue in the cramped and rolling conditions of the little ship. It might be hours – days even; and there was grave risk both to mother and child.

'I'll have us into Calais by morning,' Warwick vowed. 'Hush, Isobel, *hush.*'

Her resumed screaming went through him like knives. Flesh of his flesh, he could feel her pain. He loved his two children with a passion he had never known for any other human being, even for his wife. And his own suffering now was more intense than Isobel's. For she was quite mindless with anguished terror but he was brilliantly aware. Of guilt for the delay at Southampton. Of danger. Of total responsibility. And of the possible death of a grandchild who might be a boy – his only heir—

In his shirtsleeves, he charged back up on deck and began to harangue every seaman in sight to get the last ounce of speed out of the *Mary Exeter*.

Calais: Christ, let Calais be on the horizon with the dawn!

A misted, primrose light showed the fortifications of the port-town which England had held for so long on foreign soil, and over which the Earl of Warwick had been captain for so many years that he never doubted his welcome there.

The *Mary Exeter* was swinging around to enter harbour when the first warning shots rang out.

Puzzled, Warwick looked from the smoking cannon ashore up to his own masthead. His ensign was clearly visible there, as it must be visible to the gunners. But he hurriedly ordered another banner to be broken out, showing the Bear and Ragged Staff of his earldom.

The only recognition of this that Calais gave was to send a further half-dozen balls ploughing up the water in the *Mary's* path to anchorage. Meanwhile, several longboats filled with armed men were leaping out from the quays.

'Drop anchor,' Warwick ordered his own crew... When the rattle of the chain had ceased, the first longboat was near enough to be hailed.

'Garrison of Calais,' roared the intimidating voice of the great Earl, 'what are ye madmen about?'

'My lord—' a young officer whom Warwick himself had trained stood up amidships '—we have received orders from King Edward not to admit you here.'

Warwick stared down at him incredulously. Only his own orders had ever been heeded at Calais... 'The devil you have,' he spat. Then, 'Where is your marshal, Lord

Duras?' he demanded. 'And your commander, Lord Wenlock?' Both men were his friends: they could not have ordered the garrison to fire on his ships.

'They are within the town, my lord. They regret this action, as do we all. But we are loyal to the King, and you shall not enter the harbour.'

'Indeed...' He tried not to let his defeat and his desperation show, but there was a plea in his following words: 'Then tell my lords this without delay. My daughter, Her Grace of Clarence, is below decks of this ship, and she is in difficult travail of childbirth. I will remain outside the harbour, but I cannot put to sea again until Her Grace be delivered and rested. I ask but for the assurance that my vessels will not be attacked.'

For several days, the Exeter ships lay outside Calais' harbour, the mouth of which was constantly patrolled by the longboats while the inshore cannon pointed menacingly... On the first morning, a gift of wine had been sent out from the town 'for the comfort of the Duchess of Clarence'. But, that evening, a small bundle had been carried up to the *Mary Exeter*'s aftercastle, and prayers read over it. Then the Earl of Warwick himself had lowered the body of his infant grandson into the sea...

At the end of the week, the small ships weighed anchor and sailed off westward towards the French port of Honfleur. They were escorted by some pirate vessels that had joined them under the command of Thomas Neville, the Bastard of Fauconberg...

'If I were King Edward,' said Marshal Duras to Commander Wenlock of Calais as they watched their formidable visitors' departure, 'I would be very worried. Cousins Warwick and Fauconberg sailing together, with their heir to the English crown. And French Louis' coastline the only place where they're all welcome to land!'

14

June, 1470

IN THE JUNE SUNSHINE, King Louis was pacing the terrace of his castle of Amboise high above the River Loire. Every few minutes he halted abruptly and, shielding his narrowed eyes with the greasy brim of his hat, peered into the northern distance. His expected guests ought to be in sight by now, riding down from Normandy where he'd kept them in food and shelter this month past, and where he was yet having their womenfolk cared for. Ah, the expense of harbouring exiles!

Early this morning he'd sent half his Court out from Amboise to escort the visitors to the castle. For he still had this odd compulsion to treat Monsieur de Warwick, at least, as though he were a travelling monarch. Yet, Louis reminded himself as he began his pacing again, the English Earl was now but a landless exile; useful only if he could be made to serve French political ends. Those ends were quite clear in Louis' crafty mind (whose workings were said to be known only to his horse). They were, very simply, to keep England in a state of perpetual turmoil so that she could not attack France.

'It is good policy – but can I see it through?' His bitten nails scraped at his bluish chin. He knew Warwick well enough; they'd corresponded for almost a decade and, three years ago, they'd last met in Rouen. There, Warwick had promised Louis that he'd keep King Edward in friendship with France. He'd failed, of course. He'd allowed the damned Burgundian alliance to be made – just as he'd allowed the Woodville one previously – and, this time, he'd completely lost his hold over Edward. Imprisoning the King indeed, and expecting to run the country without one – stupid! Warwick should have learned from the bitter experience of those French nobles who'd once locked Louis himself up in Paris... Still, there was a brand new plan under discussion now and it might succeed if only by its very unlikeliness – although the present heir to the English crown, monsieur de Clarence, would hardly be overjoyed when he heard of it.

It was this: Warwick was to offer assistance to Margaret of Anjou in replacing Lancastrian Henry upon the throne of England. But, so that Warwick might not lose what he'd already gained for his own family by wedding his elder daughter Isobel to Clarence, he was to demand Margaret's consent to another marriage: that of his younger daughter Anne to the Lancastrian Prince.

Louis chuckled as he visualised Margaret's face when these proposals would be first put to her! She detested Warwick: regarded him as the prime cause of all her misfortunes. She'd be difficult – was there ever a time when she was *not* difficult? – even about the little matter of meeting the Earl. But in the end she'd come around to the sensible viewpoint which her own brother, John of

Calabria, had been the first to propose. It was her only hope of ever seeing her consort upon the English throne again, and her son heir to that throne. The price she'd pay must be submission to Warwick's wishes, now and in the future. For Warwick intended to rule England through the weak and pious Henry as he'd failed to rule it through Edward.

The Earl had always been the friend of France and the misliker of France's greatest enemy, Burgundy. So, Louis was willing to dig deep into his own coffers to help the Neville-Lancaster alliance…

Ah, here were the travellers now, coming down the Normandy road towards the bridge! Louis did a rapid count of them and, subtracting the number of his own courtiers, found that the English attendants were very few indeed around Messieurs de Warwick, Clarence and Oxford. Such a change from three years ago when Warwick alone had had six hundred people in his entourage! *Eh bien, c'est la vie…* Genially whistling up his dogs, but ignoring those courtiers who'd remained in attendance upon him in the blistering sunshine, Louis set off at a fast walking pace for the main gate of Amboise. His crooked legs looked like those of boiled crabs in their orange hose; and his battered hat seemed to be weighted down over his eyebrows by all the charms and the pilgrims' tokens festooning its crown and its brim… Louis didn't mind occasionally changing his clothes for important visitors; but he'd be hanged if he'd change his hat!

As he scrunched over the dazzling white gravel of the central courtyard, his shaded eyes raked to and fro to see that all was in order; the blue banners of France showing their Golden Lilies over the battlements; ceremonial archers and trumpeters lined up around the black arch of the gate; and, over in the castle's great doorway, the hugely pregnant Queen Charlotte standing patiently among her ladies as he'd ordered her to do, to receive her English guests... Louis nodded absently at his Queen-consort as though she were a part of the building, while the thought flickered briefly across his mind:

What will the stupid woman produce this time – another female infant more ugly and crippled than the last?

He'd ensured that the deformed Princess Jeanne would be kept out of sight today lest Monsieur de Clarence see her. For Jeanne had once been offered as wife to Clarence in a bid to buy England's friendship...

But Louis had no mental energies to waste just now on domestic matters. As he plunged under the shadow of the arch and began to stride down the hill towards the town, his main problem was how to placate Duke Charles of Burgundy. Charles was vigorously protesting at the presence of English rebels on French soil – maintaining that it was an act of hostility to himself for his brother-in-law's enemies to be harboured!

Louis knew he would have to tread carefully, as ever. Not keep Warwick here long enough to bring dangerous Burgundy thundering into France; and yet not rush the delicate proceedings with Margaret of Anjou... Ah, it was all going to be very worrying and tiresome. Especially since that Neville pirate, the Bastard Fauconberg, had begun stealing Duke Charles' ships—

Yet, one had to look beyond small difficulties. Keep the gaze fixed on England, where a lifetime of turmoil could be maintained by playing a Yorkist against a Lancastrian King.

For neither of whom, in their anointed persons, Louis cared one jot.

It took the King of France six exhausting and expensive weeks to bring about a meeting between Warwick and the ex-Queen (Margaret having proved just as intractable as he'd feared). But he'd worked on her with patience, and with the good-humour engendered by having a son of his own at last: Queen Charlotte had given birth to a boy on June 30th. This fact rejoiced Louis' heart and made him tolerant of Margaret's stubbornness. Finally she'd agreed to meet the Earl of Warwick in the castle of Angers…

It was late on the evening of July 22nd when Louis led the ex-Queen and her councillors into the room where Warwick waited with his brother-in-law of Oxford (Clarence having been persuaded by Warwick to return to Normandy.)

'Monsieur de Warwick,' Louis said, 'here is the rightful Queen of England. How do you greet Her Grace?'

Warwick replied: 'With a vow to be a faithful subject to her consort for evermore.' Then he kneeled to Margaret…

She kept him on his knees for fifteen minutes while she harangued him for his acts against Lancaster. The Earl gritted his teeth and made no reply. Louis hovered over them both, trying to put an end to Margaret's monologue in case it should prove too much for Warwick's patience. But at last the ex-Queen was satisfied with her revenge and ready to listen to terms.

Yes, she would accept the Earl of Warwick as an ally. Yes, she would give him charge of the invasion fleet. But no, emphatically *no*, she would not allow him to take the Prince, her son, to England with him on this risky enterprise: the Prince would go there only after everything had been made safe for him.

Warwick – now sitting with Oxford among the Angevin councillors – reluctantly agreed to sail without the Prince although he'd desperately wanted him as a focus for Lancastrian hopes in England. But—

'Madame,' he said, 'before I board ship, the Prince will

wed my younger daughter.' Then he folded his arms across his chest and met and held Margaret's furious stare.

In that moment they looked so alike that they might have been brother and sister: two hard, proud, handsome people who perfectly understood one another's ambitions, and who had already accounted the price each must pay the other for aid.

~

Anne Neville had kept her fourteenth birth-feast in Normandy this June past, in the harbourside house at Honfleur which King Louis had provided for her mother and Isobel and herself. It was the first birthday she'd ever had outside of Middleham Castle and there'd been no celebrations – no presents even except a cask of pirated Burgundian wine from cousin Tom Fauconberg... Anne didn't care much for wine, but she'd kissed the Bastard's red beard in gratitude for his remembrance of her. Besides, the wine might do Isobel good if she could be made to drink some.

But that was weeks ago now, and Isobel was yet weak and ailing. She'd taken childbed fever while the *Mary Exeter* was still at sea, and had later been carried ashore at Honfleur, raving in delirium. Afterwards – when George had left her for his journey to Amboise – she'd fallen quiet and apathetic. She, who had always been so lively, just lay every day in the upper chamber, staring out at the sky through the mast-tops of the ships which belonged to cousin Fauconberg and her father... Sometimes, glancing at Isobel, Anne was shocked to see on her face the same expression which old Aunt Katherine Neville's had borne when they'd told her of her boy-husband's execution. Katherine of Norfolk had adored

John Woodville. Isobel had been ready to adore George's baby...

Although she felt stifled in the sickroom, Anne spent as much time as she could with her sister. But she found it hard to keep conversation going now without mention of the stupefying order which had come from the King of France:

'The Lady Anne Neville is to be brought to the cathedral of Angers, for a solemn betrothal between her and the most noble Prince, son and heir of Henry and Queen Margaret.'

A betrothal – which would be as binding as a marriage in all but the physical act. And to a youth whom she'd never met, but who was reported to be as arrogant and as bloodthirsty as the Queen who'd borne him sixteen and a half years ago. Anne was still numb with horror at the prospect. Yet she could not unburden her mind to Isobel, who would then have to be told the whole truth: that the mast-tops she could see from her window belonged to an invasion fleet waiting to sail for England, where it would help re-instate Henry of Lancaster upon the throne. And it would be Anne's husband, not Isobel's, who would be heir to that throne... Isobel's George was to be fobbed off with the Dukedom of York. So all the perils and hardships of the past year were for nothing – the runaway marriage and the fearful childbirth, the exile and the fever— No, Anne could not tell her sister these tidings. George would have to do it after she'd left quietly for Angers with her mother...

George was sober enough now; although for three days following his sudden return from Amboise, he'd kept himself locked in his chamber with no sustenance except the remains of the birth-feast wine. Then he'd taken to prowling about the quaysides; or else sitting in a tavern, talking to a mysterious dark-haired English lady who was lodging there, while Isobel fretted at home for his company.

As they made their own preparations for the betrothal journey, Anne and her mother were almost out of their minds with anxiety over this behaviour of George's. Dear God, if he were going to be unfaithful to Isobel, did he have to choose this time to do it when she'd be wholly dependent upon him?

Anne, sitting rigidly silent opposite her mother in the litter, was thinking about Richard of Gloucester. How she'd wept for him when he'd left Middleham Castle for good, his squirehood over. And how he'd waved to her all the way down the Jervaulx road towards the Coverbridge Inn... Her cousin Dickon was the only boy she'd ever felt really at ease with. Though he wouldn't be a boy anymore, of course. He was near eighteen now, and King Edward had been heaping responsibilities upon him for a long while – he was Lieutenant of Ireland, Chief Justiciar of Wales, warden of the west march; all titles which had been taken away from his rebel kin... There was no possibility of Dickon's ever turning rebel: he was earnest, conscientious, and he had total integrity...

Heart-sick, Anne thought how confidently she would have embarked upon this betrothal journey if it were Dickon, and not Margaret of Anjou's son, who awaited her at the end of it. Because Dickon, alone, would understand one thing: that, since the fearful hours of Isobel's labour below the *Mary Exeter's* deck, she herself had been obsessed with a horror of childbirth. That demented night outside Calais, she'd felt that she was watching a protracted execution, brutal and bloody. And there hadn't even been a living infant at the end of it to make people rejoice and forget. There'd been nothing but the little canvas-wrapped bundle to be tipped into the sea.

The birth-scene had been the most terrible experience of Anne's life. And, although she knew that birth could be beautiful (for she'd often watched the animals in Middleham's stables producing their young) she felt that, for herself, it could never be anything except an act of martyrdom, undertaken for someone whom she loved as much as God – someone who'd accept and return that love. Someone like Dickon...

She expected no love between herself and the haughty Lancastrian Prince.

Her one shred of hope, now, was that the solemnisation – and consummation – of their marriage might be delayed. For she'd been told how strenuously the ex-Queen had objected to the proposed union; and how Margaret had only agreed to it finally on the sworn promise that her son would not be required to lie with the Earl of Warwick's daughter until the Earl had conquered England for Lancaster.

The invasion was to begin as soon as the ships were ready. They'd been almost ready when Anne and her mother had left Honfleur.

∼

FROM WHERE HE was sitting in the quayside tavern, George had a drink-blurred vision of the hulks of Fauconberg's ships. Soon, he himself would be a voyager on one of those vessels. It would carry him to England to make war upon his royal brother Edward.

But what was it that the dark lady had said to him, over and over again, at this very table? 'My lord, be not so foolish as to help destroy your own great House of York. For York's White Rose must wither if Lancaster be restored

– and that restoration is exactly what the Earl of Warwick is planning.'

At first, George hadn't believed her – although he'd been puzzled about many things during the conference at Amboise; not least, his father-in-law's advice that he should leave there! But the French King's sudden summons to Anne Neville, to travel at once to Angers for a betrothal service with the Lancastrian Prince, had finally convinced George that he himself was to be set aside in the new struggle for the crown.

Then Warwick had written to him, admitting this; but promising him instead the Dukedom of York 'when all England be conquered by us'.

All his adult life, George had been manipulated by stronger, cleverer people, and allowed only the temporary powers and honours of a King's deputy. He'd longed to be King – had gambled everything on the bid, and perjured his own soul in lying letters to Edward. But the prospect of being merely Duke of York could stir no flicker of ambition in him. He no longer wanted any part of the invasion enterprise. Yet—

'I am committed,' he'd said wearily to the dark lady. 'If I try to break away now, they will kill me.'

'Listen, Your Grace—' she'd leant towards him in that earnest way of hers '—you can voyage to England with the rest of the rebels if you cannot get away before. But, once there, you must go straight to the King.'

'Brother Edward would have my head!'

'*No.* I come from him, through the most noble Duchess of York who has never ceased to intercede for you. There is a promise of reconciliation held out – if you will but *ask* for it, my lord Duke, and swear to be loyal in the future. Now, how say you? What answer may I carry back with me to England?'

But he'd given her no answer to carry... Confused and vacillating, he could arrive at no firm decision about what to do: whether to cling to his father-in-law and hope for the best, or throw himself on his brother's doubtful mercies.

Edward did not like him: George knew that well enough. This courageous dark lady had either come of her own initiative or had been sent privately by Cecily of York – the King would not have troubled himself to send her...

She'd gone away now and George was alone at the tavern table. For a single instant, the wild idea crossed his mind of fleeing to Burgundy where his sister, the Duchess Margaret, would shield him from *all* his enemies—

Then he remembered Isobel. Isobel was too weak to travel and he could not leave her behind... In an odd way, he loved his young wife: she was the only possession that could not be taken from him. Except by death. And, God be praised, she'd escaped that. Although the boy-child had died...

'We buried him by Calais,' George said thickly to a group of Fauconberg's men who'd just come into the tavern.

'Who, my lord?'

'Why, my sh— my son, of course. And, anon, we'll all be voyaging over hish grave. Towards Englan' – *England*.'

To the embarrassment of the tough Fauconberg crew, Clarence put his head down on his folded arms, and wept.

'Why, he's as soft as old King Henry,' said one of the captains contemptuously.

15

Autumn, 1470

To the dim apartments in the Tower where Henry of Lancaster had been kept these five years, the Mayor and aldermen of London were making their way, led by the Bishop of Winchester.

'What condition will he be in by now?' wondered one alderman, his robes catching on the rough stones of the passage walls.

'Pray God we can make him understand what is required of him,' another said – over a shoulder from which the Yorkist collar of Suns and Roses had been hastily removed, at the report that King Edward had fled the country before Warwick's advance...

London was still in a state of tumult from both items of news: the King's flight and Warwick's march on the capital. All manner of criminals had poured out of the sanctuaries, yelling that they were 'loyal Lancastrians'. The Kentish men were massed, thousands strong, to join Warwick as soon as he arrived from the west country where sixty ships had landed him and his followers on September 13th. Beerhouses were being broken open by rioters. Foreign merchants went in fear of their lives and properties. Members of King Edward's Great Council had fled, realising there was nothing they could do in the name of a sovereign who'd taken to the high seas and disbanded his army.

Total confusion reigned everywhere. And last night, the uproar in the city had been so great that Queen Elizabeth had quit the Tower in terror... Taking her three small daughters with her she'd flown to the sanctuary of Westminster Abbey; for it appeared that the Tower itself was under siege by the Kentishmen and the Thames boatmen, who'd by then joined forces and were chanting:

'À Warwick, à Clarence, à Warwick—'

Listening to them, Elizabeth had become almost paralysed by the idea of what they might do to a Yorkist Queen and Princesses whose King had so unaccountably left his country. Yet only a few days ago, Edward had been reported marching bravely down from York to meet the rebels in battle. Then, without warning, he'd turned east; made a reckless dash across the Wash (where scores of his men had been drowned) and taken ships from Bishops Lynn on Michaelmas Day... it was an action totally out of character for Edward. Some fearful circumstance must have precipitated it. Yet, even while she understood this, Elizabeth's first reaction had been of anger with him for deserting her and the children.

Now, some said that Edward was captured – killed even – by the Hansards of whom he'd made enemies years ago. Others maintained that he was still trying to reach the low countries, hoping for aid from his brother-in-law of Burgundy. But all were agreed that his once-great army was reduced to a miserable few hundred, with only three commanders besides the King himself: Richard of Gloucester, William Lord Hastings and Anthony Woodville, Earl Rivers…

Not knowing what to believe, Elizabeth had fled the Tower under cover of darkness. She'd intended going to her mother-in-law at Baynard's Castle because she knew that that great house would be safe, Cecily being kinswoman to all sides. But when her barge tried to draw near the water-steps there, it was forced back into mid-river by a frightening mêlée of other vessels engaged in combat. The children began screaming in terror as blazing brands hissed into the water close to, and threshing bodies rocked the royal barge from which all Rose and Sun cognizances had been stripped in an effort at anonymity – although Elizabeth realised that her own face was too well-known not to be recognised, should it be glimpsed in the barbarous glow of the torches. Then, even her eight-month pregnancy might not save her from rape—

'Go on to Westminster,' she gasped to the barge-master. 'We will seek sanctuary there.' The October night was cold but sweat was trickling her spine; and the movement of the child within her, coupled with the barge's bucking, enveloped her in waves of nausea… If only she'd conceived this infant at Fotheringhay a year gone July, it would have been born and five months old by now! And she'd been so certain that night. Yet it hadn't happened. She'd had to wait for the ending of Edward's imprisonment at Middleham. Then there'd been his new, strange mood of withdrawal to get through, so that it had been February before she'd conceived his child… Last month then, Edward had installed her in luxury in the Tower to await her confinement due in November. He'd done this before setting out on his fatal journey to the north, whither he'd been decoyed by Lord FitzHugh, husband of Warwick's sister Alice. FitzHugh had raised a rebellion to lure Edward as far as possible from where the rebels would land in Devonshire. Foolishly, the King had gone chasing after FitzHugh. But when he'd looked for reinforcements from the great northern baron, John Neville, who'd aided him for years, Neville had turned upon him with the snarled reminder:

'Sire, you released the rebel Percy from prison and made much of him in your royal company. You took from me – who had earned it in arms – the princely Earldom of Northumberland, and gave it to Percy. And you expected me to be content with the paltry title of Marquis of Montagu, with only a magpie's nest of a pension upon which to maintain it – I, John Neville, who have spent my manhood fighting your wars!'

Elizabeth realised, as her barge strained on for Westminster, that John Neville's defection was probably the key reason for Edward's flight. Without Neville support the King could not survive in the north – could not even collect more forces there with which to meet the rebels from Devonshire. So, on September 29th, he'd fled the country – probably fearing not so much death as another term of imprisonment such as he'd endured only a year ago; and whose effect upon his mind and spirit none knew better than Elizabeth who'd heard his nightmare ravings...

But what now – *what now*, for her and her children? Sanctuary in some cramped quarter of the Abbey buildings at Westminster, and for God only knew how long! Without comfort – without even a change of clothing unless her ladies could follow her and bring some—

It had always been the one dread of her life, to be returned to the circumstances from which Edward had lifted her. Now that dread was reality. Even the children's hands clinging to hers reminded her of Tom and Richard Grey's long ago in Whittlewood Forest. Only she'd been so much younger then. And unburdened by an unborn infant.

As she stepped ashore and approached the dark shadow of the Abbey, she remembered her coronation within its walls: the splendour, the adulation, the luxuries heaped upon her by her adoring Edward. It was little more than five years ago that she'd been crowned Queen of England. Yet already it felt as if it had happened to another person. Or not at all. Now she was a frightened, heavily pregnant (and perhaps widowed) woman in her mid-thirties, pushing three snivelling children in front of her towards a dark, unwelcoming building. Behind her, a capital seething with riot, so that no one had time any more to read the copies of Warwick's manifesto which was nailed to church and inn doors:

'Fellow countrymen, you are called upon to rescue our most sovereign lord, King Henry the Sixth, true and undoubted King of England, from the hands of his great rebel and enemy Edward, late Earl of March, usurper, oppressor and destroyer of noble blood—'

It was on the following morning that the Mayor and aldermen came to the Tower to carry out the orders of this manifest. The Bishop of Winchester, leading them, said:

'These are Henry's apartments. Gentlemen, let us go to our true sovereign and do him homage.'

They had all dressed in their richest robes for the momentous visit. But no one had remembered to prepare Henry...

Uncombed, unshaven, and wearing a shabby gown of faded blue velvet, he was standing by the barred window, feeding the remnants of last night's supper to the birds that came to him every morning. In the changeover of the garrison, the keepers and all other Tower staff (after the discovery of the Queen's flight) even his meagre needs had been overlooked: no breakfast had been brought to him, no washing bowl.

After the civic dignitaries had all kneeled to him and tried to make him understand what was happening, they took him to those luxurious chambers which Edward had prepared for Elizabeth's next confinement. Then some of them went off to the King's wardrobe to seek rich robes that would fit him, so that he might *look* like a King when Warwick would take him out into the streets of the capital, to proclaim his re-instatement.

On October 13th, Henry entered Paul's church in the midst of a great procession, Oxford's gloved hands carrying the Sword of State before him, and Warwick and Clarence bearing his train. At the altar the crown was placed upon his head by the Archbishop of York, who had lately got through his armed guards at 'The Moor'. Then, after a Mass of Thanksgiving had been sung, the procession left the church to wend its way down towards the river, where a magnificently decked barge waited to take Henry to Westminster Palace.

It was a misty autumn day, and the crowds massed in the riot-littered streets were oddly subdued. Their cheering was ragged and spasmodic as Henry of Lancaster passed by. Henry's crowned and mounted figure had little about it to excite their enthusiasm: he looked bent and old, and his eyes lacked lustre. Many men recalled with nostalgia Edward's flamboyant progresses. Many women remembered Edward's tender, sensual mouth.

As the procession of barges moved out onto the grey Thames, Cecily watched from a window of Baynard's Castle. Her life's experiences had taught her the truth of the old proverb which she'd first heard in Dublin long ago:

'Up awhile and down awhile is the lot of all men, high or low.'

But today, her belief in the survival of the House of York was almost gone. For, although she now knew that Edward had landed safely on Flemish soil, she could see no prospect of his winning back his kingdom. He'd been too tactless while in power. He'd alienated those very men, like John Neville, whom he'd most needed and had showered his favours in all the wrong places. Well, she'd warned him; tried to advise him. But since his first fever of infatuation for Elizabeth Woodville, he'd refused to listen to her. And she'd become powerless to *make* him listen – she, who had once been his chief councillor had become a mere suppliant, pleading mainly for her son George.

She battled now against the bitter loneliness filling her heart... Of the huge family into which she'd been born at Raby Castle fifty-five years ago, there were only three survivors besides herself: these were Katherine and Ann, the Dowager-Duchesses of Norfolk and of Buckingham; and Edward, Lord Abergavenny... All her own sons were gone from her: Edward and Richard into exile, George into the hostile Neville camp, and Edmund into the grave beside his father... With her daughters she had little contact; an occasional busy letter from Margaret in Burgundy; a rare visit from Anne or Beth – the former grown worryingly thin and haggard-looking, though still defiant about her right to betroth Exeter's heiress to one of the Queen's sons, and the latter utterly absorbed in her growing family of de la Pole boys...

Once, Cecily had counted herself the luckiest woman alive for the seven handsome, healthy, intelligent children she'd managed to rear out of the thirteen born to her. Now, she sometimes felt that they were all doomed through the blood of Neville-Beaufort. It was a superstition that had lain at the back of her mind since her own betrothal day when a madwoman had screamed at her outside Staindrop church:

'Whore's blood of the bastard Beauforts! May their parents' passion be accursed in them! *Even unto the final generation.*'

Watching the barges escorting the re-instated Henry to Westminster, Cecily's thoughts voyaged with them to Elizabeth Woodville hiding in the Abbey sanctuary there, awaiting the birth of yet another child to the accursed blood.

∽

On November 2ND, the sad remembrance day of All Souls, Elizabeth gave birth to her fourth royal infant. It was a boy – the son she'd been unable to bear in the years of her haughty prosperity, and who was born now in the austere Jerusalem Chamber where King Henry the Fourth had been brought to die... The room was cold in the November morning, and there were few ladies to attend upon the Queen besides the Lady Scrope of Bolton and the Lady Berners – the latter having her hands full trying to keep the three little Princesses out of the way in their own cramped chamber.

The new baby was baptised, without pomp, in the Abbey and was given his father's name of Edward. Then he was carried back to the sanctuary where his pale mother took him in her arms and wept over him.

'Now, don't let Your Grace go upsetting herself,' the north-country Lady Scrope admonished, whisking the baby away. 'When the news gets around abroad that the House of York has an heir at last, many princes will come to King Edward's aid. And he'll return to England – you'll see!'

But Elizabeth could not be comforted. She's lost almost everything to Warwick's lust for power. Position and possessions had been taken from her. A father, a brother and many friends had been executed – the latest to go to the blow having been John Tiptoft, Earl of Worcester: he who'd murdered Desmond's children in Ireland to please his Queen... Soon, Elizabeth's title of Queen would be snatched from her, when Margaret of Anjou landed again in England to reign by Henry's side.

Burying her face in the silver-gilt glory of her spread hair, Elizabeth sobbed for Edward – the husband whom she'd never loved.

In the nearby Palace of Westminster, Henry had spent the past three weeks since his re-crowning, obediently carrying out the duties given to him by Warwick and the council. He'd signed hundreds of documents, received thousands of people.

But of all the visitors flocking to him, there were only two who were to impress themselves upon his feeble memory. These were the Tudors, Jasper and young Henry, arrived today from Wales... Jasper Tudor, Earl of Pembroke, was Henry's own half-brother; a stocky, florid-faced man, son of the late Owain Tudor and Queen Catherine. With him was his dead brother Edmund's thirteen-year-old son.

'Sire,' the Earl of Pembroke said, 'this is my nephew, Henry Tudor. I've removed him from the Lady Herbert's household where he's been brought up since infancy as a prisoner of York. Not a day too soon was the rescue either, for he was betrothed to Maud Herbert! But now he's free of all that—' Jasper gave the lad a hearty thump on the back, which made him cough.

'I pray he has not taken his father's lung weakness?' the

King whispered anxiously; recalling that half-brother Edmund, Earl of Richmond, had died coughing blood.

'No, no, Sire, he's as fit as a trout. Though thin and pale yet awhile from captivity – that's understandable.'

Young Henry Tudor looked uneasily sidelong, out of lashless eyes, at his Uncle Jasper... It was totally untrue that he'd been kept in captivity by the Herberts. For nine years, they'd reared and educated him as their own son, showing him kindness and generosity.

He was about to make a statement of this now. And also to affirm that he'd been perfectly willing, in a dispassionate sort of way, to wed young Maud – even after her father's execution by Warwick's orders last year. But he shut his pale lips on the statement. What profit was there in loyalty and gratitude? The Herberts were a broken family these days and he was quit of them. He'd gain nothing by supporting their name. The only name that mattered was that of *Tudor*.

King Henry was looking at him and stretching out a transparent hand for him to kiss... Vaguely nauseated, the boy placed his mouth against the old man's skin. He'd always hated to touch anyone – even Maud – or to be himself touched. But now as he felt the indentations of the royal signet ring against his lips, a warm feeling in his stomach quelled his nausea. He thought of the power the ring conveyed, to grant, to *grasp*. All the King had to do was sink the face of that ring into the warm wax on a document and heads fell, estates tumbled to the crown—

Yet his Uncle Jasper had forbidden him to beg the one favour he desired: that his own dead sire's Earldom of Richmond be allowed to pass to him, its heir.

'We mustn't mention that, boy,' Jasper had warned. 'Clarence has been given the Earldom of Richmond, and Clarence is our ally – though whether for good or ill, God alone knows! Still, Warwick says not to upset him. So you'll be quiet awhile about your father's title.'

Silent then Henry Tudor remained on all counts in the King's presence. And the King, with a gentle smile, commended him for this, and prophesied to his uncle a bright future for a boy who could listen and observe so intently.

'To such a one,' the King said in his queer, remote voice, 'both we and our adversaries may one day yield, and give over the dominion.'

Jasper shifted about uncertainly. He was well aware that his nephew was descended from one, if not two, bastard lines, Beaufort and Tudor; and that, although the lad had inherited his mother's brains, he'd also inherited his father's weakness of body and horror of direct violence: he'd never be a warrior in any field. But he was dogged and cunning – Jasper had to hand him that. He was also a cold, impersonal youth; odd, and without emotions... Dismissing the puzzle of his nephew's nature from his mind, Jasper began to tell the King about his own meeting with Queen Margaret at Angers lately.

The King hung pathetically on his every word; interrupting only to ask 'Did she look well?' and 'Did she seek news of me?' and 'When do you think she will land in England with our son?'

'Very soon, Your Grace,' Jasper Tudor promised his royal half-brother, 'Queen Margaret and the Prince of Wales will arrive safely from France.'

16

Winter, 1471

ALL WINTER the country lay tense under the rule of the Earl of Warwick, who was now King Henry's Lieutenant and Protector of the Realm.

'If yon Neville has his way—' some merchants were predicting '—we'll be at war with Burgundy by the spring. Then where will our trade be? In French Louis' markets, to our great loss!'

It was the merchants who were most anxious about the new government's proposed French alliance against Burgundy; anxious too about the moneys they'd all loaned the absent King because they had no hope of recovering these as long as he was in exile. Emphatically, the merchants wanted Edward back.

So did their wives and daughters. 'Everything is so tedious nowadays,' many of these ladies were exclaiming by Christmas. 'Nothing but prayers and grim faces and last year's fashions!'

London women, particularly, missed the extravagant ex-monarch whose presence had been such an excitement, for there'd always been the possibility of a kiss or a hug from him as he'd gone striding resplendently about the streets. Edward's greatest charm had been his willingness to give pleasure – his generosity with his own good-humour and joie de vivre.

But thousands of provincial folk, struggling with taxation and demands for military service, had come to realise that a change of king made very little difference to their lives; yet bad as these lives were, they did not want them worsened by foreign wars, internal strife or a return of the dreaded Queen Margaret... Tight-lipped, they went on with their own occupations, kept out of the way of officialdom and tried not to heed the growing clamour of rumour that both Edward *and* Margaret were converging on England's shores with foreign armies at their backs.

'There'll be a clash like the end of the world when these two meet,' predicted a certain Doctor of Lucena, busily packing his boxes for a speedy return to Castile... His chaplain, watching him, replied so quietly that he might have been talking to himself: 'For many, it *will* be the end...'

Edward was indeed on his way home. By February 19th, with borrowed money in his baggage and a hired fleet waiting for him at Flushing, he and his company had started out from the city of Bruges where they'd all been guests of the Duke and Duchess of Burgundy... On March 2nd he embarked in the sturdy ship of Zealand that was named *Antony*, with 500 men of the 2,000-strong army he'd collected which was composed of both Englishmen and Flemings. His brother Richard boarded the English ship *Garse* with another strong contingent of armed men;

while William Hastings and Anthony Woodville divided the rest of the army among the smaller ships making up the fleet. A few vessels were loaded only with horses, equipment and dry-food stores.

All was ready, yet for nine tedious days the wind blew unfavourably. However, on March 11th, the ships' masters met on the quayside and decided that at last it was possible to sail for England... With a good following wind, the fleet was in sight of Norfolk by the next morning.

'John Mowbray will aid us here,' Edward said confidently.

But the scouts who'd gone ashore to discover if it were safe for the main army to land, came hurriedly back. They reported that Warwick had arrested the Duke of Norfolk and all other East Anglian lords suspected of being sympathetic to the White Rose House.

So, Edward thought – memory stabbing on days of comrade-in-arms with his formidable kinsman – *Warwick is as prompt and as prescient as ever*. Aloud he said to the *Antony's* captain: 'Master Symondson, lead the fleet further north. The Yorkshire coast might be more hospitable than this one.'

Maybe Yorkshire would receive him, if only for the sake of his mighty father whom the north-country had loved. But the sky in that direction was thunder-dark and the sea roughening.

By nightfall on the 13th, the fleet was widely scattered by storm and one vessel carrying horses had foundered. At dawn, it seemed at first that only the *Antony* had survived. She limped into the port of Ravenspur at the mouth of the Humber. But Edward learned there that all his other ships had landed safely further up the coast and that the men from them were hurrying to join him.

'It is a good omen,' he told his famished troops, 'that we arrive in this port of Ravenspur. For here, seventy-two years ago, did Henry Bolingbroke make landfall when he came to claim the crown of England from King Richard the Second.'

As Bolingbroke had marched, so would he march, confident of victory over a weak monarch. And, until he had penetrated to the strongholds of the realm, he would carry Bolingbroke's famous lie upon his lips:

'I came not to claim the crown but only those lands that were my father's birthright.'

With his small army at his back, and his faithful young brother Richard by his side, Edward made for York – whose Dukedom, he still stoutly maintained, was *all* that he desired to possess, in right of his late father.

Fifteen days after landing, the invading army had doubled its numbers and was thundering towards Coventry where Warwick was entrenched. At last, within sight of his enemy's defences, Edward published the truth.

'Tell that great rebel,' he ordered his heralds, 'that *the King* has returned to England. And that he challenges the Earl of Warwick to come forth and to meet him with the sword for possession of this land.'

But three days elapsed and Warwick did not stir out of Coventry...

'Sire, what is he waiting for?' demanded Sir William Parr who'd brought six hundred men to Edward. 'Could it be the arrival of Margaret of Anjou?' Report had it that Margaret's fleet had been ready to sail from France a week ago and that only the storms of the equinox had kept it in port.

'No, Sir William,' Edward replied pleasantly, 'Warwick is not waiting for Margaret, but for my brother of Clarence whom he expects with reinforcements at any time now. I fear however that he's due for a very long wait: Clarence will not come to his aid.'

Parr, embarrassed, frowned and asked: 'How can you be sure of that, Sire?' For no one ever quite knew where they were with Clarence...

'I can be sure,' Edward smiled, 'because my brother is even now riding along the Banbury road, bringing *me* the troops which Warwick expects. Come, Sir William, help me to greet the prodigal!'

∼

GEORGE OF CLARENCE rode tensely through the April dusk from Banbury... Ever since he'd heard of Edward's landing, his mind had been in a ferment: ought he to stay with his father-in-law or go to his royal brother? For months, the entire Plantagenet family had been urging him to return to Edward's cause. His mother, his sisters Anne and Beth, had all inundated him with letters of pleading and advice. Then Margaret had begun to write from Burgundy while Edward was in exile there. She'd paid heavily to have her letters smuggled into England. Sometimes these letters had carried postscripts or enclosures from Dickon, or even a message from Edward himself... Yes, the family had certainly been united on this project, to bring George back within its fold.

He'd always known that he must give in – had known it at least since last July when his mother's emissary, the dark lady, had pleaded with him in the Honfleur tavern. But he hadn't admitted the knowledge – he hadn't wanted to proclaim the power of the family over him. Yet he was fully aware that it had always ruled his life and would always do so. Maybe it would even decree the time and manner of his death—

As he led his troops now towards Edward's camp, he considered how his emotions had been appealed to: his honour, his respect for his great father's memory! Then it had been gently demonstrated to him that he was merely Warwick's dupe – a fool to whom at first the throne itself had been promised; then less; and still less, until he'd finished up with only an agreement of being the heir if the Lancastrian Prince failed to sire a son!

God's Blood, he hadn't needed the demonstration. He'd seen what was afoot the day his sister-in-law had gone off to meet the Prince at Angers cathedral... He, George, was not stupid; it was just that he never knew precisely what to do about anything because he could see all the alternatives. There was often great confusion in his mind – a sense of fragmentation.

Maybe he was going mad. Like his uncle, Lord Latimer, who'd been adjudged an idiot after the battle of Towton and who'd died five years ago without recovering his wits – the only Neville ever to lose them, it was said! Uncle William Fauconberg had married a madwoman for her title and inheritance; but *his* son, Thomas the Bastard, was not of her blood. Although Thomas was a very wild man indeed – wilder and madder than ever poor Joan Fauconberg of Skelton had been...

George shook himself out of his wanderings and tried to decide what to say and do when he met Edward. He'd already written his abject apology; sworn his loyalty; and received Edward's assurance that all would be as before. But that couldn't be, could it? There was a royal son now whom Edward would recognise as his heir, and this sanctuary-born infant would be the next King if his father could re-seize and hold the throne. The name of George Plantagenet, Duke of Clarence, would count for as little henceforth as if the Lancastrian Prince wore the crown... Whatever happened, George was demoted – all his dreams of kingship vanished. Ah, if only Elizabeth Woodville had had another girl-child instead of the boy she could now put so triumphantly into Edward's arms! – a Prince of Wales, a future King of England; the final seal of her own success as a consort.

George frowned at the darkening road ahead. He recalled a quarrel on which he'd once eavesdropped, between his mother and Edward. It had taken place nearly seven years ago, at Reading Abbey; just after Edward's public announcement of his marriage and the subsequent arrival of Her furious Grace of York.

What were the words Cecily had used to Edward? Her voice had been so low, so thick with passion that George – fearfully crouched behind the door in the closet – had hardly been able to make them out. Yet, when she'd occasionally raised her tone, he'd distinctly heard several strange, disjointed phrases:

'Marriage indeed! Edward, you know this is no marriage.' And—

'If you have children by this woman, *they* will reap a harvest of disaster.'

Then, after a torrent containing words as 'bigamy', 'illegitimacy' and 'paramour', the final sentence: 'England *has* no Queen!'

What had his mother meant? That Elizabeth Woodville was so much Edward's social inferior that she could never be considered his true wife? Yet Elizabeth's position had been accepted by all Europe within three months of the announcement; and the birth of her first daughter had been hailed as a great royal event, at home and abroad. What else then? That the May Day marriage ceremony at Grafton had been, somehow, invalid? George decided to investigate this latter possibility, discreetly and at his leisure. Though he was certain that the astute Elizabeth and her witch-mother would have left Edward no loophole of escape from their trap – no loop-hole of which they were aware in any event, or could have foreseen at the time... Everyone knew what had happened to the Irish Earl of Desmond for suggesting a divorce: the royal leopardess had stalked, and struck, and killed him along with his children. Yet what had that word 'bigamy' signified—?

A cold finger touched the back of George's neck. He realised that, probably before this April night was over, amiable Edward would have forgiven him for his own defection, but that Elizabeth would *never* forgive him – she'd be his watchful, ruthless enemy for all time henceforward.

So he must be secretive with any questions he might ask about the marriage and must be careful in all his dealings with the Prince born of it; for Elizabeth would expect him to hate the child who came between himself and the throne, and would interpret any odd action as a threat – a threat before which every form of defence would be legitimate. *Even murder*: Elizabeth had shown that she could kill—

The spring dusk was grape-blue in the distance when George heard the first notes of the royal trumpets. His heartbeat quickened. Edward was coming to meet him! Overwhelmed with gratitude and relief he galloped forward, dismounted within sight of the King and flung himself upon his knees in the roadway. Minutes later, Edward's great height was bending over him; and Edward's voice, choked with emotion was saying:

'George – George, get up – let me embrace you. By the

Rood, brother, 'tis good to have you back. For I could not fight Warwick if you were with him, lest you be harmed.'

Stifling a sob against the royal mantle, George thought exultantly:

I'm safe now. Edward will always protect me.

Then the brothers rode off together, Clarence's troops following.

∽

SUPERNATURAL OCCURRENCES HAD ALWAYS ATTENDED Edward. Ten years ago at the battle of Mortimer's Cross, three suns had shone about his victorious army, giving him the emblem he would later adopt in kingship, the Sun in Splendour. At Towton, during a blizzard, the wind had changed to lend his men respite and advantage. And in Paul's church on the day after his coronation when he'd worn his crown there, a strange angelic shape sculptured in light had enveloped him, so it was said…

Now, on his way to London from Coventry, another unearthly sign occurred which brought more men flocking to his standard. It happened in the parish church of Daventry where he was attending Mass on Sunday, April 7th. It being Lenten time, all the statues and crucifixes were swathed in purple; and a certain statue of St Anne had been locked into a wooden shrine whose outside was draped in violet mourning cloth… Edward – praying earnestly that London would receive him as kindly as York had done – was looking at this covered shrine when suddenly its doors flew wide, revealing the gilded smiling image of the saint within.

Understanding that the capital could be his, he marched swiftly south.

On the evening of April 10th – it was the Wednesday of

Holy Week – the aldermen of London opened their gates to him and all his company. He rode through with his brothers Clarence and Gloucester on either side of him, and a great following led by Lord William Hastings and Earl Rivers.

Beaming, Edward turned in his saddle to say to the two men behind:

'Friends, we've done it – the capital is ours!'

Hastings' handsome face creased with amusement. 'Only by the skin of our teeth, Your Grace. Warwick must be well on the move from Coventry by now, and Margaret from France. Whoever arrives first, Londoners let in!'

'William, you're a cynic,' Edward laughed. 'But Londoners love *me*. And, besides, I owe them money...' Waving his plumed cap at the crowds, he rode the traditional route to Paul's church for the thanksgiving service for a safe homecoming.

Ah, how beautiful were the city women, smiling and cheering in the sunshine! Though those of the Low Countries had been delightful too, of course. Especially the young Catherine de Faro, wife of Jehan de Werbecque of Tournai – whom, he suspected, he'd left with child.[1] Well, the Duchess Margaret would see to the madam's welfare, and might even take some interest in the bastard if and when one were born – Margaret still had no child of her own by Duke Charles.

Near the churchyard wall, Edward noticed a dimpled little blonde fairly willing him to blow her a kiss as she stood on tiptoe and waved her scarf.

'Good day, Mistress Shore,' he heard William Hastings call from behind him; and realised with a stab of jealousy that it was at Hastings the blonde had been smiling so invitingly... All at once, Edward remembered who she was: Jane Shore, wife of a Lombard Street goldsmith;

Hastings had been chasing her these ten years past – ever since the time, in fact, that he'd accompanied his uncrowned King to redeem the pawned jewels of the House of York. Jane had been little more than a child then so that Edward himself had scrupled to make advances to her. But she was a grown woman now, ripe for the picking. Edward still wondering how to rob his friend Hastings of this light-o'-love when he found himself before the north door of St Paul's. Bishop Stillington was waiting to greet him there and to receive his offering... He had to break off thoughts of the goldsmith's wife in order to compose a prayer:

'I, Edward, do thank God for my safe return from beyond the sea; and I join the name of my consort Elizabeth to mine own, in gratitude to Almighty God for the gift of a son, born royal Prince of this England.'

He sought and held Robert Stillington's eye; defying the Bishop even to let the thought flicker across his mind that the child at Westminster was no lawful prince.

Stillington smiled an acquiescent smile. The King had no need to worry: his Bishop-Chancellor would never speak of what he knew.

George of Clarence, holding his royal brother's mantle aside for the offerings to be made, saw both the royal look and the episcopal smile. And he added them to his growing store of puzzles to be pondered.

After the service in Paul's, there was another matter which had to be attended to before Edward could leave for Westminster to see Elizabeth and their children. That was the matter of Henry of Lancaster who, only a few hours ago, had been escorted around the city by Warwick's adherents in a last attempt at keeping Edward out.

Clearly the attempt had failed but Henry's freedom was still dangerous. An end must be put to it before nightfall of this Spy Wednesday. Never again must Henry ride the streets of London.

From St Paul's, Edward went to the episcopal palace where he knew Warwick had ordered Henry to be left in his brother, George Neville's care... The Archbishop of York put up no resistance on behalf of his charge. He brought Henry forth and delivered him to Edward.

With cold civility, the younger monarch extended his hand to the older one. But Henry appeared not to notice the formal gesture, and spontaneously opened his arms; saying, as he embraced him who had come to take his crown:

'My cousin of York, you are very welcome. I know that in your hands my life will not be in danger.'

Startled and touched, Edward turned away; and, over his shoulder in a strained voice, gave the order for the arrest of the Lancastrian King, along with the Archbishop of York and five other bishops who were in the palace.

'Lodge them all in the Tower,' he said. 'Double the garrison there. We are going to Westminster without further delay.'

Whatever else happened, Henry must not be allowed to fall into the hands of Warwick or Margaret, who would use his goodness as a magnet for public sympathy to their own cause. As Edward boarded the royal barge, he said with a sudden burst of irritation to his brother Richard: 'Ah, why can't the saintly old fool die? We shall have to carry him around with us like a holy relic every time we leave the capital lest some rebel steal him out of the Tower!'

Richard said nothing, but he thought, *There's only one rebel who'd try that. He who makes and breaks kings. He who trained me in arms—*

To Richard of Gloucester, the imminent necessity of fighting his own great tutor-lord was a most painful apprehension; almost a negation of the motto which he'd chosen to accompany his badge of the White Boar: 'Loyalty Binds Me.'

But his loyalty must be to the White Rose House, and to Edward, forever more. He must be prepared even to *kill* Warwick, if they met on the battlefield during the final reckoning.

17

April, 1471

By midday on Holy Saturday, Edward's army was massed in St John's Fields and its commanders riding about for the last inspection before the march-out. Sir Humphrey Bourchier was there with his two nephews, Lord Berners' sons and the strong contingent they'd all led up from Kent. Lord John Howard and William Hastings' brother had arrived from Colchester with spearmen. The Lords Say and Cromwell had brought six hundred archers between them... These additions to the royal army were most welcome because the latest report was that Warwick was advancing rapidly towards London with a very strong force which included the tough northern troops of his brother John Neville.

It was a warm dry day, this 13th of April, 1471. A light wind stirred the banners and fluttered the pennants. In the spring sunshine, colours and shields and badges had clear definition; polished armour had the gleam of precious metal... The uproar from thousands of men and animals shattered the Easter Vigil air.

As the time of departure approached, Edward, armed and mounted, sat still a moment looking towards the city. He could see the tower-tops of his mother's residence, Baynard's Castle in Blackfriars. There, on Holy Thursday, he'd brought Elizabeth and the children from Westminster to join Cecily... With George and Dickon, Anne and Beth also present, this had been the first real family gathering for years and Edward had enjoyed it almost as much as his mother had appeared to do. How the old house had rung with the children's laughter! How the tables had groaned under the banquet which Cecily's stewards had produced! Ah, it had been heart-warming to go home after so much wandering; to be fussed over and made passionate love to by a wife who'd burst through her own frigid nature at last. Elizabeth hadn't asked any family favours last Thursday night. She'd seemed too conscious that her lord was leaving her again, and that he might be killed in battle this time against the desperate Warwick. All she'd begged was that the royal bodyguard should include a necromancer called Friar Bungay 'to protect you from harm, my love'. Laughing, Edward had agreed to take the so-called friar along.

Then yesterday, after the Good Friday services, Edward had persuaded his mother to move to the royal apartments in the Tower with Elizabeth and the children, lest Margaret of Anjou storm the city in his absence. Margaret had put to sea, he knew; but his scouts had been unable to discover whether she'd landed on English or Welsh soil. So he must remain in ignorance of her movements; take a chance on her coming up behind him, or seizing London, whilst he dealt with Warwick's army.

Only one thing was certain: Margaret would not find her consort Henry in the Tower. Henry was *here*, under close guard. He was to travel with the royal army along the road to Barnet; near which town, it was reported, Warwick had encamped his main force and positioned his artillery so as to cover the St Alban's highway.

An impenetrable fog was thickening the darkness of Holy Saturday night. Edward knew that he was camped very close to Warwick but it was impossible to discover the enemy's exact position: there was no sound, no glow of cooking fires – just this sensation of a great mass of men crouched beyond the St Albans road.

At an hour to midnight the enemy guns started up, roaring through the fog-blanketed dark. But it was soon evident that Warwick, too, was uncertain of his opponents' position because his gunners continued to overshoot Edward's camp. No man was hurt by them – except poor Henry who suffered from the noise and was rendered distraught with terror. But others, less sensitive, managed a few hours' sleep, happy in the knowledge that their enemies were wasting powder and shot.

By four o'clock in the morning, Edward and his commanders and men were astir, prepared for battle. Together, they recited the Easter Hymn and committed their cause to God. Then they rushed upon their foes in a sudden, full-scale offensive out of the dense mist.

Warwick's army was momentarily paralysed, its guns useless, the east end of its line overrun by the attackers. Men began to fall back there and the line to break.

Warwick himself, though fully armed, was unmounted. His brother had persuaded him to fight on foot today until the fog cleared but he was already regretting having listened to John. But now, from the ground he could not see how the battle was going or where to bring in reinforcements. Both lines were askew, overreaching one another at the ends. All he could tell was that there was serious trouble to the east...

But on the west – commanded by the Earl of Oxford – the Ragged Staff was gaining advantage. The White Rose was being routed there, scouts reported. Oxford's men were pressing Edward's into retreat – chasing them towards Barnet. The Star badge of Oxford was hammering its victory on the fleeing Rose and Sun!

One hour gone. A spectral dawn trying to break through the mist. The lines intermingled in the swaying confusion of hand-to-hand fighting. Snatches of orders, reports, comments floating eerily in the thick atmosphere—

'Reinforce the left. And centre – *centre.*'

''Tis a witch's spell, this fog.'

'Aye. The doing of the Queen's mother, likely.'

'No. Edward has a necromancer named Bungay with him.'

'Hasn't saved his west wing then – 'tis halfway to London by now.'

'*Richard of Gloucester is wounded* – Warwick will have him!'

But Warwick's only objective was Edward himself. He knew that the King must be somewhere in the centre although he could not see him; yet there was a fierce concentration of fighting there which indicated the kind of fellowship that would surround the crowned helm.

Edward must die. Warwick had no other thought in his mind as he slashed his way forward through the thinning Yorkist ranks... His brother-in-law of Oxford was trying to gather up his own jubilant troops who'd chased the Yorkist wing to Barnet.

'Raise my standard higher,' Oxford commanded his

squires. 'Trumpet the men to return – there'll be plunder enough later.'

The banner of Oxford, showing the Silver Star with Streams, swayed over a rowdy troop, drunk with victory. They'd been away from the main battle for nearly two hours. They were ready to go back now because report had it that the day was the Earl of Warwick's and they didn't want to miss the triumph.

But, unknown to them and to their commander, the positions of the ranks had altered, having swung around completely. When Oxford led his force against what he believed to be Edward's men, he was in fact leading them against Warwick's. And Warwick's main army, peering at this wild host dashing towards them, saw the Star of Oxford gleaming through the mist and mistook it for the Sun of York. Panic-stricken, they opened fire—

'Treason, treason!' yelled Oxford's men – some fleeing, some falling upon the gunners; together, making a greater confusion in their own ranks than any of Edward's attacks had done. Edward soon grasped the fact that, once more, the elements had come to his aid. Still under cover of thick fog, he pressed a new advance.

In the midst of all this, Henry slipped his guard and wandered off along the St Albans road. He was caught, brought back and bundled into his tent.

Meanwhile the Earl of Warwick was fighting doggedly on, trying to reach and kill Edward. But in the fourth hour of the battle, when news was brought to him that his brother John had been slain, the fire went suddenly out of him.

'John. Dead.' Richard Neville stood irresolute a moment, staring dazedly at the battle seething around him. It would take a great effort now, after the Oxford fiasco, to pull it to victory. And all at once, he was too tired to make any more effort, for any cause. John's life had been too high a price. Calling for a horse, he mounted and rode towards a wood some distance away. But a band of Yorkists had reached it before him – he only noticed them at the last moment as they flung themselves upon him. Then he was on the ground and they were wrenching off his black-plumed helm.

''Tis the Earl of Warwick,' one gasped. 'Run. Tell the King.'

Edward arrived within a few minutes. He'd galloped to the wood as soon as he'd heard that Warwick was taken. All at once it was the most important thing in the world to save Richard Neville's life.

But he was too late. His soldiers had killed the great Earl and had stripped him of all his armour.

Looking down upon the lean body whose life-blood was gushing from a dozen slashes, Edward knew an overwhelming sense of loss; neither for a friend nor for an enemy, but for a proud indomitable spirit against which he'd always been able to measure himself. Now he was alone. He had no other peer.

'Cover the Earl of Warwick's body,' he ordered hoarsely. 'Lay it on a wagon beside that of his brother, and conduct both noble corpses to London with all honour.'

It was eight o'clock in the morning, the fog lifting at last. There were ten thousand arrows on the field, like unlit tapers around the fifteen hundred bodies. It was already being estimated that there had not been a fiercer battle in a hundred years than that of Barnet, nor one to bring greater loss to rank and file as well as to noblemen. Sir Humphrey Bourchier was dead, and the Lords Say and Cromwell, and Lord Mountjoy's son and—

Edward passed a hand wearily across his eyes. Down there on the trampled grass was another face he recognised: that of Henry Holland, rebel Duke of Exeter – his sister Anne's divorced and exiled husband who'd begged his bread in Burgundy for Margaret of Anjou's cause.

'See to his burial,' Edward muttered to a common soldier kneeling beside the corpse. But when the King had passed by, the soldier tenderly lifted Henry Holland and ran with him towards a distant house, for he'd felt the spark of life under the shattered breastplate.

Edward ordered two of his own banners, riddled with arrows, to be carried above his army, returning to London. 'These I will offer at St Paul's church, in gratitude for my victory at Barnet this Easter Day.'

Gratitude. Aye. But he felt no jubilation for the triumph that had cost the lives of his cousin Richard and John Neville. A King needed worthy enemies whose minds and battle strategies he understood.

Now there was only one foe left: Margaret, the unpredictable Frenchwoman.

~

LIKE A CARVED FIGURE, Margaret of Anjou stood on the fo'castle deck of the flagship carrying her to England. She was unaware of the cold sea-wind that streamed her mantle and chiselled her gown to her body. Her only consciousness was that, this Easter Day, she would set foot again on the land of which she believed herself the rightful Queen.

For weeks, the sailing of her fleet had been delayed – partly by storms but mainly by her own maternal apprehensions for her precious son. If any hurt should come to the Prince, it would be multiplied a thousand-fold in her own mind and heart and body. He was her very existence, this handsome and arrogant youth. For him she'd fought and schemed, starved and courted death by land and sea for almost the entire seventeen and a half years of his life.

Those years had taken a terrible toll of Margaret's once-great beauty. Now, at forty-one, though still driven by that searing inward flame which kept her green eyes brilliant, she looked an old woman, thin, haggard and lined. But an old woman of towering dignity and indomitable will – her blazing courage legendary among her friends and foes alike. The only times that that courage burnt less brightly were when she foresaw danger to the young Prince.

The danger of being part of an invading army lay before him now, and she was sick with an apprehension so acute that it brought on one of her terrible headaches. Lights speared behind her eyes, distorting her vision... She gripped the ship's rail and breathed slow and deep. That exercise, she'd discovered long ago, at least controlled the retching which accompanied her migraines. But there was no escape from the tilting, erupting landscape within her skull. Eyes open or shut, she looked upon an inferno.

Falling to her knees on the wet deck, she prayed: 'Oh God, protect my boy. Let the English people proclaim him as their future King.' She was still on her knees when the flagship came within the shelter of Portland Bill...

Just before sunset, more than half the vessels of the fleet anchored safely off Weymouth. The rest went on to Portsmouth and Southampton, led by one of Warwick's vessels in which his Countess and Isobel of Clarence were making the voyage home.

The Countess of Warwick reached Southampton late on Easter Sunday night and became one of the first members of the Queen's party to hear about the battle of Barnet, fought that morning, with its fearful outcome. The Countess collapsed.

Her attendants carried her to Beaulieu Abbey and left her in its sanctuary, with Isobel. Then some of them travelled westward into Dorset, to bring the terrible intelligence to Queen Margaret: that she herself, the mother who had so passionately refused to bring her son to England while there was any apparent danger to him, had brought him thither finally on the very day that the cause of Lancaster had received an annihilating blow.

Margaret came near the edge of despair on hearing of Warwick's death. But once again as so often in the past, she rallied – reviewed her advantages – resolved to go on. The last of the Beaufort brothers had joined her at Cerne Abbey on Easter Monday, with Courtenay of Devon and a small force of men. With this force and the army she'd brought from France, she moved west towards Exeter.

The men of Devon and Cornwall joined her, along with forces from Somerset, Dorset and Wiltshire. Her plan now was to travel into Wales and join up with Jasper Tudor there; then march through Cheshire and Lancashire – where her cause had always had friends – gathering more troops en route before the final confrontation with Edward's army which must, she knew, be in full pursuit of hers by this time.

For days after the report of the rebel Queen's landing, Edward had tried and failed to pinpoint her position and to anticipate her movements. But she'd cleverly confused all his spies.

He had no wish to lead his own exhausted men on a wild goose chase through the west country of Wales. So he proceeded slowly, testing the ground around him in all directions. Margaret might double back and come up through Kent to assault London. Or she might approach the capital from Oxfordshire – he simply did not know. All he could do was gather men to replace those killed or injured at Barnet; and issue proclamations throughout the realm, threatening death to anyone who gave succour to 'Margaret, calling herself Queen, who is a Frenchwoman born and enemy to our land and people.'

But at last the reports hardened: *Margaret was in Bristol.* The city had let her in and had given her men, money and artillery. Soon, she'd be on the march towards Wales and would be sure to seek rest in Gloucester city for her hard-pressed followers.

Edward moved now with the speed of certainty. He sent his fastest messengers to Gloucester, ordering it to bar its gates against Margaret and warning it that he himself was on his messengers' heels to see that his orders were obeyed.

The city on the Severn kept its gates locked that Friday morning, May 4th, when Margaret asked admission for herself and her tired thirsty army and attendants. Although many of the citizens were in sympathy with the invaders' plight, they merely shouted over the walls:

'King Edward cometh. Waste no time in arguing here but *flee*.'

So, although she and her army had travelled all night, Margaret pushed on for Tewkesbury; arriving there about four of the same afternoon with the certainty that neither man nor beast could go further... She ordered camp to be pitched just outside the town, near the Abbey, in some rutted fields known as 'the Gastons'. There, she awaited Edward's coming. By nightfall, her scouts told her that he was but three miles away.

Margaret then handed over command of her weary army to Beaufort, Wenlock and Courtenay. She also gave the Prince into their charge, knowing that the youth must prove himself upon this field. Afterwards, she took the Prince's betrothed, Anne Neville, with the other few ladies of her own suite, and sheltered with them in a women's religious house some distance from Tewkesbury's great Abbey...

Before dawn on the morning of May 5th, the sound of trumpets summoning troops to battle formed a discord with the Abbey's Mass bell; and, a little later, the shouts of fighting men drowned the priest's words of consecration.

Richard of Gloucester was not yet recovered from the shoulder wound he'd received at Barnet. Nevertheless, the King had ordered him to take charge of the vanguard and to open the battle. There was no other commander whom Edward trusted now more than this slightly-built, eighteen-year-old brother of his.

Though crouched and wry-necked from the pain of his shoulder on which the armour pressed, Richard rode with a confidence that inspired the archers of the vanguard. He knew that Anne Neville was with the ex-Queen. He intended to rescue her from her forced betrothal to the Lancastrian Prince, even if it took every weapon and every legal brain in England to set her free – *free*, for himself, to whom she'd always been spiritual mistress! Like a legendary knight then, he led the opening assault; shouting to his archers to loose hails of arrows, and to fling themselves forward through the hedges and ditches of that difficult terrain where Margaret's army waited.

Rapid advance was impossible but the White Boar banner of Gloucester ploughed doggedly on. Richard could now see the Portcullis device of Beaufort, leading the enemy vanguard.

So once again – he thought – *it is to be cousin against cousin.* His heart was still heavy for Warwick's death but he'd never loved any of the Beauforts. Signalling with his sound arm, he led a concentrated attack.

Beaufort suddenly broke cover and rushed his whole

force at Richard's men. The impetus of this counter-attack was so strong that it went right through the opposition and careered down a hill towards the King's line.

Edward was taken by surprise. He saw Dickon feverishly trying to turn his troops on top of the hill but knew that there wasn't time for this re-grouping to be of much avail. Besides, Dickon was now being attacked by Courtenay of Devon; and the enemy centre was bearing down upon his own lines.

It was a bad moment for the King, floundering in the evilest battlefield he'd ever encountered. Yet his usual luck stayed with him: two hundred spearmen whom he'd left in reserve some distance away came surging to his aid. With these he succeeded in beating off his enemies.

Richard now came charging down to join forces with him while George of Clarence closed in from the left – Clarence's troops, under their banner of the Black Bull, encompassing that part of Margaret's army commanded by Lord Wenlock and the young Prince.

With fearful slaughter, the rout of the invaders began. Soon, men wearing the Queen's badge were fleeing in all directions. The Yorkists gave chase. Up and down the tortuous hillock of 'the Gastons' and through the long ditches there, they pursued their enemies to the death.

In a wooded park nearby, and across a meadow, the butchery continued... Some panic-stricken fugitives reached the Abbey and flung themselves into the sanctuary of its church. Others were drowned in the River Avon, near a mill where they'd hoped to find a hiding place.

Queen Margaret's Prince took a last, stunned looked at bloody Tewkesbury Field. No one had told him that battles were like this: obscene, barbarous – the stench of blood and entrails making one want to stop breathing the hot morning air. Fumbling off his war-helm, he pushed his way past some men stumbling towards the river. That mill over there – he remembered noticing it last night when he'd arrived in Tewkesbury with his mother and Anne. It was quite close to the town. If he could only reach some kind of civilisation—

His dark hair was saturated with sweat that ran into his eyes and dripped off his beardless chin. Never had he been in such a state in his whole life. There had always been people to attend to him. There had always been his mother (and, lately, his unbedded little betrothed wife) to lead everyone else in treating him as the next King of England when Henry, whom he hardly knew, would be dead at last.

But kings won glorious victories on battlefields; while he; the Lancastrian heir, had failed utterly. His mother's army was being cut to pieces all around him. He could hear shouts and cries – the sickening noise of metal entering flesh and striking bone.

He fled down a high-hedged lane, where some Yorkist archers behind one bank were picking off fugitives on the hills above. When a shaft lodged in his own neck, he stumbled but felt nothing for fully thirty seconds. And then, only a great weariness…

In the clearing at the lane end he sank to his knees. A mounted nobleman passing reined his horse and looked down at him. Through a red mist, the Prince recognised the man's face. He'd met him once, in France. He was George, Duke of Clarence, who was wedded to Anne's sister Isobel. So they were kind of a kind.

'Mon seigneur, help me,' the Prince murmured, reaching upward with his hands outspread. But he was dead before Clarence had dismounted to kneel by him.

'Take his body to the King's tent,' Clarence ordered a couple of spearmen nearby who were making a stretcher from their weapons. 'And tell whoever be there that 'tis

Margaret of Anjou's son. May he find with God the peace he never knew on earth.'

But the story which the spearman eventually told was, that the fleeing Prince had been on his knees, begging mercy of the Duke of Clarence, when Clarence had stabbed him in the neck... And others, who later saw his body in the King's tent being examined by Gloucester and Hastings, said that these two knights had put the Lancastrian heir to death by Edward's order...

Thus do battlefields spawn their legends.

Sword drawn, Edward entered Tewkesbury Abbey, seeking those who had taken refuge there. A priest wearing Mass vestments, and having the Sacred Host in his hands, met him at the church door and begged him not to defile the House of God with violence. But the King replied furiously:

'This Abbey church has never been granted a franchise to render sanctuary to traitors. Let them come forth or have the roof burnt over their heads.' Then he signed his armed followers to enter the holy place and search it.

They found the Beaufort Duke of Somerset, whose brother John lay dead outside on the battlefield. They found the rebel Prior of St John's, and Sir Humphrey Audley, Sir Thomas Tresham, Sir Gervase Clifton, Sir Hugh Courtenay and a dozen others – Courtenay's brother, the Earl of Devon, also lay dead outside between Lord Vaux and Lord Wenlock.

All the captured were taken into Tewkesbury town for execution, while the Abbey priests cleansed and re-blessed their violated church.

But the King who had desecrated the church was more reverent towards the bodies of the slain and the executed, his battle-anger having quickly cooled. He ordered that all should have decent burial, without quartering or defiling.

And that the Lancastrian Prince should be interred under the choir-pavement of the Abbey.

Without waiting to find the Prince's mother – but leaving orders that she should be sought most diligently and brought to him when discovered – Edward set off to attend to other troubles. The invasion had thrown the entire land into turmoil and he had many things to deal with before he might rest. Not least, the piratical Bastard of Fauconberg, who was preparing to attack London from his ships in the river; because, it was said, he refused to believe that the great Earl of Warwick was slain.

'Truly, this Neville cousin of mine is well named Thomas,' Edward growled. 'But maybe he'll be convinced that all is over when he sees his ex-Queen led captive into London.'

18

May, 1471

ON TUESDAY, May 21st, the victors of Barnet and Tewkesbury entered the capital to the sound of triumphal music and wild cheering. Richard of Gloucester led the procession with George of Clarence and Lord William Hastings. After them rode the King, heading his troops, and flanked by the Mayor and aldermen who'd come as far as Islington to meet him.

The city, though gaily decked, still bore reminders of the Bastard of Fauconberg's recent attacks. From Baynard's Castle to the Tower, the riverbank was lined with those engines of war that had been used to repel him, and the barricades of sand and gravel had been left in position. The wall of St Katherine's wharf was smashed where the city's great guns had demanded a wider range. The new Southwark gate of London bridge was burnt, with many houses nearby, and the ox-pound broken open – all the animals let loose which were kept to feed the Tower garrison.

This much damage had the Bastard caused on May 12th. Then, next day, he'd brought his ships' guns to the river edge and attacked Aldgate and Bishopgate. For three more days and nights after that he'd continued to terrorise the city. But then, Edward had sent an advance force of fifteen thousand men to London, with the promise that he himself was following with a greater army. At that, the last of his warlike Neville cousins had given up the fight against him.

The north, too, was quietening. In fact, the entire country was now settling down to the idea that Edward Plantagenet was King and would remain so until his death. Which death would more probably take place in a bed than on a battlefield, for there was no one left to challenge the supremacy of the House of York. At twenty-nine years of age, and in magnificent health and vigour, Edward could surely look forward to a long reign.

So the people of his capital cheered themselves hoarse this sunny May day as the golden monarch rode home, laughing, and waving at the girls... There was one pretty matron who waved directly back now and ignored William Hastings while she did so. Jane Shore had eyes for no one today expect the King... Exultantly, Edward blew her a kiss. Once more, he'd snatched a prize from an opponent!

But the Duke of Gloucester was oblivious of all the pretty women in the garlanded streets. His grey eyes, dark as wet slate, were focussed inward on a scene that had been repeating itself over and over in his head this fortnight past.

The background of the scene was the house of religious women at Tewkesbury where Margaret of Anjou had taken refuge during and after the battle. A party of Yorkists, including Richard himself, had found her there; and someone had blurted out, without pity,

'Madame, your son is slain.'

Until that moment, Richard had not known that he could be so appalled by the sight of human grief. But watching its devastation of Margaret – the brilliant eyes going slowly blank like the spirit leaving a corpse – the idea had suddenly taken him by the throat: 'This Prince who is dead – *He was Anne Neville's betrothed.* Maybe she loved him. Maybe she will also die inwardly when they tell her...'

He had to be the first to find Anne. The news would not come so paralysingly from a friend. So, his scabbard scraping walls, he'd gone pounding along corridors, in and out of alcove chambers, through a chapel filled with May blossoms, calling,

'My Lady Anne Neville – Lady Anne, 'tis Dickon.'

She was in the chapel. Hunched in one of the nun's pews. Staring sightlessly at a wooden statue of the Virgin and Child near the altar.

'Anne.'

Her reaction to his touch on her shoulder was abnormally slow. She turned around with a look of total disinterest on her tear-channelled face. Then she seemed to freeze in a sort of focused horror—

'Anne, don't be afraid,' he implored. ''Tis I, Dickon of Gloucester, your cousin. We were friends at Middleham.'

Her lips framed one word: 'Traitor.'

'W-what?' He tried to straighten his hunched shoulder where a bulky new bandage was supporting the re-opened wound. He tried to smooth his thick dark hair, and to rub his unwashed face with the back of his hand... Usually so neat and clean in his person, he decided he must have become unrecognisable from battle-grime when Anne did not know him. But—

'You deserted my father,' she was saying through clenched teeth. 'He was your tutor-lord and you fought against him. At Barnet. Where he died.'

The accusation and loathing in her eyes made his flesh crawl – she, who had always been so gentle and amiable – what had happened to her these months in the enemy's camp?

Then he realised that he, her childhood friend, was become more particularly her foe than anyone else who had fought at Barnet. Because she'd loved him once – trusted him... He loved her still, in the same quiet non-physical way that he'd always done even though she was become a changeling.

He stepped back a pace from her. There were no explanations, no apologies that he could proffer, except that his loyalty had been pulled two ways and he'd sided with his royal brother against Richard Neville... But how could he make that fact acceptable to a girl who was crazed with grief over her dead father? Better not to try at all... Then he remembered the real purpose of his search for her.

'Anne,' he said, 'before others tell it to you more harshly, I would break further bad news to you. The Prince to whom you were betrothed – he has been slain in the battle.'

She unclasped her hands (they were so blue-skinned and transparent that the bones showed through) and pushed back the lock of white-gold hair that had fallen on her forehead.

'The Prince?' she said remotely. 'If he be dead, then may God rest him. And may heaven comfort Madame his mother. But as for myself, I hardly knew him.'

These final words of hers, before she turned her back on him, were the only comforts Richard brought from Tewkesbury to London. If Anne Neville had not loved the

Lancastrian Prince then she'd never loved any man except great Warwick her father; nor any youth expect the Dickon of Gloucester who'd once lived under the same roof with her at Middleham... By dint of devoted patience, she might be taught to love that Dickon again.

As he rode now in the forefront of the triumphal procession entering London, Richard's mind was at the rear of the same cavalcade, where a closed litter bore the four women bereaved at Tewkesbury: the Countess of Devon, the Lady Katherine Vaux, Margaret of Anjou and Anne Neville.

For none of these would there be any comfort tonight. The gates of the Tower's prison would close as unyieldingly behind them as they'd closed behind Henry after his brief freedom during the battle of Barnet.

But Richard was determined to see Anne again soon although it seemed that she could not bear even to look at him. Whenever their eyes had met during the long journey from Tewkesbury, she'd turned her head aside. The gesture had become a barb in his soul. Yet he was willing to be wounded again. For she could still refuse to speak to him although she was a helpless, penniless prisoner – her mighty father dead, her mother locked up in a convent, and her own share of the Warwick inheritance taken into the keeping of the crown, to be disposed of at the King's will... Even so, Richard would offer his friendship once more. And it would have to be tonight because he was leaving London again tomorrow, in the royal progress towards Kent.

Tonight, then, after the homecoming banquet in the State apartments of the Tower...

King Edward was resplendent at the High Table which he was sharing with his family, and some of the sixty new knights he'd created this evening. The rest of the chamber was crammed with other knights and their ladies, and many civic and church dignitaries, in the most lavish royal entertainment since the Queen's coronation six years ago.

Edward relaxed increasingly as the meal drew to its close. He was aware of having drunk rather too much wine. But had he not more to celebrate than ever before? Total, final peace in the realm. A healthy, six-month-old son. And a captive Queen Margaret whom he should be able to ransom to the French.

Meanwhile though, there was the everlasting problem of Henry... While the Lancastrian Prince lived, it had been necessary to preserve Henry's life also, so that his heir might not inherit his claims – if he'd done so, rebels would have transferred their allegiance to a young man who'd have caused a lifetime of trouble. But now, the old ex-King was of no account, a mere nuisance. He was the last legitimate male of the Lancastrian line. Even the bastard Beauforts were all dead – unless one counted young Henry Tudor as a Beaufort in right of his mother; *he'd* escaped to France after Tewkesbury. So only Henry the ex-King remained. Edward heartily wished him dead. And many people were aware of his royal wish – it had been openly said in the streets today, as the wretched Margaret's litter had passed through the jeering crowds that 'the old King will not breathe much longer now'.

Yet Edward saw no possibility of executing a saint without rousing the whole country to outrage. Besides, there lingered in his memory a superstitious fear from what the old man had said to him in the Bishop of London's palace: 'I know that my life will be safe in your hands.' To betray that touching faith might be to invite ill-luck—

Still, one could always nudge the fates... Henry had deteriorated visibly since his walk along the St Albans road: why not edge him gently towards the grave? He had not been told yet of his son's death, nor had he been allowed to see Margaret (although it was the only request she'd made since her arrest: 'That I might talk with my lord Henry whom I have not met these seven years'.) Well, let him have both shocks in one. Let the ravaged ex-Queen tell him of the Prince's death. After that, with all hope gone, the feeble old man's hold on life must gradually loosen – but *gradually*, lest there be talk of murder...

Edward acted upon the idea at once. Leaning across to Richard, he said smilingly: 'Brother, you asked me if you might visit the Lady Anne Neville.'

'I did, Your Grace.' Richard looked at him with an almost painful earnestness: he'd imagined, earlier, that the request was going to be turned down because of a puzzling objection George had lodged to Richard visiting his sister-in-law. Richard had decided to find other means—

'Well you may go to her,' the King was saying now, ignoring George's scowl. 'But first I want you to arrange with the jailer for Margaret to be taken to see Henry. Yes – now – tonight. The couple may talk together for an hour. Though it must be in the presence of at least six witnesses, for fear of accident that may be laid to our charge. You will attend to this, Gloucester?'

'Gladly, Sire.'

'Good. Then go to the young Neville widow. She is, after all, our prisoner and cannot refuse to see you. And any ambitions she may have cherished about being Queen of England one day, are safely buried under the choir-pavement of Tewkesbury Abbey...'

As Richard got up from the table – bowing to the King, the Queen, and to the Duchess Cecily who'd followed this exchange with silent attention – Edward darted a sidelong glance at George of Clarence, who'd plotted with rebels to take his throne from him.

'Gloucester—' the King said with a curious warning note '—I have decided to give the Lady Anne into the keeping of the Duke and Duchess of Clarence because they are the only kin she has left apart from her timorous mother... Their recompense for this charge is that they will control the wealth due to her until she weds. Or enters a convent. Or dies.'

'I understand, Sire.' Richard ran a tongue around lips gone suddenly dry... So Anne was to live with George and Isobel. And they would have the arrangement of her marriage, or of her taking the veil as a virgin-widow.

As he left the banqueting chamber and made his way towards the darker, more sinister parts of the Tower, he realised that he now had more than Anne's hostility to contend with: he had George's jealousy – George's awakening suspicion that the Warwick fortune might have to be shared inside the family. That was why he'd objected to Richard's visiting Anne. Only the King had overruled him tonight. But in the future, when Anne would be a close-kept member of the Clarence household, *no* one would get in the way of George's wishes in her regard.

Richard was still meditating on the problems this would raise when he reached the guard-room. He found the five men who were supposed to be on duty playing cards and drinking. They scraped themselves to hasty attention at his entrance. Looking sternly at them, he decided that there were only three sober enough to be witnesses at the meeting between Henry and Margaret. And the jailer – who now came blustering in from his private quarters with his hosepoints still undone – yes, he was alert enough from interrupted lovemaking to become a fourth witness... The remaining two would have to be Margaret's attendants, the Countess of Devon and the Lady Katherine Vaux. Under no circumstances was Richard going to command Anne

Neville to be present at the harrowing scene. But he would not leave her alone with drunken guards about. So his meeting with her would have to take place at the same time as Margaret's with Henry.

He relayed the King's orders and paced about the stinking guard-room while they were being carried out. Four pairs of heavy-shod feet went marching along the passageway to the prisoner's quarters. The jailer, jangling keys, rapped on a door – and waited a respectful moment, as Richard had warned him to do – before entering and saying: 'Madame, King Edward has granted your request to see Henry of Lancaster. These two ladies here are to accompany you.' After what seemed like a long time, Richard heard the soft footfalls of the women following the guards' heavy tread further along the passageway and up a stair.

He had commanded that the door should not be closed on Anne Neville. When he reached its threshold she was just inside, and he saw that she'd been about to make a dash for freedom. But the gasp she gave at sight of him in the doorway was of relief, not dismay.

'Oh, Dickon – *Dickon*—'

So sudden and hysterical was her embrace that it almost knocked him off balance. 'Dickon, take me out of this terrible place – let us go home to Middleham where the air is bright and pure—' She was sobbing and gasping his arms.

As he comforted her, his heart exulted and raged at the same time, for the causes of this astonishing change in her attitude towards him. She'd been brought to the end of her control; by long exile and travelling; by bereavement; and by today's ride through the jeering city, which had ended in the dark hopelessness of the Tower.

Wordlessly, he held her tight against him. It was the

first time he'd ever clasped her whole body – her hand was all he'd ever touched before: helping her to mount her palfrey, or to cross the stepping-stones of the River Cover that south-bordered Middleham's' great park... Jesu, how long ago that all was! Anne had been but a child then. Now, he could feel the points of her breasts; and, with them, the first urgency of his own physical desire for her.

He led her firmly back into the room. He sat her on a bench near the fireless grate, under the single torch which lit the cavernous gloom.

'Anne,' he said, 'be calm and listen to me. You're not going to be kept here for long. You're to live with George and Isobel – do you understand?'

After a moment, she nodded. Her sobbing had quietened except for the odd convulsive gulp. 'I – I thank you for this news, Dickon,' she whispered then. 'You have always been a true friend to me.'

'Yet still a traitor to your late father's cause?'

'No, there was no other way for you.'

'Absolve me then of his death. Do it with a kiss, Anne, so that I may feel whether or not you shudder when you touch me.'

She said, very low, 'I did not shudder when you held me in your arms just now and comforted me like one of your own children – Richard, you have bastards, have you not?'

'Aye. Two. Katherine and John, whom I acknowledge and care for. Their mother died with the youngest. I loved her...' The grey eyes shadowed over as they contemplated an irreparable loss; and Richard of Gloucester fell silent.

In the silence, Anne remembered Isobel's labour aboard the *Mary Exeter*. She remembered, too, her own continuing gratitude for never begin bedded with her betrothed husband. Marriage and childbirth had been her terrors. Now all at once, these terrors seemed shameful, childish; because a young man still mourned the mother of his two bastards, and could say of her, 'I loved her...' To be loved like that must be armour against everything except death.

Standing up, she placed her lips against Richard's.

'Dickon,' she said, 'I absolve you of all blame for my father's slaying.'

He was about to take her in his arms again – to return her kiss – even to ask her to consider wedding him when her mourning time was over. But the sound of feet pounding down the passageway, and keys rasping against stone, made him spring to the door and fling it wide.

'What is it, man?' he shouted at the panting jailer.

'Oh Your Grace, come quick—'

'Where?'

'Henry's chamber. The old King's blood be all over it!'

Richard stopped long enough only to grasp Anne's hand and drag her with him. Whatever happened to Henry she must see, and know the truth. Together they raced up the stair and along the upper passage.

Henry's door stood upon. The sound of women's wailing flooded through with the candlelight.

Richard smashed his way past the drawn weapons of the guards and came to halt a few paces beyond them, where the Countess of Devon and the Lady Katherine Vaux wept in each other's arms. Pushing Anne towards them, he advanced on the figure in the shabby blue robe. It was lying face downward on the floor in a spreading pool of its own blood.

He looked at the silent, motionless women who stood over the body of the ex-King.

'Madame, he said tensely to Margaret of Anjou, 'tell me what has happened here.' But without waiting for her to begin, he went down on one knee beside the royal corpse and gently turned it over. The pale eyes of Henry of Lancaster stared sightlessly at the roof-beams while blood continued to ooze from his open mouth and through his nostrils as from some rupture within.

Suddenly, Margaret began to speak – her tone flat and dispassionate.

'He did not know me,' she said. 'Even when I told him that our son was slain, he did not recognise me as that son's mother, nor understand who it was that was dead. Then he asked, "When will Margaret come home?" and I replied, "I am Margaret." He looked at me then with full intelligence for a moment. Afterwards, his face contorted, he put one hand to his heart and the other to his head; and fell forward, spurting blood. He did not move again.'

Her arms hung listlessly straight by her sides. Her face remained expressionless and free of tears. The once-passionate Margaret had reached the end of all feeling, all protest at how life had used her. She went obediently with her ladies when Richard signed for them to lead her to an inner chamber.

As Anne passed by him, she took out her kerchief and tried to swipe some blood from the gold lacing on his sleeve. But he said,

'Leave it, sweet cousin. Even if I burn my garments, and soak my body in the Thames, people will still see Henry's blood upon me.'

Already he could hear the cry of 'Murder!' Because Henry's death had been the King's wish, and he was the King's man.

But Anne Neville knew the truth. And that was all he cared about.

By Edward's order, Henry's body lay openly in St Paul's amid wax candles and ceremonial guards. People passed by it in their thousands, paying their last respects to the man who had been twice King of England and once of France – whose total reign had lasted nearly fifty years. But Edward himself did not go to Paul's. Taking Clarence and George with him, he departed for Kent on Wednesday, May 22nd, jut as he'd planned to do. He saw no reason for those plans to be altered just because the last of the Lancastrian royal line had died.

But, after he and his brothers had left London, Henry's body began to bleed again in its open coffin, and had to be quickly cased in lead. Though not before many onlookers had dipped pieces of cloth in the blood that was the relic of a saint, some said. While others maintained that it was murder crying aloud.

The lead coffin was carried over the outer pavement of Paul's where the bodies of Richard and John Neville had lain only a few weeks before. These brothers were now interred in Bisham Abbey beside their parents, the late Earl and Countess of Salisbury. Henry's remains were put aboard a barge in the Thames and – with silent people lining the riverbank – taken to remote Chertsey Abbey, where no kin of his had ever lain. But it had been King Edward's order that the tomb of the last royal Lancastrian should not be made accessible as a place of pilgrimage.

'Thus will they soon forget him—' the King said philosophically as he rode south with his brothers '—and find other dramas to divert them.'

The brothers made no reply. Already they'd quarrelled violently over Anne Neville – George refusing to allow Richard to see her again, now that she'd been taken from the Tower and hidden in one of George's many residences. Which one, he refused to say. But Richard's information was that she had not left London… He intended to ask the King's permission to wed her, if she were willing. But to discover whether she were willing or not, he had to see her. And that might mean breaking into George's house when the royal party returned to London.

Well, so be it, he *would* break in. And if she were not there, he'd take the capital and, if necessary, the entire country apart until he found her!

19

December, 1471

For seven months, the quarrel of the royal brothers had been the great talking-point everywhere. Now, with Christmas of 1471 approaching and still no sign of peace between them, men who'd come to London for the festive season either brought their armour with them or sent home for it in haste. What with Clarence keeping a private army around his city residence from cellars to turret-rooms – riding the streets at all hours like a man demented, everyone was certain there was going to be violence. Gloucester was keeping a band of followers armed and mounted. He was searching, questioning, listening to every unlikely tale about where the Lady Anne might be.

Because Anne Neville had disappeared, suddenly and completely, out of the Clarence household. George and Isobel both swore that they knew nothing of her whereabouts – that she'd been free to do as she wished while living with them and had, apparently, gone off of her own choice.

'And the reason for this, I suspect—' George said maliciously when finally questioned by the King himself '—was that Richard would not leave her alone. Every day he wrote to her or came bearing some gift, although she'd neither reply nor see him, so great was her repugnance of his wooing.'

The King made an ominous humming sound at the back of his throat; then without warning shot the question at George: 'Could the repugnance have been yours, brother?'

'Indeed not, my lord! Nothing would have given me more joy than to see my beloved sister-in-law happily re-wed.'

'But to contemplate half the Warwick inheritance going with her – Clarence, how would you have regarded that? With an increase of joy?'

George's guard dropped, revealing the ferment behind the smile. '*What* half? *What* inheritance?' he demanded furiously. 'Already Your Grace has given all the northern estates of the Nevilles to Richard. And that, after promising that their administration should be mine—' His mouth trembled. Once again he had been cheated, deprived.

'Yours. Yes. For caring for Anne Neville. But you've lost her, Clarence, have you not? For undoubtedly she has vanished.'

'My lord—' George placed his clenched hands on the King's writing-table '—you gave Richard the Neville northlands while my sister-in-law was still safe with me.'

'Safe. Umm. And she disappeared immediately after the grant was made. Strange – very strange…' Edward began to busy himself with some volumes in tooled leather covers that had just arrived from Bruges. 'Well,' he continued abstractedly then, 'you and Gloucester will have to settle matters between yourselves for I can make nothing of either of you. Good morning, brother.'

Edward was weary to death of the internal strifes which had plagued his Court since Henry's death. Apart from the continuing uproar between George and Richard, there was a venomous enmity now between Will Hastings and the Queen. The cause of the latter, Edward was aware, was his own latest mistress, Jane Shore. Elizabeth dared not attack him directly about this dalliance. So she'd attacked his closest friend, Hastings, whom she maintained had 'procured the whore for the King' and was 'daily and nightly leading the King astray into evil company.' Hastings' friends had resented this reference to themselves, and had launched a vicious verbal campaign against the Woodville sisters in their brilliant marriages. The battle was now at full pitch.

Ah, women, women! Edward thought; they were at the root of all men's troubles. Yet, increasingly, he could only forget his own troubles in a woman's bed: Jane Shore's. For Jane was soft and loving, compassionate and merry – all the things that Elizabeth was not. Yet they were both equally expendable, equally his whores, if the truth were but published. Which it could never be, of course, for the children's sakes.

Momentarily, he felt the net of his own past deceits tighten about him. He had to keep that fool Stillington near him at all times although the man irritated him. He had to send expensive gifts to the Norwich convent where Eleanor Butler had died, for perpetual Masses to be sung for her soul lest she curse him in eternity. And he had to tolerate, every day of his life, the glassy brilliance of one or more of the surviving Woodvilles. Small wonder he ran so often to Jane; or spent his time hunting, dicing, drinking...

Now, in the quarrel between George and Richard, he felt himself newly threatened. He'd tried to stand aside from it. Yet knew that it was his own dependence on Richard's loyalty – his own basic distrust of turncoat George – that had precipitated events. If only he had not granted the Nevilles estates to Richard in the summer when making him warden of the west march! If only— But there, it was done and he would not undo it. Though he must now seek means of placating George, who'd said one or two things that were very odd of late, in heated exchanges. Things about 'all marriages not being what they seemed'. And about his own and Isobel's future children having 'more right than some others to the highest place'.

Edward had not queried his brother's meaning to any of these enraged utterances. But he'd finally warned George to guard his tongue in the Queen's presence. And had then at once regretted the warning.

Now however, with his usual ability to forget unpleasant abstracts, Edward threw himself into an examination of the Bruges volumes. They were beautiful – perfectly scripted and illuminated, bound and covered – as beautiful as anything he'd seen and admired and coveted during his exile... That period abroad had given him a great interest in books. And he'd recently enlisted the help of Master Caxton, the leader of the English merchants in Bruges, to procure new volumes towards a collection he intended to form at home. Caxton had agreed to choose the titles, commission the various craft-makers and ship the finished products to England. A useful, knowledgeable man, William Caxton.

Richard was at Baynard's Castle, waiting for his mother

to come up from her private chapel where she was hearing a third Mass on this last Sunday of Advent. He thought dispiritedly:

I've followed every rumour. I've searched every place, likely and unlikely. But there's no least trace of Anne…

Wandering over to the solar window, he stood – a thin, unkempt figure – staring at the snow falling on the black river. If Anne were not being well cared for somewhere, how could she survive the winter? She'd looked so fragile that night in the Tower. And he'd never seen her again.

Let us go home to Middleham – her cry haunted him. Middleham Castle was his now: he'd accepted the Clarence-disputed royal grant of it for her sake (and had been landed with the distasteful task of executing the Bastard of Fauconberg there last August, when that great rebel had been finally captured). But George could have the castle back – could have *everything* back – if only he'd reveal where he'd hidden Anne. Richard hadn't the least doubt but that George knew very well where she was. And that, whatever danger she was in, it was the direct result of George's hatred for himself.

He gazed across the river towards Southwark and remembered – with nostalgia for times changed, brotherly love gone – how he and George and their mother had once lived there while their father had been in exile in Ireland. Somehow, despite great poverty, they'd been happy together although it had been a hard life. The Fastolf house had been cold in the winter from scarcity of fuel and George had complained always of hunger—

George. Hunger. *Food.*

Suddenly, Richard had an intense recall of how his brother used to slip out of the house at night, leaving himself on guard at their chamber window. He clearly remembered watching George darting down the street, past the laundry and the brothel and the tavern; remembered the relief he used to feel when he saw him turn in safely at the pie-shop on the corner; then the tension again, waiting for him to return home without being molested or discovered... It had often been a long wait. For the pie-shop owners (a man and his wife named Roebuck) were fond of George although they'd no idea of his real identity at the time. It was in pure charity and affection that they used to give him wedges of broken pastry to eat in the shop, and some scraps to carry home to Richard... Richard now recalled George's mentioning, years later and with some pride, that he was still rewarding the Roebucks for feeding him during that lean time—

Snatching his cloak up from before the fire where he'd flung it to dry, Richard dashed out of the solar without waiting to see his mother, and went clattering down the circular stair. He put his head around the door of the Hall and shouted to his famished friends who'd just installed themselves there:

'Leave your ale. We're going to Southwark.'

'God's Nails,' said Robert Percy, 'out again – in this weather?' But he sensed his cousin's urgency and followed him at once into the snow-whitening courtyard where Richard was already calling for the horses of the entire party.

Muffled in their mantles, fifteen riders were soon crossing the bridge towards the Southwark side. It was early, the snow barely trampled except around the churches. There was a vast Sunday-morning quiet in the swirling air.

'Let us go home to Middleham,' Anne had pleaded. Now Richard prayed that they'd be able to do that. But it all depended on whether his inspiration about the Roebuck's shop-premises would prove correct.

His friends knew what they had to do. Eight of them were to attack the rear of the building and seven, including himself, the front. They were to go through the house as thoroughly as they'd gone through Clarence's and dozens of other places. And if they drew a blank – as they'd always done in the past – they were to apologise to the owners and set everything back in order. Such 'apologies' and repairs had lightened Richard's purse considerably over recent weeks.

In a simultaneous attack, the two parties entered the dilapidated building. They almost crashed into each other in the scullery behind the shop, where a girl was washing baking-tins in a trough of greasy water… Above the clatter of their drawn weapons they heard the girl scream, 'No – no – do not kill me—' before she collapsed on the beaten-earth floor at their feet. She seemed the usual undernourished kitchen drudge; her small body enveloped in a rough grey gown; a kerchief hiding her hair; her bare feet thrust into wooden clogs—

But Gloucester was lifting her tenderly up in his arms, wrapping her in his warm cloak and kissing one of the wet hands whose skin was cracked and bleeding.

'Saints!' Robert Percy muttered to Francis Lovell. 'Warwick's lass—' Neither of them had recognised her although they'd both been squires at Middleham Castle with Richard and had seen her every day there. The change in her appearance and circumstances shocked them profoundly. Had George of Clarence made her a prisoner here? If so, Richard would certainly attack him. Yet there had been no locks or bars on the rear of these premises – the wretched scullery opened into a yard which gave onto a public alleyway with only a broken down wall in between. Anne Neville could have walked out anytime—

Puzzled, Percy and Lovell followed Richard who was

now carrying Anne out through the shop. The Roebucks cowered behind the greasy counter there and were being shouted at and threatened by some of the others. But, as Richard paid no attention to the shop-owners, his two closest friends hurried outside with him to the street, and steadied his horse for him to mount with the still-unconscious girl held against one shoulder.

'Where to, my lord?' Lovell asked. 'Back to Her Grace of York's residence?'

Richard hesitated. His every instinct was to take Anne to his mother's house. But a crowd had gathered now in the snowy street, and he knew that Clarence would soon be informed of what had occurred. Clarence could lawfully remove his ward from Baynard's Castle.

'No,' he snapped. 'We go straight to the sanctuary of St Martin-le-Grand.' Weeks ago, he'd arranged for Anne to be received there if and when he found her. No one could take her from sanctuary.

Tucking his mantle more tightly around her, he wheeled his mount and galloped for St Martin's... In his heart, he cherished a cold clear desire to murder his brother of Clarence. Yet it was at himself that Anne had been staring when she'd screamed, 'Do not kill me—' as though she feared him more than she feared George.

∽

LATE FEBRUARY SUNSHINE was warming the cell-like room which Anne had occupied since before Christmas. Smiling, she looked around it now – at its bed, its crucifix, its washing cupboard and wall bench – before shutting the door on it for the last time.

In St Martin's main guest-chamber, she knew that many ladies were waiting for her, to escort her to Westminster Abbey for her wedding. She could hear their chatter as she approached in the soft doeskin slippers which Dickon had had made for her chilblain crippled feet, where the pie-shop clogs had rubbed the swellings raw on toes and heels.

'But does the Lady Anne Neville really *want* to wed Gloucester?' one high female voice was enquiring.

'Shush,' said several others. Then there were conflicting remarks of 'Of course she does,' 'She knows what's best for her' and 'Well, 'tis said that maybe not...'

Anne stood still a moment to gain composure before facing them. She knew that she'd never tell anyone in full truth of why she'd fled from the Clarence house in a covered wagon belonging to the pie-man Roebuck. Even in her own mind, she could not now recreate the terror that had finally driven her. But she knew it had all begun with a half-jesting remark of George's that she 'really ought to enter a convent, where it was safe.'

'Safe from what?' she'd asked – looking up from the embroidery thread she was holding for Isobel.

'From our brother of Gloucester, of course. Now that he's been granted all the northern holdings that were your father's, he wants you out of the way – lest you should wed some strong-armed husband who might dispute the properties with him! So you'd best take the veil, sister-in-law – set Gloucester's restless mind at ease...'

She'd glanced at Isobel, who was steadily winding bright thread into a ball around her thin finger-tips... Often, she'd begged Isobel to have letters of hers taken to Richard. But her sister had always snapped: 'Don't be a fool, Anne. He's made not the slightest attempt to contact you since you came to live with us. Obviously he does not want you now – he's received all he needs from the King without you! The Yorkshire and Cumberland territories and castles of our father...'

After that, there were repeated references by George to the desirability of Anne's taking the veil.

'I have no wish to be a nun,' she always replied.

There the matter uneasily rested until the fearful night when she heard servants whispering near her door – saying it was common rumour that Gloucester wanted the Lady Anne Neville 'out of the way – maybe in the grave like poor King Henry.'

After that, though she well knew the innocent manner of Henry's death, Anne began to feel threatened inside the imprisoning walls of the Clarence house. Little by little, as the lonely weeks went by with no word from Richard, she came to believe that he, who'd sworn friendship, wanted only her death, lest there be any dispute about the lands which the King had given him. Then, one early morning in a dark corridor, a man had grabbed her and tried to hurl her down a flight of stone steps. She'd escaped his grip – but not before she'd seen the badge of the White Boar on his sleeve... So Gloucester's henchmen were here, within the very walls that were supposed to protect her!

Blindly, she'd run down to the courtyard. There was a covered wagon there which she'd seen several times before. Its owner – also familiar to her – held a lantern as though guiding her to him... She, Warwick's daughter, cowered beside Roebuck the pie-man – talked incoherently to him – listened to his mad proposal that she should leave here at once in his wagon and go to stay with him and his wife in Southwark.

'Very well. But I want to work for my keep,' she'd said.

'So you shall, lady. And, in a little while, none will recognise you. Then you'll be able to go out free on the streets, without fear of Gloucester's spies.'

She'd been waiting for this total change in her appearance – indeed, hastening it by personal neglect and backbreaking work, while overhearing customers in the shop discussing how Gloucester was combing London for the Lady Anne Neville – when the armed men had burst into the scullery. And, recognising Richard as their leader, she'd believed her last hour to have arrived.

But what kindness and understanding he'd shown her during his daily visits to her in the sanctuary! He'd convinced her that he'd written to her every day during her time with Clarence – that he'd tried to see her but had always been turned away by the message that she did not wish it.

George – Isobel – to be parties to such a conspiracy! Yet Anne could never believe that it was they who'd tried to frighten her out of her wits, with whispering servants and an assassin disguised as a Gloucester follower. Nor that it was George who'd bribed Roebuck to come repeatedly to the courtyard, so that a terrified girl might eventually run to the shelter of his wagon.

No, nothing would ever be proved except that her mind had become slightly unhinged during the months of her unconsummated marriage to the Lancastrian Prince. And she herself would never speak of the Southwark business expect to say (as she'd said to the King himself when he'd questioned her):

'I went to Southwark of my own free will. I was not kept a prisoner by the Roebucks.' That was all anyone would ever get out of her – particularly Richard, of whom she'd never admit the shameful doubt she'd entertained.

She trusted him now. She thought of him with great tenderness and gratitude. It was possible even that she loved him.

Confidently she walked forward to the guest-chamber

and went in to receive the greetings and wedding gifts of the ladies.

With a sigh of relief, the Duchess of York slipped into her pew near the altar of Westminster Abbey, and watched the sixteen-year-old Neville bride advance to stand beside her own youngest son, who would be twenty this coming autumn... How thin and frail Anne looked in the wedding finery which Cecily herself had chosen for her! But how radiant was the face she was turning towards her bridegroom, who had eyes for no one but her.

Ah, Cecily thought, *they're going to be happy together at last, after all this time of turmoil.* They were to leave for the north almost immediately after the ceremony, and were to make their permanent home at Middleham Castle. That would at least put the length of the country between Richard and George!

There had been a final, fearful quarrel between the royal Dukes after Richard had placed Anne in sanctuary. Then the King – nervous for the peace of the realm – had called them both before his council, where they'd continued to argue their property and marriage rights with such passionate brilliance that their respective lawyers had fallen silent.

It was early February before Edward himself had managed to make some kind of peace between his warring brothers. Clarence had finally agreed that Gloucester might marry Anne Neville, provided that he and Isobel should receive back most of the Warwick and Beauchamp inheritance which had been settled on Gloucester; and also that the titles Earl of Warwick and of Salisbury should be added to the Dukedom of Clarence.

To this Richard had agreed, insisting only that Middleham Castle should remain his; and that he should be allowed to bring there the widowed Countess of

Warwick, Anne's mother, who was still under armed guard at Beaulieu, and quite penniless.

Immediately he'd secured these assurances, Richard had arranged his wedding with Anne; and had refused to await the Papal dispensations for the marriage of cousins.

'Yet they're only cousins in the second degree,' Cecily told herself now to quiet certain misgivings she'd entertained all along; for she'd seen many times in the course of her own life how the children of near blood-kin often inherited weaknesses from both parents which, intensified in one body, killed the child... Both Isobel and Anne Neville were fragile women. And Richard, though heather-tough now, had been so frail an infant himself that his survival had been regarded as a miracle... But would Anne ever be able to bear him *any* children? She was reed-thin, and light, and had a hollow cough—

Cecily tried to give her full attention to the marriage service just beginning, but a final thought edged itself into her mind:

Maybe she'll strengthen when she gets back to the north. And she'll have her own mother there to care for her, thanks to Richard's thoughtfulness.

Yes, all was going to be well for the Gloucester marriage. It was the Clarence one which really worried Cecily.

Isobel of Clarence had moved to Warwick Castle, leaving George alone in London. And George had made the very curious remark in an alehouse there recently that, when he and Isobel got a healthy son at last, the boy might well expect to wear England's crown one day.

Queen Elizabeth (who was expecting another child soon) heard of this indiscreet statement which seemed to threaten her own infant son, and at once turned her animosity away from Sir William Hastings and concentrated it upon her brother-in-law. She now watched every move of his with a fixed intensity of malice which sent shivers down Cecily's spine even to contemplate... Elizabeth was dangerous, George reckless and foolish. He would not find in the Queen the generous and honourable opponent he'd had in his brother of Gloucester. But Cecily doubted if her second son appreciated this fact of his increasingly quarrelsome life. Sometimes indeed, he reminded her of the Fool on the Precipice in the tarot cards: a man indivertibly bent upon his own destruction.

All through the Nuptial Mass for Richard and Anne, she prayed for George. He was as dear to her as any of her other children although he had never believed this. In his own mind, it seemed, he always came third to Edward and Richard, even in their mother's love... He was the middle-in-age brother, permanently crippled between the elder and the younger; and always futilely struggling against his own impotence.

20

December, 1477

A December storm was howling around Warwick Castle. Icy draughts, finding their way through the high shuttered windows, flickered the fire and candle flames, and even stirred the heavy curtains around the bed of Isobel of Clarence.

Cecily, keeping midnight vigil by her daughter-in-law's bedside, hunched deeper into her fur-lined cloak as she fingered her girdle Rosary beneath its folds. There was nothing she could do for Isobel except pray for her soul's peaceful passing. Isobel was dying. The only person who would not believe that fact was her husband George, who prowled endlessly around the dark fortress – harassing the servants, drinking overmuch with visitors.

For the moment, Cecily was peacefully alone with George's wife. The Household chaplain had just left; and she'd previously ordered the nurse, Ankarette Twynyho, to rest awhile in the anteroom. The aged resident physician had shuffled off to his own quarters, to mix another useless potion for the dying twenty-five-year-old Duchess.

It seemed to Cecily now that her own life was calendared solely by births and deaths – that, at past sixty, she was no longer capable of involvement in wider issues. In the five years since Dickon and Anne had married, there had been political excitements aplenty but she'd felt herself increasingly remote from them: Edward's armed invasion of France that had been bought off by Louis' golden bribes so that not a blow had been struck. This, followed by the Treaty of Picquigny, and the ransoming of Margaret of Anjou by Louis for 50,000 marks. But intimate family affairs were all that had begun to matter to Cecily of late. Especially since she'd moved out of London, to live in a small manor house she'd had built near St Benett's busy Abbey at Holm, in the Norfolk parish of Horning. Edward had given her the land at her own request – because she liked the sea air there and the wide, open prospect – and she'd always cherish the document of the royal title deeds which concluded:

'For so much as our dearest lady mother hath sued unto us for this matter, and for so much also as our very trust is in her' – with, on the reverse of the parchment in the King's own hand: *'My Lord Chancellor, this must be done.'*

Ah yes, these were the little things that defended an ageing heart against greater sorrows – even against greater joys...

Shortly after the Gloucester wedding, the Queen had given birth to another daughter. But the infant had died within a few weeks; of convulsions; brought on, Cecily was convinced, by Elizabeth's' ill-temper during pregnancy. But Isobel and George had had a daughter, Margaret (now a healthy three-and-a-half-year-old) while Dickon and Anne at Middleham rejoiced in the birth of a son. This

Gloucester heir had been christened Edward for love of the King, who himself was father of another son by this time, Prince Richard, and another daughter, Anne of Westminster, born last year... Then the Clarences had had a boy who was nearly two years of age now. But it was this boy's infant brother, born last month at Tewkesbury Abbey, whose birth had shattered Isobel's always-precarious health.

George should not have brought her here from Tewkesbury, Cecily thought for the dozenth time. There had been no point in bringing Isobel back to Warwick Castle from her reckless pilgrimage to the Abbey of which she was patroness. But she'd begged to be returned to her ancestral home and George had given in to her fevered request. Though he'd had the sense to leave the infant in the Abbey's infirmary where it was yet being cared for...

Hearing of her daughter-in-law's illness, Cecily had set out from Norfolk with a few of her own more competent retainers to help the stricken household. But she'd known within an hour of her arrival yesterday that there was nothing that could be done to save Isobel. Cecily had seen the death signs too often, too closely, to have any doubts... She'd nursed her best-loved sister, Katherine of Norfolk, until that vital spirit had departed at last, having outlived four husbands. Then she'd attended the funeral of Katherine's grandson John Mowbray, Duke of Norfolk, who had left but one small girl as heiress to all his wealth and estates. And it was only eleven months ago that Cecily had watched over the last hours of her own eldest daughter Anne, Duchess of Exeter – 'the merciless Duchess' as people had always called this divorced wife of Henry Holland who'd sold her only child for betrothal to the Queen's son, Sir Thomas Grey, for 4,000 marks.

But Cecily remembered nothing of her daughter's

hard, intractable nature as she'd held her in her arms at the end She'd remembered only her birth in Fotheringhay Castle thirty-six years previously, the firstborn of the thirteen children of York. And it was for the baby and the memories of that babyhood, that Cecily had wept until it seemed she could have no more tears... Anne's former husband, Henry Holland, had been drowned from one of the King's ships a few months earlier. He'd been rescued from Barnet field in '71, and later pardoned by Edward after a term in the Tower. But his wife had never pardoned him for siding with Lancaster against York.

Cecily sighed now for the obstinate, passionate children she had brought into the world. Maybe it was a mercy that their father had been cut off in his prime, else his great heart might have been broken over them.

Beloved lord and husband, Richard of York! – finally, he was at rest in a fitting tomb. For, last July, the King had had his body reinterred at Fotheringhay with that of Edmund of Rutland. The coffins of father and son had been brought down from Pontefract – where they'd lain these sixteen years since the battle of Wakefield – in a procession of unparalleled magnificence. Cecily remembered every detail of the occasion when the mighty gathering of mourners had reached Fotheringhay at last, where she herself waited with many priests and nobles around her.

It was a day of clear summer sunshine; a light wind stirring the trees around lovely Fotheringhay church and sleeking the grass of the water-meadows by the River Nene. Ah, how many such days had the young Richard and Cecily of York spent here with their small children! – for Fotheringhay had been their favourite castle...

Blinking back stinging tears, Cecily watched the funeral chariot enter the churchyard. On it was laid a wax effigy of her husband, garbed in ermine and purple under cloth of gold; on his head a crown, as statement that by right he had been King of England; at his feet his shield, his sword and his helmet.

One on each side of the chariot walked George and Richard, followed by a multitude of their attendants all in deepest mourning garb; and before it paced the King, with tears streaming unashamedly down his face... Edward held out his arm to his mother and led her into the lofty light-filled church.

There, after a solemn service, the coffin of young Edmund of Rutland was interred in the Lady Chapel; while that of his father was placed in a vault under the chancel. Beside the Duke of York's coffin a significant space was left: at Cecily's request, her own body was to lie there eventually. She and Richard of York would be together again at the last—

She was aroused now from her thoughts by a new scurry of draughts from the passageway. George came into the bedchamber. She smelt the sourness of too much wine on his breath as he bent towards her, to ask thickly:

'Is there any change?'

'No, my son.'

'But there *must* be a change sometime – she can't lie like that forever! Nearly four weeks now...' He swayed close to the bed and stood looking down at his wife's face, in which the fine bones were scarcely covered with flesh and the closed eyes were darkly ringed. He said softly then: 'Isobel, the children cry for you in their sleep. And so do I – so do I. *Christ, why must it always be Clarence who loses?*' Suddenly, he had crumpled to his knees, sobbing; a big handsome man who looked like the King but who had none of Edward's defences.

Cecily drew his fair head down on her lap and began to

stroke the thick fine hair. Then, absently, her fingers strayed to the skin of the neck that was exposed above the loosened collar. At once, George stumbled to his feet, muttering, and backing away from her.

'George – I'm sorry—' she said; dismayed at having forgotten how he hated the back of his neck to be touched... In more communicative times, he used to explain that it gave him nightmares – about an executioner's axe, feeling for the place to make its first incision.

'Where's that damned nurse?' he shouted now, as Isobel stirred and moaned. 'Why isn't she here with the doctor's new potion?'

'The potion is not needed, George—' Cecily was gently raising Isobel's shoulders, trying to ease the ominous struggle of her breathing '—and I sent Ankarette Twynyho to rest. She was exhausted, poor woman.'

'Exhausted – bah! She never learned how to work in the Queen's over-staffed household, that's all. I told Isobel not to accept her from there. But Isobel feared to offend Elizabeth by refusing – *Nurse, curse you, come here!*'

Ankarette Twynyho bustled in from the anteroom. 'I was just coming, Your Grace.' She was a plump, fairish woman with eyes that had caught, curiously, an expression of the Queen's: a hostility veiled by a half-smiling indifference... She'd been under-nurse to the Queen's children for several years, during which time she'd tried to model herself on her royal mistress. She'd succeeded so well as to make the Duke of Clarence instinctively dislike her.

'The Duchess needs new medicine,' he said harshly now. 'Get it for her from the physician's rooms. And be quick if you value your life.'

Still holding Isobel, Cecily sighed for the uselessness of Ankarette's journey. But she said nothing that might further agitate George, and quietly waited for the nurse to return. In a surprisingly short time, she heard her outside the door again — a spoon chinking on a cup as the heavy door-handle was turned... At that moment, Isobel's eyes opened and focussed full on George, who was bending over her.

'My love—' Isobel whispered '—save yourself — for our children's sakes. Promise me — you will not pursue—' Her lips moved over some following words but no sound came. Her eyes had closed wearily again by the time Ankarette had reached her side and begun spooning a liquid into her mouth.

Some ten minutes after she'd swallowed half of the draught, Isobel died.

The physician of Warwick Castle later told her grief-stricken widower that he had handed out *no* potion to the nurse after twelve o'clock on that night of December 21st. When questioned, Ankarette admitted that it had been a concoction of her own which she'd brought to the sick-room: ale mixed with honey and plant juices. A medicine which she'd often given previously to the Duchess, to ease her breathing.

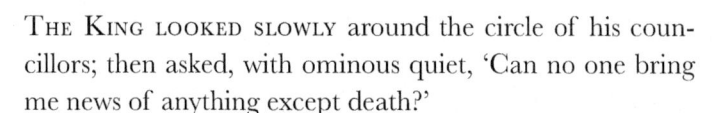

~

THE KING LOOKED SLOWLY around the circle of his councillors; then asked, with ominous quiet, 'Can no one bring me news of anything except death?'

In January his brother-in-law Charles, Duke of Burgundy, had been killed at the siege of Nancy. In January, too, the Clarence infant had died at Tewkesbury Abbey, little more than a week after its mother's death at Warwick. All events had combined to bring about strange and disquieting results.

The passing of the great Duke Charles had made his

only daughter, Mary of Burgundy, the most sought-after matrimonial prize in Europe – a prize which the heiress's stepmother decided must go to her own favourite brother, George of Clarence, so recently and conveniently bereaved. But King Edward had sent a prompt, terse message to his sister Meg in Bruges: *'We have no intention of letting Clarence go beyond our gaze, nor of giving him power overseas, so near to France. Sister, if you value our friendship, drop these proposals.'* The Duchess Margaret had dropped them – and was now busily arranging the marriage of her stepdaughter to the Archduke Maximilian of Austria.

So, once more, Clarence had been rejected; thwarted in a high ambition. And either that, or his recent bereavements, appeared to have driven him partially out of his mind. Since January, he'd paid only a few brief visits to Court; had maintained an almost total silence while there – even at council meetings – and had so steadfastly refused to eat or drink under the King's roof that it seemed he feared poisoning.

These oddities of his brother's behaviour Edward had endured patiently enough. But the report now before him was another matter altogether – a matter so serious that he had to read its details through twice before its full import penetrated:

'On the 12th day of April, at Cawford in this county of Somerset, a band of fourscore and two men wearing the livery of my lord of Clarence came to the house of one Ankarette Twynyho and broke down the door; then by force did carry the woman off to Warwick town and did cast her into prison there. Later, she was brought before the justices of the peace and indicted, at my lord of Clarence's suit, on a charge of having given to the late Duchess of Clarence venomous drinks of ale mixed with poison, which drinks caused the Duchess to sicken and die. The accused pleaded her innocence; but the jurors, for fear of their lives and goods, returned a verdict of guilty; and the

accused was sentenced to be drawn from the jail through the town, unto the gallows of Myton, there to be hanged until she was dead. The sentence was carried out without delay. And was also hanged alongside the woman one John Thuresby of Warwick, found guilty of having poisoned the infant son of the Duke and Duchess of Clarence—'

'By the Holy Rood,' Edward breathed, flinging the document aside, 'so my brother acts as though he has the King's own power! He interferes with the course of justice, and orders executions without writ or signet-seal from me. Jesu, I did well to mistrust him all along.'

Now all of Clarence's past transgressions, great and small, rose up before Edward's mind. His alliance with Warwick and his runaway marriage with Warwick's daughter. His part in the French-financed invasion of '70, and his convenient repentance before the battle of Barnet. His embarrassing public quarrels with Richard over the yet-mysterious Anne Neville business... Aye, and there'd been other matters too! Clarence had been up to his neck in some new plot with Archbishop George before that wily Neville priest had been dispossessed of all his fine goods and clapped into Hammes prison – where he yet rotted and would continue to rot until Edward's hatred of him had abated; which would be never... Then there had been George's conduct in France two years ago – and his tiresome sulking afterwards when Edward had had quite enough trouble to face at home for a French war that had turned into a carnival— Ah, the crown had never received any support from this treacherous, covetous brother who'd once been its heir apparent! On the contrary: Clarence was probably at the bottom of half the rebellions that still shook the realm from time to time. He had a strong following of ex-Lancastrian malcontents and other eccentrics who were astrologers, necromancers and God alone knew what – his own oddity was a magnet which drew every crank in the kingdom to him! If he'd been anyone except the King's own brother, he'd have been a headless, disembowelled and quartered corpse long ago. But he knew – or, rather, he believed – that he was inviolate. Well, let him be warned once more. Just once—

Yet Edward did not see what could *ever* be done with Clarence. Except to make the warnings sharper, closer. Bring them much nearer home…

There was a notorious trial going on at Westminster just then which involved a servant of Clarence's, one Thomas Burdett. Burdett stood accused – alongside old John Stacy the astronomer, who'd foretold the Duke of Suffolk's execution aboard the *Saint Nicholas of the Tower* long ago – of having cast the horoscopes of the King and the Prince of Wales to foretell when they should die; and of having proclaimed to the common people, by speech and writings, that both would die soon; and that the King's successor on the throne would be one whose name began with a letter G… In other times, Edward might have smiled upon it all as nonsense. But when, on May 19th, he heard the trial verdict of 'Guilty' he signed the execution warrants with grim satisfaction.

There! Let George see his faithful servant hang tomorrow at Tyburn.

It was an uneasy summer. The Queen constantly nagged Edward to have Clarence imprisoned lest he make another marriage and, all that time, the evidence mounted that the Duke was a dangerously reckless man. There was an armed uprising in Cambridgeshire of which he seemed to be the instigator. Now came French ambassadors bearing poisonous tales from Louis: that, while George had still had hopes of wedding the Burgundian heiress, he'd boasted of what he would do to France and *to England* when this power was his. And that he was conspiring with his sister Margaret of Burgundy against King Edward, whom he had called 'a bastard, sired by a captain of archers in Rouen'.

Louis' poison, strengthened by Elizabeth's urgings, finally worked in Edward's mind. He summoned his brother to Westminster Palace. There, before the Mayor and aldermen of London, he accused the Duke of committing acts which violated the laws of the realm and threatened its security.

'Place him under arrest,' Edward then ordered his guard, 'and lodge him in the Tower.'

As the news raced through the city, many predicted that the day of final reckoning was already in sight for Clarence; while others maintained that the King would not – *could* not – execute his own brother on any charge while Cecily of York still lived. The King revered his mother too much to give her that heartbreak. And 'proud Cis' would plead, even on her knees, for George's life although he had impugned her own honour by calling the King a bastard...

Aye, but the Queen? – would she not press the balance the other way? It was common knowledge how much Elizabeth hated George of Clarence. And she still had the King in the palm of her hand even if he *did* sleep with Jane Shore.

The betting began on how long George of Clarence would be allowed to live.

21

January, 1478

ON THE SURFACE, no royal occasion had ever been brighter. St Stephen's Chapel, Westminster, was lavishly decorated for a wedding service this January morning of 1478. The King's second son Prince Richard, Duke of York, aged four, was to marry the six-year-old Anne Mowbray, sole heiress to the duchy of Norfolk.

But a dark cloud was hanging over the entire House of York, and everyone in the party awaiting the bride's arrival was aware of its shadow. Especially Cecily, who stood under the golden canopy with the little groom, his royal parents and sisters, and the seven-year-old Prince of Wales... It was a cloud grown larger and darker these six months since George of Clarence had been locked into the Tower. There, he still awaited an unknown punishment for a list of charges against him that lengthened, week by week, as enquiries were pursued at home and abroad into his past activities. His mother's frantic pleas had done nothing to halt this relentless inquisition.

Her hand tightened on the shoulder of her grandson, Prince Richard. The child twisted around to look up questioningly at her. Holy Virgin, how like George as a boy he was! May God protect him from his uncle's fate—

The little bride was coming into the chapel now from the Queen's chamber with a great retinue of lords and ladies. In her splendid new clothes, she looked vitally pretty – just as her great-granddame, Katherine of Norfolk, used to do! Her chief escort was Beth of Suffolk's eldest boy, John de la Pole, Earl of Lincoln.

King Edward was stepping out from under the canopy to lead Prince Richard to the altar. When Anne Mowbray arrived there, he moved her close to the Prince with a paternal gesture before signing to the Bishop of Norwich to begin the ceremony. Then he returned to the Queen's side, and Cecily understood the glance of glowing triumph which Elizabeth gave him: the huge Mowbray estates were now secure within the family, after the years of negotiation since the third Duke of Norfolk's death.

Ah yes, Cecily thought, *there was a time when I, too, planned and plotted thus for my family. But fate defeated me on most counts...*

When the Mass was over, the huge throng of wedding guests congregated in the King's apartments for the banquet. They were led thither by the cousin-Dukes of Buckingham and of Gloucester – Richard having come down lately from Middleham for the Parliament which was to open tomorrow...

Richard's presence was a ray of comfort to Cecily. If any solution could be found to the Clarence dilemma, her youngest son would find it. In his quiet way, Dickon always knew what to do in a crisis.

But there was nothing anyone could do for George –

that was clear as soon as Parliament opened and a bill of attainder for treason was brought against him, the King himself being his accuser. George protested his innocence on all charges but finally fell into a despairing silence after his ancient right of wager by battle had been refused.

Vainly then, Richard argued on his brother's behalf the various accusations that had been made (no one except himself daring to question the King's charges). These were:

That the Duke of Clarence had plotted to destroy the position of the King and his children – not just once, in 1470 when he had been generously forgiven, but on several more recent occasions.

That he had sent his servants into all parts of the realm to stir up riots and risings and general discontents.

That he had spread a report of the King and Queen practising sorcery, and using poison to do away with those subjects who displeased them. Also, that the King was a bastard who had no right to reign or have his sons by Elizabeth Woodville succeed him.

That he, Clarence, had preserved a document issued under the Great Seal of Henry the Sixth, promising that if Henry and his son died without heirs, then Clarence and *his* sons should rule over England.

That he maintained a secret army of followers who had sworn upon the Blessed Sacrament to make war on King Edward.

That he had plotted with Burgundy for the invasion of England.

That he had repaid 'with heinous, unnatural and loathly treason' the many favours showered upon him by the King; and had, at the time of his arrest, been engaged in a new plot against the throne, even more unnatural and malicious than hitherto—

'What plot, my lord?' George challenged from the ranks of the jailers who guarded him.

'You know it, brother, and I know it,' thundered the King. 'But we will not give tongue to it here lest it poison the very air we breathe.'

Edward's fixed stare, full of menace and rage, defied George to speak again. And in its threat was included Dr Robert Stillington, who had chosen to sit as near as possible to the prisoner. The Bishop of Bath and Wells had been a close friend of George's for several years, a fact which had impressed itself upon Edward's memory and given a sinister twist, in his mind, to many of George's utterances and pretensions.

Edward now demanded of his Parliament that Clarence be attained of high treason. There were many members present who felt that the charges, as made, were vague and unproven – that there was much more here than met the eye. And all members were genuinely puzzled by the ferocity and vindictiveness of their usually-merciful King... Still, they acceded to his demand: the bill of attainder was passed, declaring George Plantagenet a traitor and depriving him of his freedom, his titles and all his properties and estates.

Despairingly, Richard watched the haggard, prison-pale captive being taken away. There was only one sentence for treason: death. And Edward himself would have to give the order for that to be carried out. Could he do it? Until today, Richard had believed not – had even convinced his mother that the King would not take matters to such an end. But now there was a passion tinged with fear blazing behind the royal gaze; almost a madness—

Suddenly, Richard saw both his brothers in one frame of vision. They'd always been physically alike, Edward and George – large, fair men, blue-eyed and fresh complexioned. But imprisonment had blurred George's outlines: his body had grown thick and loose from lack of exercise, and the greyish skin of his face hung heavy, dragging eyes and mouth into an unaccustomed mould. *Yet he was still extraordinarily like Edward* – or was it that Edward's appearance had begun to mirror George's? There was a flabbiness about the King now that hid the angle of his jaw, bulked his waist, took the spring out of his step. When had this change begun? Perhaps in France in '75 when, amid all the pleasures supplied by Louis, Edward had fallen grievously ill... Yet he'd taken no extra care for his health since then. Indeed, he'd gambled and whored, overeaten and overdrunk, slept less and worried more than hitherto. It seemed now that he had never really recovered from his French illness, and that it was slowly progressive. While under it smouldered the same fear that was consuming George: *the fear of death*.

On February 7th, sentence was formally passed upon George Plantagenet by a special court presided over by his cousin Harry Stafford, Duke of Buckingham – he who was wedded to Catherine Woodville...

Ten days went by without royal order for the sentence to be carried out – days that were tortured years to Cecily who, without food or sleep, kept up a barrage of petition both to God and to the King, to spare her son's life.

But, on February 17th, the Commons sent their Speaker into the House of Lords, to ask that whatever was going to be done to the traitor should be done without further delay. Then Edward knew that he must act – must show the impartiality of his justice. Yet it seemed that his tongue had turned to stone when he tried to give the order for his brother's execution on the morrow...

'Only the King can destroy the King,' Jacquetta Woodville had once stated. Did the process begin when he cut down the brother who was his mirror-image? George could not be allowed to survive: he knew too much, and was fatally indiscreet when in his cups. Which was too often—

'Where's Gloucester?' the King asked dully of Sir James Radcliffe, one of his own intimate attendants, who was standing nearby. He'd formed the question with some idea that Richard's presence could hold back the darkness threatening to engulf him.

'He went to the Tower, Your Grace,' Radcliffe replied, 'as soon as Speaker Alyngton left the House of Lords.'

'Eh? What for? I gave him no leave—'

'He went to see that a gift of his was safely delivered to his brother.'

'A gift? What gift?'

'I hear it was a butt of malmsey wine, Sire.'

Edward stared with haggard eyes at Radcliffe; then muttered, half to himself,

'Malmsey... aye, 'twas always George's favourite drink. What was it he used to call it? "The prized vintage of Malvasia". Well, trust Dickon to remember... But I think he's been over-generous. For even George cannot get through a whole butt before the axe falls on his neck.'

For George Plantagenet however, the axe never fell. He was found dead in the Tower on the morning of February 18th. He was just over twenty-eight years of age when his life ended.

Some believed the popular story that he was actually drowned – or drowned himself – in the butt of malmsey wine. But others, less literal-minded, took it that he simply drank himself to death at the last, when the order for execution, finally signed by the King, was shown to him.

George Plantagenet, once Duke of Clarence and Earl of Salisbury, Great Chamberlain of England and King's

Lieutenant of Ireland, was laid beside his wife Isobel in a vault behind the high altar of Tewkesbury Abbey, quite close to the last resting-place of Margaret of Anjou's son. His two surviving children were made wards of the crown.

Three days after his body had been carried out of the Tower, Robert Stillington was arrested and imprisoned there, on a charge of violating his oath of fidelity by an utterance prejudicial to the King. The arrest of the Bishop of Bath and Wells, who had so long enjoyed royal favour, seemed strange to many; and none knew what the 'utterance' in the charge could have been.

Expect, perhaps, George Plantagenet, who would never speak of it now.

22

September, 1478

Cecily's bones ached from five days in the saddle; but even when a November wind knifed across East Anglia, she refused to ride in the litter with her younger grandchildren. The extra burden might slow the litter's progress, and only God knew whether the journey had taken too long already: plague was spreading out from London in every direction.

The dreaded symptoms had first appeared in the capital at the end of September. King Edward had promptly given up his autumn hunting around Greenwich and had moved to Eltham where Elizabeth was awaiting yet another confinement. She'd had a third son last year. That child had been christened George before the Clarence scandal had exploded.

Resolutely now, Cecily put Clarence's death to the back of her mind. It had aged and embittered her; but its crying wound healed a fraction every time she managed to banish all thought of it and concentrate upon the present. For months after the funeral, she'd made the sad mistake of never stirring out of Baynard's Castle. Ironically, it was the arrival of the plague in London's streets that had brought her forth at last.

All her life she'd had a terror of infection. But when news of the plague's ravages had finally penetrated her mourning, her sudden fear was not for herself but for her beloved grandchildren living near London – the offspring of Edward and dead George and Beth. These were the ones who mattered now, the youngsters growing up around the Yorkist throne. On them depended the whole future of the White Rose House.

Springing to furious activity, she'd organised her London household for a winter move to her manor house in Norfolk. She'd sent servants ahead to prepare the place which had been uninhabited these two years. Then, leading a great train of horsewains loaded with food supplies and clothing, she'd set out from the plague-stricken capital; keeping close by her as many of her grandchildren as she'd been able to coax from their parents.

Edward had given into her care the Princesses Elizabeth, Mary, Cecily and Anne. After some debate, he'd also given her Prince Richard and the Prince's little wife, Anne Mowbray... Then Beth of Suffolk had handed over three of her de la Pole boys, with a stammered plea to Cecily that they should be kept safe at all costs. Finally, the two orphaned children of Clarence, who were now the King's wards, were allowed to travel to Norfolk with their grandmother... So, presently, Cecily had eleven high-titled and high-spirited youngsters in her charge. And despite the worry and responsibility of them, and the ever-present dread of the plague's catching up or even lying in wait ahead, she was feeling happier than she'd done in years. The children's company had renewed her youth.

For the first time, she could entirely forget for long

periods the terrible drama that had been enacted in the Tower last February. She could cease tormenting herself with questions as to how and why it had all occurred, whether it could have been prevented, and if Richard's wine-gift to George had been but a compassionate offer of escape from reality – or had the younger brother *known* that the older one could actually drink himself to death? In any case, George had been saved from his lifelong terror of the axe. The whole truth of the matter would never be discovered. Though it didn't really matter now – any more than it mattered whether it was Louis of France or Elizabeth Woodville who'd actually brought about George's death by whispering in Edward's ear. Cecily found it impossible to keep a rage of grief and regret and suspicion seething in her own heart while boy and girl cousins giggled and teased one another just behind her ageing, dignified back.

Half-smiling, she urged the entire party on for Norwich with the reminder that St Benett's was only a day's journey beyond; and that there was no plague reported from either place, so that everyone might eat heartily in the city... Food, she recalled, had been her own main preoccupation and pleasure in early youth. Her fiancé had once given her an apple that had tasted like ambrosia; she'd eaten it before the evening meal at Raby on her betrothal eve, over fifty years ago, but its memory was still as clear as the shape of the white primrose pressed in her Book of Hours... Ah, she must cease dwelling so in the past!

That Christmas of 1478, Cecily went to unaccustomed lengths to have a festive household. She gave the children the pleasant task of decorating the manor – hanging it all over inside with evergreen boughs and berries and coloured ribbons. She told the servants that there was to be no economy in the use of candles, torches and tapers; and that the great log fires which blazed at each end of the Hall were to be kept going from early morning until late at night for the whole of the Twelve Days. Then, on Christmas Eve, she went down to the cellars with her steward and arranged for a reckless amount of food to be sent to the kitchens for preparation.

'Your Grace,' the steward warned grimly, ''twill be a lean spring at this rate!'

She knew that he was right, because no outside supplies were being brought from markets, now that the plague was moving rapidly northward: the household was living entirely on its stores from granary, buttery, cellar and ice-house.

'That may be,' she replied. 'But I want the children to remember this Christmas as a time of happiness and plenty...'

∼

THE FESTIVAL DAWNED bright and crisp with hoar-frost. There was still a sickle moon hanging low in the sky when everyone set out for the nearby Abbey to hear the Second Mass of Christmas Day – the Midnight Mass having been celebrated in the manor house's private chapel.

The younger children romped ahead, reminding Cecily of journeys down to Staindrop Church from Raby Castle long ago. It seemed to her that it was only the fashion in clothing that had altered; the young faces and voices were unchanged from those of her own Neville hearth-kin – sisters and brothers and cousins, most of whom were now dead – or from the Plantagenet family which she and Richard had reared...

But the older girls were walking sedately beside their granddame. The Princess Elizabeth, aged twelve, was already a beauty, tall and rosy fair – the gentleness of her nature giving an increased loveliness to her face. She looked every inch the Queen she must be one day: she was betrothed to Louis' son, the Dauphin Charles of France, and there was a rumour that Louis was slowly dying. Young Charles would succeed him as King, and Elizabeth would be Charles' consort... Beside her was the pretty Princess Cecily, who was to wed the heir of King James the Third of Scotland. And alongside her was the Princess Mary, for whose hand in marriage the young King Frederick of Denmark was asking. Truly, Edward was making great matches for all his children. Lately, he'd betrothed the Prince of Wales (who lived in Ludlow Castle surrounded by Woodville tutors and attendants) to lame little Anne of Brittany, the heiress of Duke Francis. May God forbid it ever leaked out that all of Edward's brood were bastard-born, for that would be the end of their high marriage hopes, if they could bring with them no claim to England's throne.

Cecily glanced around her to see where George's orphans were; they had a habit of keeping themselves apart from the others. Ah yes, there was solemn, pious little Margaret Plantagenet walking between her cousin-fiancé John de la Pole, Earl of Lincoln, and her four-year-old brother Edward, the new Earl of Warwick. Margaret was holding her brother tightly by the hand, guarding him against anything that might cause him to stumble – he was a slightly backward child, slow of speech and awkward of movement. Cecily always thought that the great Warwick title, with which the King had invested him after George's death, sat rather pathetically upon him.

Still, she couldn't deny that the King had done his best for George's dependents. He'd given Margaret a household of her own; and he'd paid all his late brother's servants to the end of the year. Yet these deeds had not salved the royal conscience, it seemed. Report had it that nowadays, whenever the King pardoned a wrongdoer, he'd turn his head aside afterwards and, weeping, mutter:

'Ah, unhappy brother, for whose deliverance no man asked!'

Edward had quickly forgotten Richard's and her own pleas for George's pardon – pleas to which he himself had remained deaf because Louis of France had been whispering insinuatingly in his ear, trying to enmesh the Duchess Margaret of Burgundy in a quarrel with England. Only it was George of Clarence who'd been brought down by the net spread for Meg… 'Christ, why must it always be Clarence who loses?' Thus George had sobbed in Warwick Castle on the night of Isobel's death. And Cecily recognised now that George had been born to be a victim; of others; of his own temperament; of circumstances and of fate. *And George had known it.* Was this the knowledge, foolishly admitted, that had been the real cause of his condemnation? Had Edward been afraid to pardon him because of it? The only possible source of that knowledge was Robert Stillington, and he'd been imprisoned within three days of George's death. Yet the Bishop of Bath and Wells was now free again and, to all appearances, a good friend of the King's; though some maintained that beneath the Bishop's quiet smile a lively anger blazed, because of the months spent in a dungeon and the large fine exacted at the end – all for an unspecified offence!

By February, the pestilence was raging throughout Norfolk. Several monks of St Benett's had died, and no member of Cecily's household went to the Abbey for Mass anymore. The manor gates remained shut, denying admittance to any who called – even the arrival of a royal messenger on St Valentine's Day failed to open them: the man had to shout his tidings through a grille.

'Our lady Queen has been delivered of an infant Princess who has been christened Katherine.'

A sixth girl, Cecily thought, as she went out to question the man after he'd been handed wine and food over the wall. Ah well, she'd be useful in the marriage market like all the rest. Her eye fell on the four-year-old Princess Anne toddling along beside her. Anne was promised to Philip, the infant son of Mary of Burgundy and the Archduke Maximilian.

'Are Their Graces, the King and Queen, in good health?' Cecily asked the messenger through the grille – keeping her face as far as possible from his and holding a kerchief over her mouth and nose.

'Aye, Madame. The King has received a dispensation from the Holy Father which allows him to eat meat in Lent, so that he may keep up his strength against the pestilence.'

Cecily smiled slightly. Trust Edward to find justification for his appetites! Her own household was still healthy, God be praised, though living mainly on dried fish and oatmeal.

'What other news?' she asked then; wishing that Edward's terror of the plague did not forbid him to write and receive letters.

The messenger hesitated a moment – just long enough for her to understand that she must prepare herself for ill tidings. 'Sad news, I fear, Your Grace. A month ago, the plague struck the convent at Barking—'

'My sister – Jane, the nun?'

'Aye, lady. God rest her.'

'Aye, indeed,' was all she replied as she turned sadly away…

One more plague victim, the Neville sister next in age to herself. Sweet Jane, whom she'd visited so often over the years for advice and aid of prayer… Yet it was not those visits she remembered as she made her way towards the manor chapel. It was a journey long, long ago from Middleham to Raby. Across the flooded River Tees at Wynston. When Jane had still been wearing her novice's habit of white serge—

Cecily's tears flowed for her sister as she knelt and prayed for the repose
of her soul.

Easter came mild and wet, and now the entire country was in the plague's grip. So many died that death became unremarkable. The routines of State and commerce were pared to the bone – no courts or parliaments were held, no English exports made because of lack of buyers abroad – indeed, English ships had difficulty finding a harbour anywhere outside their home ports; some had been burnt at foreign moorings. Back in England, this year of 1479 came to be referred to, simple, as 'the plague year' in the scant records that were kept.

In March, the sixteen-month-old Prince George of Windsor had died. Later, death came threefold to the Paston family of Norfolk; young Walter, studying for the priesthood, was fatally stricken in August; his grandmother Dame Agnes, widow of the judge, died the same month; and in November, Sir John was laid to rest by the White Friars of London.

But Cecily's household remained free of infection throughout that terrible summer and autumn. And when December came in with sudden, intense cold, the plague abated so much everywhere that she felt it necessary to return her precious charges to their parents.

She'd had a year of their close company – a year of growing to know and love each one as though it were her own child. And none of them would ever forget her; she would live forever in their memories as the regal granddame who taught them how to preside at imaginary banquets and receive invisible ambassadors; and who then played rope and ball and marble games with them – told them stories about things that had *really* happened – and taught them songs and rhymes and old north-country sayings.

'I love you, grandma'am,' Prince Richard stated solemnly as he bade her farewell. 'When my brother comes from Wales, we will make him envious of the times we've had in your house – will we not, Anne?' he appealed to his child-wife... Pretty Anne Mowbray nodded so vigorously that she shook her dark curls free of her fur-lined travelling hood; then she kissed her great-grandaunt Cecily and moved reluctantly towards the waiting horses. Her sisters-in-law, the three elder Princesses, were already mounted, with Clarence's two children sitting their own palfreys a little way off as usual, attended by faithful John de la Pole. The tiny Princess Anne was in the litter with two of her de la Pole cousins.

All white Roses, Cecily thought. *God keep them – oh God keep them!*

After they'd gone – with a great troup of servants attending them – she became aware of the biting cold and of the old arthritic ache in her joints which she'd hardly noticed this year past. Still, she went on with her preparations for a journey to the north: she was to spend the springtime with Richard and Anne and their little son and the old Countess of Warwick at Middleham Castle. She felt, now, that she could no longer live apart from one or other member of her family.

Richard was most dear to her; but dearest of all was Meg in Burgundy. Some day before death called her, she had to see Meg again.

But Dickon first; for she'd never laid eyes on the little son whom Anne had borne him six years ago.

'Young Ned is not strong enough yet for long journeys,' his father had smilingly told her. But the confidence of the smile had been belied by one gesture which Dickon always used when he was anxious and worried: the nervous twisting of a ring around and around on his finger.

23

February, 1480

'The north is colder than it used to be...' Cecily remembered her father, Earl Ralph of Westmorland, making that remark several times on his final visit to Middleham and Raby castles before his death. Now, as she herself rode towards Middleham, and felt the cold like a menacing presence over Wensleydale, she wondered if it were an augury of her own last journey. She was near sixty-six, a great enough age for the times. And at Northampton Abbey recently she'd taken solemn religious vows, offering what was left of her life, in place of Sister Jane's, to God's service; so that she now existed most frugally, with much prayer and penance, and wore only a black gown and veil without ornament – she, who'd once assured herself so vehemently:

'I could never be a nun – never – *never!*'

Yet she hadn't foregone her freedom to travel. That

freedom she intended to maintain until all her joints stiffened completely.

The noonday bell rang out from Jervaulx Abbey in its wooded setting on the River Yore. Pausing with her attendants by the gate of this great Cistercian House to recite the Angelus, Cecily thought she'd never seen the trees look so starkly bare, so stricken by the intense cold, against a sky drained of all colour.

The Angelus over, she crossed herself and urged her mount forward over the frozen track towards the Coverbridge Inn. From just beyond there, the towers and battlements of Middleham Castle would be visible near the high western rim of the dale.

Never had she so looked forward to a journey's end as on this bitter February day of 1480 when the fields were too hard with frost for ploughing to have begun at Candlemas... it would be a poor harvest from the late sowing. And the brutal cold that had rid the land of plague had already destroyed vines and fruit trees, and caused birds to fall frozen-winged out of the sky. There would be widespread famine – for which, as for all disasters, people would blame the King! Poor Edward, who was even now having to struggle hard to maintain his peace with France and with Scotland...

As she rode up the steep track towards Middleham Castle, Cecily was engulfed in a lifetime's memories of this place over which the shades of mighty Salisbury and Warwick still seemed to brood. But then she saw Richard surrounded by a throng of people, coming out over the drawbridge to greet her and, suddenly, it was *his* domain – his presence alone that dominated here... As she dismounted and walked with him under the great arch that framed the castle's interior buildings, she tried to analyse the change that had come over him but found it too subtle for quick assessment. All she knew was that now, at twenty-seven, Richard of Gloucester was totally mature, totally in command of himself and all that came beneath his authority. Never had he reminded her so strikingly of his father, after the uncertainties of youth had been swept away.

Now Anne was approaching with a small boy by her side. Cecily kissed them both, and remained stooping a moment to look better at her grandson. Like Dickon, this young Edward was small and thin and dark. But she noted with dismay that he also had his mother's and his late Aunt Isobel's air of fragility in the too-fine skin, the flush high on the cheekbones, and in the birdlike hand that still reposed passively between her own. Involuntarily, she thought of the tiny corpses that had fallen out of trees along the road—

Anne and Dickon were smilingly helping her up the grand staircase towards the Presence Chamber and all their friends were crowding merrily behind, transforming the once-austere atmosphere of this most formal part of the castle to one of friendly warmth... Clearly, Richard was much respected by all the young lords who were visiting him from northern estates: there were Scropes here, and Percys and Metcalfes and Dacres, Plumptons, Ogles, Greystokes and Conyers – all youthful, eager, vital men who showed Richard great love without presuming too much upon his quiet friendship, but whose manners entirely rejected the rigid forms of Warwick's day, and the present stale frivolity of the royal Court.

Looking around the crowded Presence Chamber, Cecily realised that she was in the sort of company she'd known all her married life: the company of active soldiers. And that her youngest son was as much their natural leader as her husband had been until his death in battle, nineteen years ago.

The bitter spring gave way at last to summer weather, making a burst of May blossoms throughout the dales.

Cecily took her little grandson Edward for walks and gentle rides. Sometimes his mother, Anne, or his granddame, the widowed Countess of Warwick, would accompany them; or his nurse, Joan Collins, a bonny girl from Kettlewell. Also, as often as possible, his father made time to come.

The shining affection between Richard of Gloucester and this only wedlock-born son of his was both joy and pain for Cecily to watch, because she was convinced by now that the child's health would no more strengthen than Anne Neville's had done – Anne was a frail woman, unlikely ever to bear another infant... The death of his sole heir could utterly crush Richard.

Still, for the present, Richard was joyous in his son, full of plans for the future. Cecily believed that everything he did these times was done with an eye to the lad's growing up. 'When Ned is old enough—' he would preface a discussion of many an ambitious project; like the current one of transforming the parish church of Middleham town into a chantry-college.

Cecily had often tensed herself to warn Dickon: 'Do not love this child of yours too much.' Yet she knew she could never say the words; never cloud for even a moment the bright, tender hope in those grey eyes of his.

Then, quite suddenly, there was no more opportunity for discussion of any kind. In mid-May, England declared war on Scotland. Richard of Gloucester was nominated the King's Lieutenant in the north, and was bidden to collect troops there with all haste and to lead them across the Scottish border. King James the Third was to be taught a sharp lesson for recent armed incursions by some of his subjects into England.

'Though I reckon James be hardly to blame,' Richard said privily to his mother as he bade her farewell before his departure. 'It is my belief that French Louis' forces are behind all the northern unrest.'

'To lure Edward up from the south?' Cecily asked sharply. She knew it was one of the oldest military ruses, outplayed and outworn; yet Edward himself had once been precipitated into exile by it. 'You cannot credit that France means to invade us.'

'No. Louis is too sick in his body now for that. But the spider's mind is as active as ever. It plans to keep England, Brittany and Burgundy immobilised on three distant sections of its web; for if they come together actively, they can destroy the centre were Louis sits... Mother, listen, you must go to Edward. Tell him I will keep the north for him – he must not distract himself by leading an army up here. Let him instead aid Burgundy, which is so sore pressed by France – our sister Meg there will give him wise council on what to do. And let him finally settle the marriage treaty between the Prince of Wales and young Anne of Brittany, and between the Princess Katherine and the Spanish heir. That way, he rings France with his own interests and alliances.'

'B-but his daughter Elizabeth – her betrothal to the Dauphin?'

Richard's eyes narrowed as though warding off a blow.

'Must we fling our loveliest rose to a deformed idiot?' he asked, his voice vibrant with passion. Then, more quietly, 'I'd sooner see my fair niece in her grave than wedded to Louis' son Charles.'

But the control had taken over the voice a sentence too late. With pity, Cecily realised that Richard loved young Elizabeth of York; not as a niece but as the healthy, golden, ideal of womanhood (like his dead mistress, the mother of the robust bastards John and Katherine) which pale Anne Neville could never be... Yet he would be wholly faithful to Anne; ever gentle with her, while he burned out his Plantagenet passions in service to the King.

It was eighteen months since Cecily had last been to London. On her return there in early June, Edward came at once to visit her at Baynard's Castle. She was in her solar when he arrived and he went alone up the steep, winding stair, leaving his attendants in the Hall.

Always in the past, he'd run up that stair. Now – although she was expecting him – his mother hardly recognised his slow heavy tread. When he entered the room, he was barely able to speak from shortness of breath. And she remembered how, long ago, this had been the first real sign of middle-age in his father.

But there was more than middle-age afflicting Edward. With a spasm of the heart which she struggled not to let show on her face, Cecily noted the physical deterioration of her royal son.

Even allowing for the new, hugely-padded shoulders just coming into fashion, Edward's girth had increased visibly. Gone was the supple waist, the slim athletic hipline. Instead, a general thickening of the body swelled his doublet all around. And the long legs that had been so slim, firm and shapely bulged now in their rich hose.

Yet it was his face, when he approached to kiss her, in which Cecily noted the greatest change. The brilliant blue eyes were dulled and diminished by encroaching circles of puffed flesh; and the once-splendid jawline was entirely blurred. The King's face had become that of a dissolute man who drank and gambled and whored far into the night. And the sunshine of his yellow hair was dimming behind an overall greyness that repeated the new pallor of his skin.

'Edward—' she held him against her so that he would not see her shocked expression '—have you kept well? And Elizabeth?' The latter question was purely a matter of form; she was not interested in Elizabeth's health.

He laughed. 'Bess is expecting again. November or thereabouts, I think. She's gone to Eltham to look after herself... As for me, well, I escaped the plague; what more can one ask? But there's been a slight recurrence of my damned "French fever" lately.' This was the mysterious ailment he'd first taken five years ago, when he'd led an army over to terrorise Louis into paying the huge annual sums to stay out of France in the future.

'So you are not fully recovered yet?' Her maternal gaze tried to rationalise the obvious signs of ill-health.

'Of course I am. Long since.' He propped one foot on a bench-end and leaned his elbow on his knee. 'Only I've been too occupied with papers and delegations to take enough exercise... Mother, come and sit by me. Tell me all about affairs in the north – is Richard on the move towards Scotland yet?'

'Yes, before I left Middleham, he rode out with a great force to join Northumberland. You need have no worries for the safety of the marches, Edward, while your brother is your Lieutenant there.'

'Ah, I know that; I'd trust Dickon with my life. Nevertheless, I shall ride north in person as soon as a few matters here have been settled.'

'What kind of matters?' She hoped they'd be complicated enough to keep him from his military saddle for some time. Now, at the age of thirty-eight, he did not look like a King who could fight another battle and hope to survive the exertion.

He closed his eyes. 'Mainly the usual bickerings with France,' he said. 'Louis has finally paid off Margaret of

Anjou's ransom, but not one penny of young Bess's marriage-moneys can I extract from him.'

'Has he arranged the formal betrothal between her and the Dauphin?' For an instant, Dickon's anguished face rose before her mind's eye.

'No, he has not,' Edward replied testily. 'And when I tried to push him to it a few weeks ago, Dauphin Charles fell diplomatically ill. Though the delay is all purely a question of money, of course...'

Is it, Cecily wondered? Or could Louis be having second thoughts about wedding his only son to the Princess Elizabeth of York? But surely not. The lovely young Bess had been known as 'Madame la Dauphine' for a long while now. And her sister Mary's betrothal to the King of Denmark was still being delayed, because Mary had been offered as a substitute bride for France should anything happen to Elizabeth before her wedding with the Dauphin. Therefore, two of Edward's girls were tied up in this matter. Small wonder he was impatient of its settlement by Louis...

Edward opened his eyes and, heaving his leg off the armrest, sat up straight. 'But I'm going to put the fear of God into cousin Louis,' he said pleasantly. 'Because I'm about to have further talks with young Mary of Burgundy and her Austrian Duke – Meg has been making this request on her stepdaughter's behalf for a long while.'

'Meg? You've heard from her recently, Edward?' Cecily had received no letters from her daughter in Burgundy for several months, although she herself had written often from Middleham.

'I have. Many times. And replied to all. In fact, we've been arranging something which I think will greatly please you, Mother.'

'Y-you've agreed to send aid to Maximilian?' It was what Dickon had advised.

'No, not quite – not yet anyhow. Though the betrothal of his son to my little Anne makes me look favourably upon his pleas for help against France. Still, such matters take a deal of discussion. And who better to talk them over with than my sister Meg, the mighty Dowager-Duchess of Burgundy?'

Cecily jerked her head around to look at him half-incredulously. Meg – her dearest daughter – coming home to London after all those years! Edward stood up and held out his hands to help her rise. Abstractedly, she noted how the many rings he always wore were becoming embedded in his flesh...

'Mother,' he laughed, 'put away this crow's garb of yours for a while, will you? I want everything and everyone to be bright for Margaret's coming, when we'll feast and hunt and dance just like old times!'

Edward was unaware of change in himself or his surroundings. For the moment, he'd even forgotten that Margaret's favourite brother George was dead.

∼

IN THE PALACE OF GREENWICH, a royal banquet continued long into the July night to honour the King's mother and the visiting Dowager-Duchess of Burgundy.

Cecily had put aside her nun's robes for the occasion and, dressed with all the splendour she'd once so enjoyed, sat proudly beside her daughter. It was easy to be proud of Meg. At thirty-four she was an immensely handsome woman, strong-faced and regal; and her twelve years of power in Burgundy had given her a presence which made her the equal of any mighty lord, including Edward himself... She'd been bargaining with Edward and his council during the three weeks since her arrival and was gradually winning all the concessions she needed for her stepdaughter's husband, Duke Maximilian.

Cecily marvelled that Meg showed no signs of strain. But then, energy and the love of a good fight had always been a characteristic of the York children: Neville and Beaufort and Plantagenet blood had endowed them with rare strengths.

When the meal was over, all the minstrels and many of the guests wandered out into the lantern-hung gardens by the river. Dozens of brightly-lit barges were moored along the banks, with the royal barge conspicuous among them; its master and twenty-four oarsmen resplendent in new liveries. These royal servants waited to take Margaret back to Coldharbour House – the old Neville residence near Baynard's Castle which Edward had had sumptuously prepared for her visit.

'Is all going well, Meg?' Cecily asked as, near midnight, she walked towards the barge which would carry both herself and her daughter home.

Margaret squeezed her arm. 'Splendidly, Mother. Edward has promised two thousand archers and fifty men-at-arms for Burgundian defence against France. And he's to ratify the marriage treaty between little Philip and Ann – look, I have the rings here with me.' From her bodice she drew two small circles of gold set with diamonds and pearls in a rose cluster and threaded on fine chains to be worn about the children's necks.

Cecily smiled: 'You're a good matchmaker, Meg. But when are you going to begin thinking about another marriage for yourself?'

Margaret's laugh rang out. 'Oh, I have many proposals. The latest – from King Louis – offers me a rich and powerful Frenchman in my bed if I will prevent an alliance between Burgundy, England and Brittany! Louis lives in daily terror of invasion. And I know not which agony I wish the most upon him: the waiting fear or the bloody reality.' She walked on a few paces in silence; then added, 'Both, in due season, for the man who destroyed George.'

It was the first time she'd mentioned her dead brother, apart from a request to have his children visit her in Thames Street. Cecily made no reply. By now they'd reached the mooring of the royal barge. Margaret stood, looking sightlessly down into the black water astern of the vessel and said, very low,

'I have a boy in my household service at Bruges. His name is Perkin. He is the son of one Jehan and Catherine de Werbecque of Tournai – Catherine was much admired by Edward during his exile ten years ago. But the boy resembles George more than Edward – he reminds me heartbreakingly of George as a child; and I favour him so much that gossip has it that he is my own son by some adulterous liaison!' She swung her gaze up from the water and fixed it on Cecily. 'Mother,' she said, 'I love this child who may be of the blood of York; but I would not hesitate to use him against the enemies of our House.'

By September, Margaret had obtained a sheaf of documents signed by King Edward, making many promises and concessions to Mary and Maximilian of Burgundy. It had been a hard ten weeks' work; but she was well satisfied with its results as she set off on her homeward journey. She'd received a gift of ten palfreys from her royal brother, with a gorgeous pillion of blue and purple cloth of gold fringed with Venice lace. And her mother had given her many pieces of rich, old jewellery; because, as Cecily had said,

'I am unlikely to have need of them from henceforth, and they suit neither Beth of Suffolk nor Anne of Gloucester.' To Elizabeth Woodville, Cecily had never offered any of her personal ornaments, although the Princesses had received many pieces of the York collection from their granddame.

The jewellery Cecily would not miss, for she'd re-adopted her nun's garb. But her heart would ache with loneliness for a long while after Meg had sailed from Dover in the *Falcon*.

24

April, 1483

UNDER AN EASTER MOON, Westminster Palace lay sleeping at last after the hubbub of King Edward's sudden return from Windsor. No one knew why he'd left Windsor, his favourite springtime castle. Maybe there had been another quarrel between him and the Queen. But then, His Grace had been moody and unpredictable for some months. Rumour was that he was again suffering from his 'French ague'; and that the present recurrence of it had hit him harder than in the past because his mind was irritated by so many troubles.

First, the Scottish war had exhausted his kingdom – a realm already weakened by famine after two bad harvests since the plague year. Then Prince Richard's wife, little Anne Mowbray had died, so that her great Norfolk inheritance had passed out of Crown control. And, a few months later, the Princess Mary had breathed her last at the eminently marriagcable age of fifteen.

But these disasters were small by comparison with what the New Year of 1483 had brought: *the rejection by the Dauphin of France of the Princess Elizabeth's hand.* Louis had now betrothed his Dauphin to the Burgundian heiress after signing a peace treaty with her father, Duke Maximilian – who might have remained England's friend if only King Edward had dealt honestly with him. But Edward had deceived even his own sister, the Dowager-Duchess Margaret, by holding secret negotiations with Louis while swearing friendship to Maximilian.

Out of the tangle of this web of deceit had emerged the Treaty of Arras: peace and a marriage alliance between Burgundy and France, to the total exclusion of England. Well might England's King be sick in his mind these times as well as in his body.

Edward lay alone in the great bed. By his pillow was a copy of 'The Recuyell of the Histories of Troy', presented to him by William Caxton from the new printing press here in the city. But Edward did not have a light by him tonight for reading. His head ached, and he'd told his attendants that he wanted solitude and darkness.

Through a gap in the bed-canopy curtains he could see the moonlight on one of the Westminster Abbey's towers. He'd been anointed and crowned in that Abbey twenty-two years ago this coming June. And he'd had Elizabeth crowned there the year after their marriage. But would their eldest son – who'd been born within that Abbey's precincts – receive the regalia of kingship at its altar? The lad was but twelve-and-a-half years old yet, and not as handsome nor as outward-going as Edward would have wished him to be. A pox on those Woodvilles, who'd always surrounded the Prince. They'd infected him with their own preciousness – their own negation of real life, real feeling. The boy must be taken away from Ludlow Castle and from his tutor-uncles and half-kin, the Woodvilles and the Greys, there. A spell with Richard in the north might do the heir to the throne a power of good; remove that whining note from his voice – give him more of a sense of robust humour and less of his own apartness. The people of England preferred a king who was also a man, a human being, not a mere collection of Woodville attitudes, suspicions and petty jealousies.

'By the Rood, how sick I am of it all!' The pain at the back of Edward's head made the down-filled pillow feel like a log of blazing wood, but he was too weary to move or call a servant to change the pillow.

If Janey had been here, she'd have attended to it for him; given him many other comforts besides and asked nothing. But he hadn't sent for Jane Shore on his return to the capital this time. He didn't know why except that he was tired. Tomorrow perhaps or the day after he'd invite her to come to him.

Elizabeth had known all about him and Jane for years – the wife had even cultivated the mistress's friendship! But then, it was quite in character for Elizabeth to do whatever would most benefit herself; and a friendship with a younger woman who enjoyed the King's bed could be nothing but instructive. By this means, Elizabeth had got a last royal child: the Princess Bridget, born two years ago at Eltham when the Queen was already forty-four and permanently heavy-breasted and thick in the waist... Well, she'd have to find other occupations for her physicians now, for there'd be no more pregnancies!

Jane had never had a child, either by her husband or her royal lover or—

'Speak it, Edward, the name of your best friend: *Will Hastings.*'

Hastings, aye; companion in all sports and

debaucheries. And so beloved of his King that a tomb was being prepared for him beside the royal one that was yet unfinished in St George's Chapel, Windsor, on the north side of the altar... For a moment, Edward fretted about this uncompleted work. Men of foresight prepared their own tombs well before middle-age – he'd be forty-one at the end of April and he hadn't learned foresight yet in anything, it seemed...

But he was impatient of certain predictions of disaster that had come to his ears lately. These had followed a parliamentary vote of thanks he'd had made to his brother of Gloucester for great services in the north. He'd granted Richard some of the marcher lands won back from the Scots; and he'd created him and his heirs forever wardens of the west march, keepers of the city and castle of Carlisle and of all other Crown possessions in the county of Cumberland, with the right to appoint the sheriff of that county. He'd also given to Gloucester and his heirs permission to hold, with palatine rights, all further lands that might be won over a certain wide area... All this had seemed to Edward little enough recompense for a brother who'd virtually exiled himself in the north-country, to remain the courageous guardian of his sovereign's rights there. But the grumblers maintained that an hereditary principality had been founded; and that, though it was subject to the English Crown, it still had so much power under a strong and popular man like Gloucester that it might well prove a grave danger to the throne itself one day.

Edward moved his head painfully on the burning pillow.

'Dickon would never threaten *me* – he's loyal, honourable and, above all, content. Happy mortals neither plot nor blackmail...'

Feverishly, Edward thought of the Woodvilles with their endless, petty intrigues. Ironic, was it not, that he'd once credited Elizabeth with high-mindedness? Yet he'd lived to discover that she was a totally unprincipled woman, immoral in the deepest sense... So what if their eldest son took after her and her ilk? What if he failed, as signally as the Woodvilles had done, to win the love of the people, high and low – *to win his Uncle Richard's love?* For he could not survive without those mighty buttresses of affection even if he were the most lawful king since time out of mind. Instead of which, he was but one of the multitude of bastards whom Edward had sired—

The pain in the King's head became acute. For the first time in several weeks of feeling vaguely ill, he acknowledged the possibility that he might be dying. *His Will* – he must remake his Will... The old one, drawn up before he'd gone to France in '75, had Elizabeth's name heading the list of executors. If he were to die now, with his heir still under age, Elizabeth might manoeuvre herself into the position of Regent, which would give her and her family further years of influence over the young King. And suddenly, Edward was as determined to free his son from the Woodvilles as he'd once been to free himself from the Nevilles; though at least the Nevilles had been noble enemies, not common upstarts forever apprehensive of being plunged back into poverty.

That was the fatal flaw in the Woodville character: greed – for power, possessions, vengeance. It was their only deep passion; they had few feelings besides. But it was a passion that would always keep them from the upper air of true honour, wide vision.

Edward admitted now that these things were also lacking in himself, though for different reasons. And their lack had brought about the ruin of his entire life. The son must be saved from the blunders of the father...

Yes, in the morning he'd make a new Will. And this time he'd leave no room for argument about who should guide the heir and protect the realm: Richard of Gloucester's name would be clear for all to read. And Richard would carry out his duties with the courage and conscientiousness which he applied to everything he did.

Richard would never learn the truth about the Prince of Wales' illegitimacy. There was no proof anyhow. Eleanor Butler was long since dead; reckless George (who'd somehow stumbled on part of the story – Edward had never discovered how) George had been silenced. And Robert Stillington was yet so chastened by his term in the Tower, and his expensive release, that he'd developed a total blank in the mind concerning the marriage he'd once performed.

No one else knew. Except Cecily of York. But would *she* damn her own royal-reared grandson in order to put George's obscure heir upon the throne, and maybe revive the ancient scandal coupling her own name with the 'archer of Rouen'? Not proud Cis, who'd given a lifetime to consolidating the dynasty of York!

Convinced that his mother would remain silent, and his brother in perpetual ignorance of the truth, Edward fell into a deep sleep on the bed that was soaked with his sweat.

But somewhere in the pit of oblivion, he met the ghost of an old woman who shrieked at him until his head began to ache again. 'Who are you?' he managed to ask at last. 'I am Margaret of Anjou,' she replied. 'You killed my consort and my prince.' 'But—' Edward whispered '—you're dead also. We had a report from France last year—'

The realisation that the figure of the ex-Queen was a

fantasy jerked him awake. Carefully, like a drunken man, he began to recall the facts:

On August 25th, 1482, Margaret had died at the age of fifty-two years in her castle of Dampierre. It was just over six years since she'd been ransomed out of England by King Louis for 50,000 crowns. In exchange for this sum – the cost of her release from imprisonment in England – Margaret had signed over to Louis all her rights and claims to titles, lands, possessions and parental inheritance in Lorraine, Anjou, Bar and Provence. As a poor pensioner of Louis' then she'd lived out her last heartbroken days. In her Will, she'd begged to be interred in the cathedral of Angers, near her royal ancestors. And when she was dead, Louis had sent at once to claim whatever small possessions she had left behind. These turned out to be a few dogs; of which her sole heir, the King of France, became owner.

The ironic story had once amused Edward. Now it terrified him.

Frantically he rang the bell at his bedhead; and the entire palace sprang to wakefulness with the dread news that the King was sore sick.

~

FOR THREE NIGHTS AND DAYS, Cecily had been at the Palace of Westminster. She'd received word of Edward's illness on the evening of Low Sunday, and had gone up river at once by barge from Baynard's Castle. She'd been with her son most of the time since then.

Now she sat in the anteroom nearest the royal bedchamber. All the anterooms were crowded with people, yet there was hardly a sound because everyone moved softly, spoke in whispers. The King was alone with his confessor who was preparing him for the Last Rites.

Cecily felt dazed and remote. The acute part of Edward's illness had come on so suddenly, progressed so quickly since a hearty meal he'd eaten on Good Friday evening, that she still felt she might wake up from a nightmare. Her cold fingers moved automatically from bead to bead of the black Rosary which she wore with her nun's garb, but she was not praying; she couldn't pray.

'He must not die,' she'd told herself over and over again as she'd sat by Edward's bedside. Yet, every time she'd looked at him, his great body had seemed diminished a little more, like something being consumed by flames. Today he'd appeared no larger than the child she'd borne in Rouen, forty-one years ago this month of April.

God, it was not right that an old woman who'd outlived her usefulness should survive, while the one man England needed slipped away into death's shade.

Who would control the country? – keep the wheels of government turning until a new reign began? The one experienced soldier and administrator, Richard of Gloucester, was far away in the north. He, and he alone, would have adult royal authority, since Edward had named him Protector of the Realm in his Will and he was the last male of the original Yorkist line. But how long would it take messengers to find him on the wild marches towards Scotland? And how long more before he could reach the capital, to assert his position as head of affairs there? The Woodvilles would almost certainly challenge his Protectorship; and his delay in arriving would give them time to entrench themselves, and to have the Prince brought from Wales for immediate crowning as King Edward the Fifth.

For the first time, Cecily faced the reality of her own dilemma in the matter of this coronation. Could she stand silently by and let it proceed? – let the Holy Oil be poured out on a boy who had no more right to its sanctification than any other of Edward's many bastards? 'Woe unto you, oh land whose king is a child,' the prophet had cried in the Old Testament; but greater woe, surely, if his anointing where an act of injustice to the true heir? And yet, to put George's slow-witted eight-year-old son on the throne was to beg for even greater national disaster. The land needed a grown man—

Tormented in her mind, Cecily wished for only one thing apart from Edward's recovery: that Dickon were here. She'd be able to talk to Dickon; tell him the whole truth and let *him* decide what must be done. He ought to have been put in possession of the facts long ago so that he'd be prepared for such a crisis as this. Instead, he'd been left in ignorance of a position which his brother George had suspected, and died for. Cecily turned an anguished gaze towards the door of the King's bedchamber.

Ah, Edward, Edward, she thought, *you sowed rashly all your life. May God forgive you the deceits you allowed to flourish. And may He aid the reaping of this bitter harvest which you have escaped.*

The chamber door opened and the confessor came out.

'His Grace is truly repentant of all his sins,' he announced, 'and is ready to meet his Creator: God be praised.'

'Amen,' replied the hundreds of courtiers, ministers and officials crowded in the ante-chambers... Lord William Hastings was there with his followers in one open room; a hostile gathering of Woodvilles in another; and a group of clergy in a third, with the Bishop of Bath and Wells standing a little apart from them, staring fixedly towards the King's chamber. On Robert Stillington's face, the usual nervous, placatory expression was giving way to one of relief as realisation penetrated that the King was indeed dying... Cecily saw the Bishop's shoulders straighten and the firmness of decision harden his countenance. In that moment she knew that he had made up his mind to publish the truth: that young Edward of Westminster could never lawfully inherit the crown, nor Elizabeth Woodville remain Queen of England – Elizabeth must be demoted to the crowded ranks of the royal mistresses.

Cecily knew a moment of blind panic as she watched the Bishop cross over the central aisle between the anterooms and, with deliberate tread, approach William Hastings. *Ought I to try to stop him* – she wondered – *crave him for his silence?* Then she glanced back at the Woodvilles; noted the tense, greedy faces waiting, without sorrow, for Edward to pass away. And she knew that she would not interfere with the Bishop's decision.

Hurry down from the north, Dickon. Only you will know what to do, and have the courage and the power to do it. She spoke aloud, but her words were drowned by the sudden surge of the throng towards the open door, beyond which hovered the presence of royal death.

She stood up and moved forward. Deferentially, everyone made way for her... Black-robed and slow and regal, she entered the living presence of King Edward the Fourth for the last time.

NOTES

Chapter 16

1. Note: The date of birth usually given for Perkin Warbeck (one of the several pretenders to the English throne during the reign of Henry Tudor) is 1474; but there is doubt about this, as about his true parentage. He claimed to be the second son of King Edward and Elizabeth Woodville (born 1473). Rumour said he was a bastard of the Duchess of Burgundy, sired by the Bishop of Tournai. In his confession before execution, he stated he was son of Catherine de Faro and John Osbeck (Werbecque or Warbeck) controller of the town of Tournai. But his physical resemblance to the Plantagenets was so striking that many people supported him as Edward's (or as Clarence's) son; and Edward *could* have sired him in 1470/'71.

BRIEF BIBLIOGRAPHY

The Life and Reign of Edward the Fourth, Cora L. Scofield, Frank Cass & Co. Ltd., new edition 1967. Two volumes.

The Fifteenth Century, E. F. Jacob, Clarendon Press, 1961.

The Yorkist Age, Paul Murray Kendall, Allen & Unwin, 1962.

Lancastrians, Yorkists and Henry VI, S. B. Crimes; Macmillan, 1964.

The End of the House of Lancaster, R. L. Storey, Barrie & Rocklife, 1966.

Margaret of Anjou, Queen of England, J. J. Bagley, Herbert Jenkins, 1948.

Later Medieval Europe, D. Waley, Longmans, 1964.

Richard III, Caroline A. Halstead, Longmans, 1844.

The College of King Richard III, Middleham, J. M. Melhuish, booklet issued by The Richard III Society.

English Costume of the Later Middle Ages, Iris Brooke, A. & C. Black, 1956.

The Paston Letters, edited by James Gairdner, the three-volume edition published in 1872, '74, '75 by Edward Arber.

Religion and the Decline of Magic, Keith Thomas, Weidenfeld & Nicolson, 1971.

Anatomy of Witchcraft, Peter Haining, Souvenir Press, 1972.

The Dictionary of National Biography.

An Age of Ambition: English Society in the Late Middle Ages, F. R. H. Du Boulay, Nelson, 1969.

The Betrayal of Richard III, V. B. Lamb, Mitre Press, 1959.

Archaeologia, Vol LXXXIV, 1934, feature on investigation into the fate of the Princes in the Tower by Lawrence E. Tanner, Professor William Wright.

The Later Plantagenets, V. H. H. Green, Edward Arnold, 1955.

The Tower – 880 Years of English History, John E. N. Hearsey, MacGibbon & Kee, 1960.

The Spider King, Lawrence Schoonover, Collins, 1955.

Author's Note:

For most events, I have given the modern form of dating although in the fifteenth century these would have been given as saints' days, vigils, etc. followed by the year of the King's reign.

READ ON FOR THE FINALE OF CECILY'S STORY IN 'WINTER'S ROSE'

London, England, 1483

King Edward IV is dead, plunging England into chaos. His brother Richard rides from the cold North in an attempt to take the reins of government and restore order, only to be crowned King Richard III...

Cecily of Neville, famed matriarch of the House of York, is powerless to prevent the rapid turn of events – the inevitable battles, betrayals and murders that haunt her son Richard in his short-lived reign. And at the heart of it all are two young princes confined in the Tower of London, their fates a mystery to this day...

Winter's Rose is the final novel in Eleanor Fairburn's famed quartet on the Wars of the Roses, and a touching end to her masterful representation of Cecily Neville, the Rose of Raby.

WINTER'S ROSE

The dying Edward roused himself in the great bed.

'More pillows,' he muttered. 'Raise me up.'

It took four men to lift him. When he was propped, the Sun in Splendour device of the bed-hangings was crumpled behind his huge shoulders.

He tried to focus on the crowds pushing into the royal apartments but his swollen eyelids had narrowed his vision to a slit, like the view through a war helm's vizor. He swayed his head in the practised motion of tournament and battle. After a while, he managed to frame a familiar face amid the swirling confusion of the Palace of Westminster's State bedchamber. But it was Tom Stanley's face, not the one he sought. Who'd want Stanley, the Lord High Steward, in a dark hour? – so miserable and long-visaged that he was known as 'Merry Tom'; his crossed eyes betokening his devious mind!

Wearily, Edward continued searching for the other face. He found it at last, quite close to his own: that of William Hastings, who was his Lord Chamberlain and also his Captain of Calais as well as being his closest friend.

'Will—' He tried to stretch out a hand to Hastings but the hand felt cased in steel; it remained on his chest until the kneeling Chamberlain had lifted it between his own palms.

'Will,' the King urgently repeated his friend's name, 'I desire that you and your party shall make peace with the Woodvilles.'

He sensed how Hastings stiffened; yet there was no edge, except of tears, to the voice that answered.

'Aye, my lord. Anything you desire.'

Anything you desire: how often had Will said that to him in the past! Concerning a day's hunting or a night's whoring or— But it was all over now. The King could see the signature of the reckless years scrawled across the other's face as clearly as he felt it in his own body: deep lines on the toughening skin, lids hooded over world-weary eyes, the hair grizzling...

'Then summon the whole hornets' nest here before me, Will. But not Elizabeth.'

'You don't wish to see the Queen, Sire?'

'*No.*' He clenched his teeth on the obscenity he'd been about to add. Newly shriven of his sins, he'd soon receive the Holy Eucharist for the last time; there must be no blasphemy in between. Anyhow, he was too tired now even to hate Elizabeth, as he'd hated her since his brother's death in the Tower. It was Elizabeth and her rapacious family who'd engineered the fearful end of George, Duke of Clarence... 'Hurry, hurry,' he gritted to Hastings. 'There's little time left me.'

His illness had been sudden in its onset, swift in its fatal course. During the initial fever, following a chill caught on a fishing trip, his mind had been too confused for action. But as his body had ceased its struggle to live, inward vision had grown intense. He knew now what he must do to secure the future of his heir and the kingdom's safety, if only he were given time…

A woman's hand was smoothing his forehead with thin, cool fingers that wore no jewellery except for a plain gold ring.

Edward shifted his vision sideways, grimacing with pain as his eyes moved. He knew that the hand belonged to his mother, Cecily, Princess of England and Dowager-Duchess of York. He had a great longing to look at her once again: an old woman now but still remembered as young, vital, beautiful; the 'Rose of Raby' that used to be.

Their eyes locked. He saw the scald-marks of weeping on her ravaged face, within its linen coif that held the black veil of a religious order. Yet suddenly, Edward envied his sixty-eight-year-old mother. She'd been given leisure to repent her sins and set her affairs in order. But he, the great sinner, was being dragged from life before his forty-first birthday at the end of this month of April, 1483.

Full awareness of the chaos he'd leave to his successors dismayed him to his very soul. He yearned for help and comfort. Death was a lonely enterprise.

'Maman.' His lips formed the childhood title learnt long ago in France where he'd been born. He felt no shame at using it now. He'd seen brave men, mortally wounded on battlefields, sobbing for their mothers.

Cecily's hand faltered in the act of smoothing his hair. For her, that one word crystallised their relationship; swept away all the defensive obscurities of the years since Edward's union with Elizabeth Woodville.

'My beloved son,' she whispered, 'may God be good to you.' Then she saw William Hastings re-entering the chamber, and knew that this was the last intimate moment she'd ever spend with Edward. The King's mother must not monopolise the King. Kissing him, she arose and moved away...

Two groups of people approached the royal bedside.

One was composed of the Queen's relatives, all of whom had been advanced to wealth and power far beyond their merits, by the lavishness of the King while he had loved Elizabeth. The Queen was notably absent now. But her eldest son by her first marriage was well to the fore: Thomas, the profligate Marquis of Dorset, Constable of the Tower. He was a young man of dissolute countenance and lounging gait. By reputation, he was utterly without virtue or decency; and the fact that the King was his stepfather had not deterred him, of late, from laying siege to one of the royal mistresses, Jane Shore... Behind him was his brother, Sir Richard Grey, with the Woodville uncles Sir Edward, military commander, and the haughty Lionel, Bishop of Salisbury. Many other supporters of the Queen followed this quartet; notably the Lord Lyle, brother of Elizabeth's first husband, Sir John Grey of Groby...

The second group, led by William Hastings, was a tight knot of members of the oldest and noblest families; men whose sires, grandsires and great-grandsires had held high office under the Crown after distinguished service in arms; men who resented and despised the upstart Woodvilles.

Edward stared hopelessly at both groups. Now that they were before him, he realised the emptiness of the gesture he was about to demand of them.

'Clasp hands, across the chasm that divides ye.'

Hastings was the first to move. He grasped the arm of the red-headed Sir Edward Woodville. Reluctantly the other lords followed his example with the rest of the Queen's kin.

Gazing at them all, Edward continued wearily and without conviction,

'If ye love one another, all may yet be well. For my royal heir. And for the Kingdom of England.'

He sank back against the pillows, rolling over on his side so that his face was half-hidden. His swollen eyes closed against the empty mummery of the reconciliation. He knew it was but a play, enacted to humour a dying man. As soon as he was gone, the actors would resume their enmities and their opposing ambitions. Even Hastings, so faithful a supporter of the royal will and pleasure in all things, Edward recognised as a politic animal, expedient, and having many skins... Oh God, if only Richard of Gloucester were here! That one unshakable pillar of the throne; that one man who could be relied upon, absolutely, to put country before self. But Richard was far away in the north. It would be days before he even heard of his royal brother's death; weeks before he could reach the capital. By then, the Woodvilles would be entrenched around the boy-King.

Still, Richard must be given full power, and the authority to assume it. He must be formally named as Lord Protector and Defensor of the Realm, even if it took Edward's last breath to do it.

He whispered: 'Call the executors of my Will. There is a codicil I would add to which you must all be witness.'

When they arrived, the eight executors formed a new group close to the bedside. There were five prelates and three lords. Once, among the executors of the King's Will, the Queen's name had taken precedence over all others. But later, that of Thomas Stanley the High Steward had been substituted for Elizabeth Woodville's, and every reference to the Queen had been removed from the King's testament.

Edward was now gasping: 'Add this to what has been written – that our most beloved and royal brother Richard,

Duke of Gloucester – shall become Protector and Defensor of the Realm – immediately upon our decease. He shall also have the care and guidance of our eldest son – Edward, Prince of Wales – who shall be King after us by the Grace of God.'

In the silence that followed, the dying man heaved a sigh of vast relief. The worldly weight of government had been lifted from him at last. Richard must bear it now. And Richard, faithful and earnest, would accept it as a sacred trust, unquestioningly, until the young King grew up to take it from him in his turn. Richard need never know about the flaw in the right of succession; a knowledge which had brought death to that other royal brother, George of Clarence. Better that Richard remain in ignorance.

'I would now see my youngest son,' the King whispered to one of the executors, John Russell, Bishop of Lincoln.

The tall prelate hurried out to an anteroom and returned, leading a small, bewildered boy by the hand.

'Dickon,' the boy's father said, 'come close.'

The fair head of the little Duke of York bowed under the faltering royal hand. He strained his ears to catch his sire's last words...

The April evening was drawing darkly in as the priests came from the Abbey of St Peter into the Palace. They bore the Sacred Host with taper and bell for the final comfort of Edward Plantagenet, King of England, the fourth of his name since the Norman conquest.

Away to the south, thunder rolled. Afterwards, it rained in torrents all night while the King sank deeper into unconsciousness...

Two days later, on Wednesday April 9th, the bells of Westminster Abbey began to toll. Their lament was soon echoing from St Paul's Church on Ludgate Hill, and from

St Dunstan-in-the-West, St Martin-in-the-Fields, St John at Clerkenwell and St Olave's across the Thames at Southwark: *the King is dead – dead – dead...* These tidings fell like hammer blows, stunning folk in their tracks. Few of the ordinary people had even known that Edward was ailing.

Their genial Edward, of the mighty laugh and the mightier appetite, he could not be dead! It was a false rumour, cruel; spread no doubt by the damned French.

But a hundred other churches, both within and without the city walls, had now taken up the funeral clangour. Only a King's passing could give rise to such a concerted lament.

All at once, citizens began to feel afraid of they knew not exactly what. Change. The future. Unknown masters. Even a return to the wars of a decade ago.

All at once, too, the past became a golden time, of prosperous seasons under blue skies: spring, summer, harvest. Savage taxes and peremptory calls to arms were forgotten, as brief thunderstorms during a sunny spell. With the death of Edward, the weather must permanently turn. There could only be hard winter ahead; for did not Scripture say, 'Woe to thee, land, that thy King is a child'?

Edward's heir was but twelve and a half years old, and a Woodville born and bred. By the insistence of his mother's kin he was being reared in remotest Wales, far from the influence of the old English nobility. This had always caused great displeasure to many.

Now the crowds, thronging the narrow streets of the capital, exchanged forebodings above the din of the bells. Twice, in little more than a hundred years, England had crowned a boy-king; and twice, disaster had resulted, both for the sovereign and his people. From today, the plague of a minority was to be visited upon the land yet once again; and all the actions of the Crown could be manipulated by the ruthless Woodvilles, whom very few had cause to love or trust...

In the Palace of Westminster now, the King's body was already exposed to public view. Naked except for a loincloth, it had been stretched upon a bare board an hour after death, in compliance with ancient custom: that a royal corpse should be displayed for all to recognise and examine. That way, there could be no doubt about identity or cause of death; no rumours of substitution or murder to disturb the country's peace later on.

The Mayor and his Aldermen filed slowly past, followed by lords, merchants, clerics and courtiers...

When John, Lord Howard, reached the bier, he stood quite still for several minutes; his big shoulders hunched, his weather-beaten face suddenly aged beyond its fifty-two years. He'd been the King's friend – though never the companion of his idleness – since the beginning of the reign, when he'd come to the battle of Towton with a sword in one hand and a bag of gold in the other. At Barnet, and Tewkesbury too, he'd fought for Edward. Since then, he'd been his councillor at home, ambassador abroad, champion on land and sea. Only last year, all England had rung with John Howard's fame, when he'd led a fleet of ships up the Firth of Forth to destroy a threatening Scottish navy.

Yesterday, he'd arrived in London from his home manor of Stoke Nayland in Essex. On the way, he'd heard that the King was abed of a chill but had thought nothing much of it: in recent years, Edward had been prone to sudden brief indispositions, from which he always emerged shouting for action and amusement!

Howard's intention had been to pay his usual visit to the King after he'd been down to the docks – there, he'd wanted to watch some cargoes of arms being shipped for

Newcastle-upon-Tyne, where Richard of Gloucester had need of them for the Marches' defence. But a message from Will Hastings had sent him hurtling up-river instead, his barge lanterns lit before five of the clock because of the thunder darkness.

He'd spent the night pacing the Palace corridors, and conferring with Hastings and other lords: ought they to send letters, *now*, to Richard of Gloucester, advising him to hurry southward, or decently await some last-minute miracle which would restore Edward to health?

Finally, in his own hand, Hastings had scrawled a brief letter; sealed it; placed it in his gipsire. Then they'd all waited. Only when the King was assuredly dead had the letter been dispatched by fast messenger to the north. By God's grace, Richard would be found at his home-castle of Middleham in Yorkshire's Wensleydale, not several days' journey further along the Marches towards Scotland.

John Howard had listened to the Chamberlain's horseman clattering out of the Palace yard; in his saddle-bag, the missive which would bring Richard such intense grief.

Howard had always respected the young Duke of Gloucester, and had grown to love him during the Scottish campaign of last year on which they'd both fought so energetically for the King's peace. Richard was a man after his own heart: plain-spoken, decisive; having a great affection for his home and family but never allowing domestic comfort to keep him from official duties. He was also a man with a real passion in his soul for music, and for the sea. These things, too, were Howard's inspirations. Their sharing had drawn the two men together. Now they had a mutual affection; and their wives were also close friends of one another.

If Howard had not had to defer to William Hastings as

his superior in council, he himself would have written the letter to Richard. Aye, and sent it sooner too! His seaman's mind was better attuned to the wind of danger than was that of the easy-going Lord Chamberlain.

He stood now, looking down upon the body of the man whom he knew that Richard of Gloucester had blindly worshipped.

'Ah, reckless Ned,' he thought, 'so to have abused such a mighty carcase...' Bending forward, he dutifully examined it for signs of violence or the known symptoms of poisoning. But it was clear that this royal death had been induced by excess of food, drink, women; by sudden bouts of outdoor activity after weeks of cocooned lounging indoors, just to prove that the King could still keep up with younger, fitter courtiers; and by a rage, sustained at furnace-heat since Christmas, against the French King who'd broken off both the English alliance and his Dauphin's betrothal to the Princess Royal. It was madness ever to have trusted Louis the Spider. As Ambassador to France, John Howard had warned Edward about Louis long ago.

Sighing, he moved away from the bier. The shuffle of feet resumed. The bells continued to toll.

Howard left the death-chamber and trod his ponderous way through all the crowded anterooms. There was no sign of the Queen, but members of her family and party were everywhere, looking busy and alert. All night, while Edward had been sinking, they'd been shamelessly canvassing support from anyone who would listen to them. Now they seemed to be concentrating their efforts on churchmen, great and small. For the most part, the great were ignoring them – Howard saw the Archbishop of Canterbury brush past Lionel Woodville without a glimmer of recognition – but there was a noticeable drift towards them of lesser men. Morton, Bishop of Ely, for instance, Master of the Rolls to the late King, and a member of the royal council on which Howard himself sat; but too unpleasant a man for anyone to have recommended for further advancement. Then there was old Rotherham of York, the Chancellor. Powerful enough once while his wits held together, he was now a mere cipher under the direction of Dr Alcock, Preceptor to the Prince's household in Wales. Rotherham was presently deep in conversation with the younger of the royal stepsons, Sir Richard Grey, who also spent much time at Ludlow in Wales...

John Howard was certain that the Woodville party had long since sent their fleetest messengers posting westward, to apprise young Edward's guardians that their charge was now King of England in all but the crowning.

The crowning— Howard halted so abruptly in a doorway that a gentleman usher, bent on some urgent errand, cannoned into him from behind. The solidly-built East Anglian lord paid no attention to the collision, but continued to stand motionless and frowning while he examined a point of law inside his head.

The crowning of a new King put an immediate end to any Protectorate, unless the office had been previously extended by Parliament. What if the Woodvilles hustled their charge to London, and had him crowned there before Gloucester could reach the capital? The Duke would be powerless then to break through the Queen's vast army of relatives and favourites, barricading the throne and holding all key positions in the southern part of the country. He'd never have the least chance of taking over the guidance of the young King's person; for the Woodville's disliked the Duke of Gloucester as much as he disliked them, although he'd always avoided an open quarrel with them. Still, the enmity was there. And Parliament could not assemble in time to strengthen the Duke's hand.

John Howard decided to write to Richard about these misgivings. But he'd sent the letter to York, not to Middleham; for surely Richard would leave his castle at once on receiving Hastings' news, and hurry south – pausing only at York to collect reinforcements of the armed band he'd bring with him? *'Come strong,'* Hastings had urged.

Thoughtfully, John Howard vacated the doorway he'd been blocking, and moved massively onward, to the relief of the gentleman usher.

A coronation, he reasoned, was a big undertaking, requiring weeks of preparation, and also sanction by a council of peers. Even the Woodvilles wouldn't be arrogant enough to override the hereditary lords, who would certainly object to a hasty ceremony without the presence of the Protector.

Still, there was no guessing what such a faction might not attempt, under the urgings of a jealous and power-hungry Queen who had killed enemies before now.

Aye, fair Elizabeth knew how to have murder done!

Lengthening his stride, Howard made for St Stephen's chapel where the lords had agreed to meet.

ALSO BY ELEANOR FAIRBURN

THE WARS OF THE ROSES QUARTET:

White Rose, Dark Summer

The Rose at Harvest End

Winter's Rose

OTHER HISTORICAL FICTION:

The Green Popinjays

The White Seahorse

The Golden Hive

Crowned Ermine

WRITING AS CATHERINE CARFAX:

A Silence With Voices

The Semper Inheritance

The Sleeping Salamander

To Die A Little

WRITING AS EMMA GAYLE:

Cousin Caroline

Frenchman's Harvest

WRITING AS ELENA LYONS:

The Haunting of Abbotsgarth

A Scent of Lilacs

WRITING AS ANNA NEVILLE:

The House of the Chestnut Trees

Printed in Great Britain
by Amazon